Jaime Faber is an American woman

She is finally beginning to put down roots and pursue a career. She is ready for the monthly bills and the daily paper, grocery shopping and laundry. After a nomadic childhood spent with her flamboyant, artistic mother, Jaime can hardly wait to settle into a normal, secure life. At twenty-five she has reached the age of responsibility.

Jaime's move to New Orleans is a logical first step. She begins a new job as a social worker and rents an apartment that she slowly decorates with loving care. At twenty-five Jaime finds strength and satisfaction as she carves out her version of the American Dream. But she also feels a growing need to share it.

Dear Reader,

This is indeed a special year for American Romance: it marks our fifth anniversary of bringing you the love stories you want to read. Stories of real women of contemporary America—women just like you. This month we're celebrating that anniversary with a special four-book series by four of your favorite American Romance authors. Rebecca Flanders, Beverly Sommers, Judith Arnold and Anne Stuart introduce you to Jaime, Suzanne, Abbie and Marielle—the women of Yorktown Towers.

They've been neighbors, they've been friends, but now they're saying goodbye, leaving Manhattan one by one, in search of their lives, in search of happiness, carving out their own version of the American Dream.

Jaime, Suzanne, Abbie and Marielle: four believable American Romance heroines...four contemporary American women just like you.

We hope you enjoy these special stories as much as we enjoyed preparing them for you for this occasion. It's our way of saying thanks for being there these past five years. We here at American Romance look forward to many more anniversaries of success....

Debra Matteucci
Senior Editor

Search the
Heavens
Rebecca Flanders

Harlequin Books

TORONTO • NEW YORK • LONDON
AMSTERDAM • PARIS • SYDNEY • HAMBURG
STOCKHOLM • ATHENS • TOKYO • MILAN

Published August 1988

First printing June 1988

ISBN 0-373-16257-X

Chapter One

New Orleans. The very phrase conjured up visions of Mardi Gras, steamy Creole dishes and antebellum mansions secluded behind lacy wrought-iron gates. Jaime Faber had discovered all that and more in the two weeks she had been in the city. But the two things the guidebooks generally didn't mention were the heat, and the traffic.

Jaime had known of course that the climate in New Orleans was subtropical, but after two years of New York winters—not to mention the stifling New York summers—she thought she was prepared for anything. Not true. In mid-June the heat that wrapped around the city was like a wet blanket; it dripped from the eaves and rose up from the streets in foggy waves. Her toothbrush never dried, and ten minutes after her morning shower she was already sticky with sweat. By noon the heat was so debilitating that most natives had learned to leave the streets for a cool drink under a ceiling fan, or a well-deserved siesta in an air-conditioned room. Jaime had found that habit an easy one to adopt.

As for the traffic . . . for two weeks, in a very touristy way, Jaime had barely noticed it. She had walked where she needed to go, or taken the St. Charles Trolley when she was in the mood for exploring. Today, however, she was driving her first car, and she could not believe she had been so foolish as to try to negotiate a moving vehicle through the French Quarter.

The car had not exactly been Jaime's idea, and she still had mixed feelings about it. Jaime was twenty-five years old and she had circumnavigated the globe at least twice, but she had never owned her own car. She had had her driver's license since she was seventeen, but had simply never stayed in one place long enough to see the benefits in owning a car. It was Jaime's mother who pointed out that New Orleans was not like New York, and in the South *everyone* drove. Besides, since her new job would require a good deal of fieldwork, she would need a car to get around.

Jaime listened to her mother's long-distance advice as she always did, told her she would think about it, and the next morning a grinning automobile dealer knocked on her door and handed her the keys to a brand new Mazda XL. Jaime supposed wryly that she should be grateful it had not been a Rolls-Royce limo that was parked outside her house, and a liveried chauffeur who had knocked on her door. Jaime's mother did like to go to extremes.

Jaime loved the car, of course. It was smart, black, absurdly luxurious and far more expensive than anything she could have afforded on her own. It was simply that the entire concept made her uneasy. It had been her mother who recommended her for this job in New Orleans, her mother who had found the adorable little carriage house in the Garden District that was actually within Jaime's budget, her mother who had paid the shipping fees on the few possessions

Jaime had brought with her from the New York apartment. Jaime was too much accustomed to the luxury of being Leona Faber's daughter to object to such gestures, but she had to draw the line somewhere. And it seemed to her the car might have been a good place to start.

The truth of that suspicion was borne out to her as she sat locked in traffic on Bourbon Street, surrounded by milling pedestrians, honking taxicabs, huge delivery vans and the occasional flower-draped horse carriage, which plodded by with a maddeningly superior air. The blue digital numbers on the dashboard clock flashed nine twenty-eight, and Jaime groaned out loud. Her first day on the job and she was already twenty-eight minutes late. Whatever had made her think life in the Deep South would be slower paced than New York City?

In the side mirror she spotted a break in the traffic and lost no time. Counting on the Mazda's much-lauded high-performance engine and blind luck, she whipped the wheel, gunned the accelerator and dashed around a delivery van to a chorus of squealing tires and blaring horns. Narrowing her eyes grimly and gripping the steering wheel, she made a reckless left turn into Esplanade and hoped for the best.

Victory House, her destination, was less than half a block away. She could see its dull yellow facade peeping through a curtain of Spanish Moss, and she felt like a marathon runner entering the home stretch. As a matter of fact, she probably would have made better time if she had run.

Esplanade was divided down the middle by a wide grassy median, and Jaime had to wait in a crossing lane to get to the other side. Just ahead she could see an empty parking space in front of the house, marked by a Reserved sign, and she thought her luck might be changing. She inched toward the space, uncertain of her parallel parking skills but determined to try, when a movement from the corner of her eye sent her heart lurching to her throat.

From out of nowhere, a dusty blue motorcycle whipped in front of her just as she was entering the parking space. There was no way she could keep from hitting him. It happened too quickly for her to do anything but slam on the brakes and envision, in a horrifying flash of living Technicolor, the accident that was about to happen.

But when her car came to a screeching stop, half in and half out of the parking space, it was without the sound of twisting metal and broken glass. She cautiously opened eyes she had not even been aware of closing and saw that the motorcycle was nestled securely against the curb not half an inch in front of the bumper of her car, and the motorcyclist was climbing off, apparently unharmed.

Jaime was shaking as she got out of the car. She didn't know whether to be furious or relieved, and she wasn't at all sure what the correct protocol was for a situation like this. But she was surprised at how calm her tone sounded as she called, "Excuse me—but I think I was here first."

The man glanced at her curiously as he got off the motorcycle and removed his helmet. The first thing Jaime noticed about him was that he was very young. The second thing was that he was rather good-looking in a careless, rumpled sort of way. His light brown hair was tousled by the helmet in curls and spikes, and his jaw was stubbled by the trace of a blond beard. His jeans were faded and worn and his shirt, with its old-fashioned, thin brown stripes, was wrinkled from the wind. He looked back at the relative positions of their vehicles, and pointed out, "Doesn't look like it to me."

His tone was not unfriendly, but it did occur to Jaime that in this area of town, with a man who looked like he did and rode a motorcycle, it might not be a wise idea to start an argument. Though she knew it probably wouldn't do any good, she was persuaded to try reasoning with him.

She came around the car toward the sidewalk, trying to look pleasant and nonthreatening. "I believe there's a law of physics," she said, raising her voice a little to be heard over the sound of traffic, "that states two solid objects cannot occupy the same space at the same time."

He grinned. "Wouldn't be the first law I've broken."

Jaime could well imagine. A horn blared in her ear as an angry driver tried to get past the protruding fender of her car, shaking his fist at her. She took her courage in hand and objected, "But, this parking space is reserved for cars—"

"Where does it say that?"

Another horn blared and Jaime was becoming frantic. "It doesn't have to *say* that—"

He unfastened a satchel from the back of the motorcycle and swung it over his shoulder. "You're not from around here, are you?"

"What makes you say that?"

He grinned again. "You talk funny."

Jaime didn't know how to respond to that, and it was just as well because just then another blare of horns and a string of angry expletives from a passing driver drowned out whatever she might have said. The motorcyclist cupped his hand around his mouth and called back, "Don't mind her, she's from out of town!"

Then he glanced at Jaime's car and commented, "Nice set of wheels. I'd be careful about parking it in this part of town, though." He touched his fingers to his forehead in a small salute and, incredibly, he started to walk away.

"Wait!" Jaime cried. "I can't just leave my car here like this—"

He turned back to her, unconcerned. "Then move it."

"Wouldn't it be easier for you to move your motorcycle?"

He looked thoughtful. "Tell you what," he agreed. "Because you're new in town, and to show you what Southern hospitality is all about, I'll share the space with you."

"But—"

"Don't worry about my bike," he assured her. "If I need it, I'll just take it over the curb."

"I wasn't worried about your bike," she stated adamantly. She knew she was pushing her luck, but sometimes a show of strength was necessary. "I *was* here first."

He seemed to consider that. "All right, how about this?" he suggested. "If your hubcaps are still intact by the end of the day, the parking space is yours. Now I couldn't be fairer than that."

"But—"

"By the way," he tossed an easy grin over his shoulder as he turned to go, "welcome to New Orleans."

Jaime just stood there, openmouthed and speechless, until he disappeared around the corner.

A moment later Jaime couldn't believe that she'd taken on a man who, considering the part of town she was in and his appearance, could well have been a junkie or worse, and she decided that, all things considered, she had probably gotten off easily. *Good God*, she thought despairingly, *he'll probably come back and slash my tires, at the very least. Mother, next time you want to give me a present, just send a box of candy.* . . . But it was nine forty-five and she did not have time to move her car, or even to worry about the bizarre incident any longer. Pausing only to snatch her purse from the front seat and lock the car doors, she hurried up the steps to the settlement house.

JAIME'S INITIAL INTERVIEW for the position had been conducted with the board members over lunch—being Leona Faber's daughter, what else could she expect?—and she had never had a tour of the facilities. Her first impression of the inside of Victory House was a mixture of scents and sounds: pine disinfectant and the clatter of dishes, library paste and the scuffle of feet on a wooden floor as someone chanted out aerobic instructions to the background of a swing tune. A television was on somewhere, and another voice was occasionally interspersed with that of the aerobics instructor from the open door of a classroom, which apparently had something to do with tenants' rights. The faint scent of coffee wound through the various sensate impressions like a unifying thread.

The narrow hallway down which she walked was painted pale yellow, the floors covered in peeling gray linoleum. A big room opened on the left, a staircase shot sharply upward to the right, and the hallway branched at either end toward more rooms. Before she got herself thoroughly lost on top of everything else, Jaime paused to get her bearings.

The walls were dotted with United Way posters advising against the hazards of drug abuse and teenage pregnancy. A bulletin board was littered with notices of upcoming community events and services offered by Victory House. On one wall was reserved a space for drawings by preschoolers, which ran the gamut from horrifying to beautiful. Hand-lettered signs with arrows pointed the way to "Social Security and Welfare Checks," "Counseling" and "Childbirth Classes." Jaime followed one of these signs to "Office," which was located up the stairs, making what repairs she could to her appearance along the way.

She was wearing a Laura Ashley dress in a cocoa-rosebud print with an intricately tucked bodice and a dropped waist, a long peach-colored gauze scarf and a hip-length khaki vest. All of her clothes were oversized, ankle-length and loosely styled in a vain attempt to disguise figure flaws that no amount of dieting or exercise could seem to correct.

Jaime was short and squarely built, with broad shoulders, large bones and firm, compact proportions. All her life she had felt like a tall person squeezed into too small a body, and no matter what she wore she always felt fat. Even her fingers were short and stubby, and her calves were as round and muscular as a gymnast's. Her jawline was square and distinct, her hazel eyes wide spaced, and her mouth broad and generous—all of which would have been striking on a taller, slimmer person, but which on Jaime merely looked out of place.

Of course none of that probably would have mattered nearly as much if Jaime's mother hadn't been so unequivocally lovely, and if Jaime hadn't felt like the ugly duckling every time the two of them were together.

Jaime was aware that, if she really wanted to, there were ways to change her unsatisfactory appearance. She had tried Weight Watchers, and was probably the only person in the history of that esteemed organization to actually gain weight while on the program. She had tried streaking, frosting and dying her nondescript mousy brown hair, with utterly unimpressive results. She had even gone to a makeup specialist but was never able to achieve the same effect when she tried the wizard's methods at home. She had finally decided that it was the fate of some women to be forever plain, and had come to an uneasy peace with the fact that she would never be as beautiful, as glamorous, or even as tall as her mother.

One glance at her compact mirror told her that today the situation was even more hopeless than usual. She was forty-five—no, fifty—minutes late, her carefully pressed and starched dress was already a mass of wrinkles, and her makeup was beginning to cake and run with sweat. Only her hair, a tightly permed mass of shoulder-length curls, was bearing up well against the New Orleans heat and humidity, but even it clung damply to her scalp and was too heavy against the back of her neck.

She was still flustered and more than a little disturbed over the incident with the motorcyclist, and if she had gone out of her way to create a more disastrous beginning to her new career she could not have done a better job. For a moment, her most cowardly instinct almost persuaded her to go home, call in with some convincing excuse—a sudden attack of malaria might do the trick—and try again tomorrow.

But it was too late. She had reached the top of the stairs with its scents of mimeograph ink and stale cigarette smoke. A telephone was ringing down the hall, and a young woman with an armful of manila folders barely paused as she rushed by to inquire, "May I help you?"

"I'm here to see Ms Campion?" The questioning inflection came from anxiety, confusion and a small amount of hope that her new supervisor would not be in, and therefore not realize how late her newest employee was for her first day of work.

The woman called over her shoulder, "Daphene!" and hurried away.

A moment later the most beautiful black woman Jaime had ever seen emerged from an open door across the hall. She was at least six feet tall, as svelte as a Parisian model and moved with the kind of fluid grace that made walking seem like an art form. Her hair was clipped close to the scalp, accentuating her high cheekbones and large almond eyes, and her skin was flawless. Just looking at her made Jaime feel short, fat and clumsy, and about as competent as a puppy.

Daphene Campion had a pipe wrench in one hand, but she extended the other to Jaime in a strong, firm handclasp. "You must be Jaime Faber," she welcomed her warmly. Her voice was rich and mellifluous, as only befitted her stature. "I'm Daphene

Campion, and welcome to Victory House." She pronounced her last name Campi*one*, and Jaime was glad she had not embarrassed herself further by mispronouncing this elegant woman's name in her presence.

Jaime rushed quickly into an apology, "I know I'm late and I'm so sorry, but the traffic—"

Daphene waved it away negligently. "You'll find we keep a fairly flexible schedule here. If you drove I'm surprised you made it at all."

But for all the other woman's graciousness, Jaime could feel herself being scrutinized from head to toe, and more than anything in the world she found herself wanting to please Daphene Campion. Not because Daphene was her boss—just because she was Daphene.

Then Daphene said suddenly, "I don't suppose you know anything about plumbing?"

Jaime relaxed cautiously. "I spent two years in a New York apartment where the pipes were purchased after the builders ran out of money, and scheduled maintenance was a hit-or-miss proposition. I learned plumbing the same way other people learn street fighting—out of self-defense."

Daphene Campion smiled and handed her the pipe wrench. "You've just received your first assignment."

Daphene gestured her to a small, bile-green bathroom with a rust-pitted tub and dingy, water-swollen tiles. A carpet of damp towels was spread under the sink, where the problem apparently was.

"Disgusting, isn't it?" said Daphene cheerfully. "But it still beats running up and down the stairs when you want to go to the john. And since we hold a lot of our preschool programs up here, that could add up to some wear and tear on the stairs."

Jaime weighed the pipe wrench in her hand and, sparing one brief regretful thought for her hand-washable-only dress, sank down on the floor and peered under the sink. She saw the difficulty immediately.

"There's a hole in the J-bend drain. It's rusted through."

"That's right," Daphene said, with apparent surprise. "I've already got the replacement part. I just couldn't figure out how it all fit together."

"No problem. It just twists apart here..." Jaime lay down beneath the sink and applied the pipe wrench, unable to shake the feeling that more than her skills as a plumber were being tested. After a moment, Daphene's slim black legs disappeared, and Jaime suppressed a wry smile. She had not spent six years of her life obtaining a degree in Social Services to lie beneath a dripping sink and twist a pipe wrench, and Daphene Campion knew that very well. She merely wanted to see how the rich-girl neophyte reacted to the nuts and bolts, as it were, of inner-city social work.

Fortunately, Jaime was accustomed to such tests and had learned to take them in good humor. And she couldn't blame Daphene. There were distinct disadvantages to being the daughter of a woman as flamboyant and successful as Leona Faber, the most common of which being that no one ever took her seriously.

Leona Faber had made her fame and fortune in one of the most difficult, competitive fields in the world—art. Her life-style was eccentric, haphazard and free spirited...not to mention well publicized. Her national and international showings were media events, and even her prints were beyond the income of the average upper middle-class family. She had absolutely no qualms about using her name or her money to assure the best of everything for herself and her daughter. So with an inside edge like that, why was Jaime Faber lying on a wet floor in a two hundred dollar dress wrestling with a pipe wrench?

That question, and a dozen like it, had become rote to Jaime over the years and she had a handful of stock answers. The truth was, most of the time she didn't know.

Daphene Campion came back just as Jaime was fitting the new washer over the old pipe. Jaime saw through the corner of her eye that she had a file in her hand. "Well," Daphene commented with a note of admiration, "I can't accuse you of false advertising. I've been fighting with that fool thing all morning."

"Experience," Jaime told her. "And if the rest of the plumbing is in as bad shape as this bathroom, you're going to have plenty of it before much longer."

"Life is full of little challenges, isn't it?" She sat down on the toilet lid and opened the file. "Now, let's get down to business. No," she said as Jaime started to get up, "you keep working. I'll talk."

Daphene slipped on a pair of magnifying glasses— the kind one buys at the drugstore for six dollars—and glanced over the file. "Your transcript looks very good. Your field supervisor speaks very highly of you. And there's a glowing recommendation here from Abigail Jarvis of the New York District Attorney's office."

Jaime smiled a little, embarrassed. "Actually," she felt compelled to explain as she busily fitted the washer on the new connection, "Abbie and I were friends. We lived in the same building in New York, and we once worked on a case together."

"Still, it's quite impressive. I see your first field assignment was in Harlem. That could come in handy. We have some pretty rough characters around here, too."

"I know," Jaime murmured, fitting the J-bend in place. "I almost ran over one of them with my car on the way in."

Daphene lifted a graceful eyebrow. "My, you have had a busy morning, haven't you?"

"All in a day's work." Jaime tightened the slip nuts and reached over the basin to turn on the water, keeping a careful eye out for leaks. When none were apparent, she gave a satisfied nod, turned off the water and wiped her hands on a towel. "That should do it."

Daphene looked her over once more, though with a new air of appreciation now. "Miss Faber, you may just be the most valuable member of my staff."

It was all Jaime could do to keep from beaming her pride as Daphene extended her hand to help her up. "Come on," Daphene said, "let me show you around."

They walked through a converted bedroom that Daphene wryly referred to as the "administrative offices." Three desks, a wall of filing cabinets and a portable copy machine served five regular staff members, including Daphene. "We try to avoid paperwork as much as possible," Daphene explained. "It only slows down the process." Jaime opened her mouth to object, somewhat appalled that a service as complex as Victory House could even attempt to function efficiently without the proper bureaucracy to back it up, but restrained herself just in time. She was hardly in the position to offer criticisms or judgments—not yet.

They peeked into a room where a class on mothering was being held, and Daphene went on, "As you know, a place like Victory House exists for the community it serves. We have programs for senior citizens, new mothers—most of whom, incidentally, are under seventeen—we have play therapy in the mornings for preschoolers and after-school groups later on. Three mornings a week we serve a light breakfast out of the kitchen, and I'm sorry to say that sometimes that's the only hot meal many of these people ever get. We even have our own medical clinic around back, and we work very closely with Dr. Gerreau, whom you'll meet before the day is out.

"We are entirely privately funded. We have an arrangement with Charity Hospital and Tulane University, who train interns here for a fee, but most of our funding comes from churches and private donations. We therefore have to be very creative about how we manage our expenses, and sometimes—" Daphene smiled dryly "—about how we acquire our funds."

"As you might have guessed," Daphene continued as they descended the stairs, "most of the time we're short-staffed. For that reason, everyone does a little bit of everything around here. You'll be expected to do some outreach work, as well as take over one or two of the programs. One day you might be working in the kitchen, another counseling a pregnant twelve-year-old who's run away from her pimp." Daphene cast a sidelong glance at her. "Not very glamorous, is it?"

Jaime met her gaze steadily. "I didn't get into this line of work for the glamour, Ms Campion."

Daphene smiled. "I didn't suppose you had. And for right now, just to show you what a sweetheart I can be, I'm not going to ask you why you did choose this line of work. I imagine you get rather tired of answering that."

"Sometimes," agreed Jaime. Though she was grateful for Daphene's tact, she had already prepared one of her stock answers, just in case.

They had reached the front hallway, with its coffee smells and classroom voices, and Daphene turned to look at her. Jaime was struck again by strength of personality behind the beautiful face. "So," she said, not unkindly, "I've shown you my better side, now I have to play bad cop for a minute. To be perfectly honest with you, I was against taking you on here at Victory House. I don't care how bright you are or how highly recommended you come, or how big a donation your mother has promised us. You're young. You're inexperienced. And frankly, our work here is too important to encourage dilettantes."

She lifted her shoulders slightly in a gesture that could have been resignation. "But, as I said, we're understaffed, and we don't have the luxury of turning our backs on a warm body and a pair of hands. We have a rather large turnover here," she said, fixing Jaime with her penetrating gaze. "We get some tough cases, and burnout comes quickly. You'll find that Victory House is not exactly what they taught you to expect in social work school, and a lot of young save-the-worlders find out they just can't hack it. In other words, if you're looking for a way to prove yourself or assuage your social conscience, I wish you'd go someplace else. We just don't have time for it here."

Jaime responded simply, "I could have gone into any field I wanted to, Ms Campion. Or I could have done nothing at all. I chose social work because it's what I do best. I don't have anything to prove except that I can do my job. And if I fail at that, you'll let me know, won't you?"

Daphene smiled. "Damn right."

The two women held each other's eyes, and for a moment an agreement was reached. Then Daphene reached into the file she carried and brought out a slip of paper. "Now," she said briskly, "your first assignment is beating the streets. And no, it's not punishment—we start everyone out this way, and everyone on staff spends at least one day a week outside the House. We've got to keep in touch with the community. I want you to start making home visits to everyone on this list—"

The door opened with a powerful thump, and the man who strode into the hall cast a shadow that would have dwarfed a professional wrestler. He weighed at least three hundred pounds and was so tall he walked in a perpetual stoop, massive neck arched forward, jaw thrust out. He wore a frayed vest that left his arms and most of his chest bare, and his ebony skin gleamed with perspiration. The buttons strained over his stomach, and the vest was trimmed with various pieces of sharp-edged metal. His head was shaved and he wore a string of safety pins in one ear; the carved handle of a knife protruded boldly from a scabbard on his belt. The big man moved toward them aggressively, and Jaime's muscles instinctively tensed for fight or flight—mostly flight.

He stopped before Daphene and thrust a rather large wad of crumpled bills into her hand. "Here's this week's take, Miz Daphene." The man's voice was as deep as the rumble of a train. "A hunnert dollars more'n last. I told you that bastard was holding out on us."

Daphene flipped through the bills appreciatively. "He didn't give you any trouble, did he?"

"Hell, no." He thrust his thumbs into his belt and rocked back on his heels, scowling. "Ole Deke knows better than to mess with me and my boys. We done teached him one lesson too many."

Daphene looked at him warningly. "I told you I don't want anyone hurt, Armand."

"Hell, Miz Campion. You got to hurt folks ever now and again. It's the only way they learn anything."

Jaime listened to the interchange with growing horror, and at last she couldn't be silent any longer. "Excuse me," she said tentatively, staring at Daphene. "But—do I understand you just collected... protection money?"

Daphene smiled, totally unconcerned. "In a way. Deke has been shaking down local businessmen for years. Armand and his boys are bigger than Deke and his boys, so now Armand shakes down Deke and puts the money back into the community."

Jaime let the information sink in, hardly able to believe her ears. She opened her mouth for an incredulous protest, but then jumped as Armand's voice growled, "Who's de pussycat?"

Daphene smiled and patted Armand's arm. "Armand, I want you to meet Jaime Faber. She's working for me now, so you be good to her, you hear?"

Armand fixed Jaime with a glare that made her want to hide behind Daphene, and then said abruptly, "Any beer?"

"In the kitchen," Daphene said, and Armand strolled off.

Jaime was still reeling, and when Armand had disappeared, all she could manage to say was, weakly, "You give him beer?"

"Armand used to be a junkie," Daphene explained patiently. "Now he drinks one beer a week, in the kitchen, with members of my staff, and it's the highlight of his week. It's little enough for all he does for us."

"But—" Jaime tried very hard to form a coherent sentence. "But . . . don't you think the proper procedure would be . . . the police?"

Daphene looked confused, then glanced at the money in her hand. "Oh, you mean this?" She laughed. "Honey, even if we could get the police involved in this community, the residents wouldn't stand for it. Most of them are living on the fringes of the law anyway, and anything representing authority scares them to death. As for the money—well, they're used to paying somebody. It makes them feel safe. They *want* to do it. If we ran off Deke—which I suppose we could—there'd just be someone else along to take his place, not only because this community breeds that sort of thing, but because it demands it. So we do the next best thing. We keep Deke honest, and we take a portion of the proceeds and put it back into the community . . . sort of like income tax, when you think about it. Only perhaps a shade more efficient."

Jaime's shock must have been apparent, for Daphene smiled at her kindly and patted her arm. "I see

I've offended you, and I'm sorry. But the culture of this community is a unique thing, and we cannot live apart from that culture—otherwise we're less than useless. Perhaps after you've been in the field a few days, you'll understand."

Jaime cleared her throat a little. "It's just...that I'm used to doing things a little bit more . . . by the book."

Daphene laughed lightly. "You'll get over that soon enough! Now—" she slipped her arm companionably through Jaime's and took out the slip of paper again "—about this list...."

Chapter Two

Jaime had been on the job for less than half an hour and already she was beginning to suspect she had made a mistake. As she left Victory House with the list of names and addresses clutched in her hand, she was still stunned over the incident with Armand—and too thoroughly intimidated by Daphene Campion to admit to herself just how shocked she really was.

All her life Jaime had worked hard to develop a live-and-let-live attitude; having grown up with Leona Faber and her constantly fluctuating band of eccentric friends, what choice had she had? But she had gone into social work expecting to spend her days in a dull, orderly government office, surrounded by rules and regulations and bound head and foot in red tape, knowing exactly what the restrictions were and abiding by them happily. She told herself she wasn't morally offended by Victory House's method of alternative financing, merely somewhat nervous. Jaime had never been comfortable in unstructured situations, and she wasn't even certain this was legal.

She was beginning to understand why her mother had pushed this particular job on her so anxiously. Leave it to Leona to take a nice, safe, perfectly run-of-the-mill career opportunity and turn it into something out of *Crime Story*.

When Jaime came out of the building she noticed that her car was still crookedly occupying the parking space in which the motorcyclist had left it, but the motorcycle was gone. The rear fender was still partially protruding into the street but traffic seemed to have no trouble moving around it, and the way Jaime's luck was running today she didn't dare try to move it. She dug into her tapestry canvas bag and came up with her street map of New Orleans, checking it against the addresses on her list. Happily, she noticed that all of the addresses were within easy walking distance.

The first four on her list took her back through the Quarter with its boisterous crowds and colorful street fronts, across Jackson Square with its peddlers, street artists and panhandlers, and into a somewhat seedier neighborhood. Here paint was peeling from low shotgun houses, mongrel dogs pawed through garbage cans and teenage boys of varying nationalities eyed her sullenly. The windows were covered with sheets, and toddlers in baggy and stained diapers played on the sidewalks—sometimes with supervision and sometimes without.

The building before which Jaime stopped was not a row house and not a tenement, but a cross between both. Actually it was two old houses that had been divided into apartments, joined by a flat-roofed breezeway across the courtyard. It was a far cry from the modern, Upper East Side Yorktown Towers where Jaime had spent the last two years of her life, but she had seen worse.

After some time spent squinting over the faded mailbox labels in the front hall, Jaime ascertained that the first person on her list lived on the second floor. According to the notes Jaime had scribbled in the margins of the list, the Franklin family consisted of an eighteen-year-old mother of three named Cara, and her grandmother Pearlie. Cara and the children had made regular use of the facilities at Victory House until about two weeks ago, and Daphene wanted to know why they had stopped coming.

Jaime made her way down a hot, narrow hallway that smelled of mildew and onions, around scurrying palmetto bugs and broken toys. She paused to blot her neck and her face with a tissue and knocked on the door of apartment twenty-two.

Inside the apartment she could hear the television blaring *The Price is Right*, and a baby was wailing. It never ceased to amaze her how even the poorest families always managed to afford television. She had seen homeless families hook up color TV sets to car batteries in the ghettos of New York.

She knocked again, louder, and after a moment heard a scuffling and the click of a bolt. The door opened to the length of the chain, and one brown eye peered suspiciously out at her. "Who are you?" an unfriendly voice demanded.

"My name is Jaime Faber, from Victory House. Are you Cara?"

"I don't know you," the girl returned, and started to close the door.

"Do you know Daphene Campion?" Jaime said quickly, and the door hesitated.

After a moment the door closed, the chain rattled, and the door opened again, revealing a young girl with mottled café-au-lait skin and stringy black hair caught at the nape with a rubber band. She was wearing a pair of frayed shorts and a faded T-shirt, and a little girl of about three clung to her bare leg. She looked Jaime over critically. "Miz Daphene really send you?" she demanded.

"She was worried about you." Jaime smiled. "May I come in?"

"Did you bring any coupons?"

Jaime's puzzled expression prompted an impatient snort from Cara. "You know, food coupons. You got any?"

"Why, no. You have to pick those up yourself, Cara, from the office downtown—"

"And just how'm I suppose to do that with three brats and a sick gran'ma?" she retorted belligerently. "Miz Daphene always brings me my coupons. I swear if we don't all starve to death... Well, don't just stand there, you might as well come in." She opened the door wider and snapped over her shoulder, "Carena, shut off that set! That racket's 'bout to drive me out of my mind!"

She turned back to Jaime. "You tell Miz Daphene about my coupons. And I ain't got my check this month, either."

She strode over to the television set—a nineteen-inch color portable on a rickety old table—and flicked it off, snatching up a pack of cigarettes from the top of the television on her way. She spoke sharply to the two children who sat on the floor in front of the blank TV. "You kids go on outside and play. We've got company. Here, Jacob..." She detached the little girl from her leg and pushed her toward the boy. "You mind your sister, now. Don't let her go wandering off."

Jaime smiled at the children as they filed toward the door. "Why don't you bring them down to Victory House this afternoon? There's plenty of room to play there."

"I done told you, girl," Cara said, lighting a cigarette and shaking out the match. "I got a sick woman here. I got to stay and watch her."

"Your grandmother? Do you mind if I see her?"

Cara shrugged and gestured toward a curtained-off room. "I called Dr. Quaid already," she said. "Won't do no good, though. She says she's under a spin and sinking fast."

Cara held aside the curtain for her, and Jaime entered a small, low-ceilinged room that was almost completely filled by a four-poster bed. The one narrow window was open to the street noise and the flies, but covered with a sheet to keep out the light. The woman on the bed was big, gray-haired, and obviously ill.

Cara's tone gentled as she entered her grandmother's room. "Granny? You got company. Miz Daphene sent her to visit with you."

The woman opened her eyes weakly.

"Mrs. Franklin?" Jaime walked forward and extended her hand. "I'm Jaime Faber. We've been worried about you over at Victory House."

Pearlie Franklin gripped Jaime's hand weakly. Her hand was hot and dry and her breathing sounded labored, with a faint rattle to it. "Lor', child, that's kind of you. Sit a spell, help a dying old woman pass the time."

Jaime felt the woman's forehead, and she was burning up. She glanced at Cara. "How long has she been sick?"

"She's been right poorly for a week now, but took a turn for the worse last night. That's how come I called the doctor."

Pearlie started to speak but began to cough, and it was a terrible, wracking sound. Cara hurried from the room to put out her cigarette, and Jaime, alarmed, sat on the edge of the bed and supported Pearlie's shoulders with her arm. Jaime was no expert, but she had worked for a while in the social services department of a hospital in New York, and the cough sounded very much like pneumonia to her.

Cara came back with a glass of water, and Pearlie took delicate, gasping sips. Her color was terrible.

Jaime said, "Mrs. Franklin, you should be in a hospital. I'm going to call an ambulance now, and—"

"No." Struggling to breathe, Pearlie weakly waved away the water glass and Jaime's words. "Won't have no—doctors. I got the voodoo, chile, and ain't no doctors gonna help me now."

Jaime stared at Cara. "What did she say?"

Cara took the edge of the sheet and blotted her grandmother's face. "Voodoo," she responded matter-of-factly. "Somebody's done gone and put a curse on her."

"But . . ." Jaime looked at Pearlie, who lay weakly against the pillow with her eyes closed and her lips parted for dragging breaths, and then at Cara. "But that's ridiculous! You surely don't believe that!"

Cara shrugged. "I don't. But she does."

There was a knock on the outside door, and Cara grumbled, "Probably one of them blame kids, back up here already. You sit with her, I'll be back."

Jaime took the old woman's hand between both of hers and patted it soothingly. This was definitely one thing the textbooks hadn't covered. But wasn't one of her most valuable skills the ability to gently reason, to persuade people around to her way of thinking? Wasn't that what her field supervisor had most complimented her on, and wasn't that how she had been able to convince the New York District Attorney's office to decline to prosecute a desperate young mother charged with child abandonment?

Jaime said gently, "Pearlie, I know you don't know me, but I want to be your friend. Can you believe that?"

The old woman smiled weakly. "Lord child, I ain't so rich I can afford to turn away friends anyplace I can get them."

Jaime squeezed her hand. "Good. Now, I'm your friend and I'm not going to do anything that's bad for you. You need medicine, Pearlie, and people who know how to take care of you." Pearlie began shaking her head and trying to pull her hand away, and Jaime went on quickly, "I'll go with you. I'll go with you in the ambulance and I'll hold your hand every minute—"

"No, no doctor." Pearlie was growing more and more agitated, her breathing was more erratic, and she slapped feebly at Jaime's hand, pushing her away. "You keep them doctors away from me, can't do nothing to help poor Pearlie now. You keep them away, you hear, I've got the voodoo...."

Pearlie was so upset that Jaime was afraid she was only aggravating her condition, so she assured her quickly, "All right. Nobody's going to hurt you, I promise. You just stay calm. Rest."

Jaime stood up and straightened the sheet Pearlie had disarranged in her thrashing about, then walked away from the bed, biting her lip. Obviously the woman had to have medical attention, no matter what her objections or personal beliefs to the contrary. Of course, Cara said she had called a doctor, but the girl didn't seem too reliable to Jaime, and it went without saying that no doctor would make a house call even if Cara was telling the truth. No, the only thing to do was to call an ambulance. She wondered if there was a phone in the apartment. And what had happened to Cara, anyway?

Jaime could hear voices in the outer room, one of which was male, and she frowned a little in annoyance. Cara might claim that she could not leave her sick grandmother's side, but chances were she didn't mind taking a little time off to entertain her boyfriend.

Jaime pushed through the curtain and stopped still. Standing in the center of the room, chatting amiably with Cara, was the motorcyclist who had stolen Jaime's parking place.

He was still tousled, still windblown, and still unshaven. His jeans were pushed into the tops of scuffed motorcycle boots and in deference to the rising morning heat he had rolled up the sleeves of his rumpled shirt and unbuttoned the top three buttons over a beige T-shirt. He wore a large leather pouch, like a purse, over one shoulder.

He noticed Jaime before Cara did, and he tilted his head toward her inquisitively. "Don't I know you?"

Cara glanced at Jaime. "This is the girl from over at the settlement house I was telling you about. What's your name, honey?"

He snapped his fingers in recognition. "That's right! The black Mazda."

Jaime said cautiously, "What are you doing here?"

Cara frowned impatiently. "This is Dr. Quaid. I said I called him, didn't I?"

The man moved forward with an easy, ebullient step, his hand extended. "Quaid Gerreau's the name. And yours—?"

Jaime ignored both the question and the proffered hand, staring at him. "Did she say...doctor?"

"That's right." He dropped his hand, cocking an amused eyebrow. "Don't tell me you've got doctor phobia, too? I'd better move fast, this stuff must be catching."

"But—but..." Jaime felt foolish for stammering but she couldn't help it, and she blurted out, "But you're too young to be a doctor!"

He grinned. "Bless your heart." He turned to Cara. "Now where's this patient of ours?"

Jaime didn't move away from the curtained door even when Cara gestured the way, and she couldn't stop staring at the ill-dressed, easy-going man whom, until three minutes ago, she had characterized as a twenty-year-old street bum and who now called himself Dr. Gerreau. *Gerreau*... An awful, sinking feeling started in the pit of her stomach and she said, "You wouldn't by any chance be the same Dr. Gerreau who runs a clinic out of Victory House, would you?"

"The same Dr. Gerreau with whom you were told to cooperate implicitly?"

Jaime nodded weakly, growing more miserable by the second.

"The same," he pronounced agreeably. "Cara brings her kids to me for their checkups. So far we haven't been able to do anything about getting Granny in, though."

Jaime was wretched with embarrassment, and more flustered than she had possibly ever been in her life. The best she could do was try to save what she could, and with a stern effort, she collected herself. She said in her most brisk, businesslike voice, "I'm Jaime Faber. Mrs. Franklin has a fever and chest congestion, and seems very weak. She won't let me call an ambulance. She says—" Jaime glanced at Cara. "She says she's under a spell."

"I told him that, girl," Cara said irritably, and pushed aside the curtain. "Now get out of the way and let the man do his job."

Jaime quickly stepped aside, and Quaid Gerreau, as he brushed against her skirt on the way past, winked at her.

Jaime hovered in the background, feeling like a child at an all-adult dinner party. She saw Quaid move toward the bed, speak a few gentle words to Pearlie and take his stethoscope from the safari-type bag on his shoulder. She noticed Pearlie's initial objections but she never quite saw how Quaid convinced the woman to allow him to examine her, because Jaime was too busy thinking over and over again, *A doctor!*

And not just any doctor, but the doctor from *her* new place of employment, which made him more or less her superior. Frantically she tried to remember whether or not she had insulted him that morning, but all she could really remember was his lazy, rather insolent grin, his musical drawl, and the way he had stood on the sidewalk in his faded jeans and tousled curls, looking her over with the same appreciative sweep of the eyes with which he had admired her automobile.

Above her embarrassment—or perhaps because of it—she was angry. How was *she* supposed to have guessed who he was? He didn't look like any doctor she had ever seen, and he certainly didn't act like one. Even now, sitting on Pearlie Franklin's bed, holding her hand and talking quietly with her, with his sleeves pushed up and his shirt unbuttoned, he looked like nothing more than a friend who'd stopped by for a casual visit. No, he didn't. He looked like a wind-blown, devil-may-care, rather appallingly sexy motorcyclist.

Quaid was saying to Pearlie seriously, "You got any idea who would want to put you under a spin?"

Pearlie shook her head against the pillow, moaning, "No, it's everywhere. The voodoo is everywhere. Ain't no use fighting it, it's just everywhere."

Quaid nodded and patted her hand. "You just take it easy for a bit, Miss Pearlie. I've got to think what to do."

"Bless you, young man, you're a sweet thing. But there ain't nothin' you can do for poor Pearlie. Not a thing in this world."

Quaid picked up his shoulder bag and stood, going over to Jaime. Anxious to be of help, Jaime inquired, "Do you want me to call an ambulance?"

Quaid shook his head thoughtfully. "No, that won't do."

"What's wrong with her? Is it pneumonia?"

Again he shook his head. "Voodoo," he said.

Jaime stared at him, for a moment speechless. When she did find her voice all she could say was, very carefully, "You're joking, right?"

He lifted his eyebrows in mild surprise. "Voodoo is serious business, *chérie*. Nothing to joke about." He pronounced the endearment as *cherry*, with a lilting inflection that was both sensual and charming.

For a moment Jaime felt herself drawn into the enchantment of his voice, then she whirled and started to push through the curtain. "I'm calling the hospital, right now."

He caught her arm lightly, his expression full of forbearance. "Ah, now, I wish you wouldn't go doing that. I've got enough problems with the board as it is, I don't need any more trouble. And believe me, there's nothing the hospital can do for Pearlie Franklin."

Jaime hesitated, looking at him closely. His eyes were green, she noticed. Emerald green. "Are you really a doctor?" she demanded suspiciously.

His lips quirked upward at one corner lazily. "Only the best that's ever been," he admitted modestly.

Jaime glanced at Pearlie and at Cara, who was sponging her grandmother's forehead solicitously, and then she lowered her voice deliberately. "You can't mean to tell me," she said distinctly, "that you really believe in this—voodoo nonsense."

"Why not? Next to Catholicism, it's the biggest religion in New Orleans." He pronounced New Orleans like a native—*No-luns*, with a melodious, lilting twang. It would be easy to be completely captivated by his drawl, if the things he said were not so outrageous.

Jaime swallowed hard, searching for some scraps of logic in a world in which reason seemed to be rapidly whipping away. "Well, I'm not a doctor," she began after a moment, "but even I can tell that poor woman is sick, and I don't think it has anything to do with a spell."

"Spin," he corrected absently. "It's called a spin." Then he frowned thoughtfully and turned back into the room. "Cara," he said, "where's your grandmother's hairbrush?"

Cara handed him a hairbrush from the rickety nightstand near the bed, and Jaime watched in growing incredulity as Quaid plucked a few hairs from it and deposited them in a small plastic bag he took from his satchel. *All right,* Jaime thought blearily, *this is it. I've walked through the looking glass and there's no turning back now....* But her amazement threshold was elevated another step as Quaid took a pair of suture scissors from his bag and carefully clipped two of Pearlie's fingernails. The clippings he placed in the plastic bag along with the hair.

But perhaps the worst part was the dawning hope that slowly broke through the pain on Pearlie Franklin's face. "Lordie, chile, you gonna find the witch doctor for old Pearlie? You gonna get her to take me out from under this voodoo?"

"I'm going to do my best, Miss Pearlie," Quaid assured her soberly. He placed the bag inside his satchel and buckled it. "I'll be back as soon as I can."

"Oh, praise be, praise be," intoned Pearlie, her face wreathed with joy as Quaid left the room.

Jaime followed him out. "Psychology?" she said hopefully, yet without much real hope.

"Nope." He arranged the strap of his bag diagonally across his shoulder and reached for his helmet. "Voodoo."

Jaime closed her eyes briefly and helplessly. Yet one more thing no one had bothered to teach her in social work school: what to do when the inmates take over the asylum.

When she released a small breath and opened her eyes again Quaid was looking at her with a peculiarly studious air. "Come on and go with me," he invited suddenly. "There's something I want you to see."

Jaime didn't have time to think about it even for a moment. "No, thank you." Quickly, she went for her purse. "I have other calls to make."

"They can wait."

"No they can't."

He laid his hand upon her arm again. Jaime had been fumbling through her purse for her list, but with his touch, she stopped. Even being around him made her nervous; when he touched her she felt positively quivery.

She raised her eyes to him and found he was grinning again. "Believe me, *chérie*, almost anything can wait down here," he drawled. "No sense in getting into too much of a hurry. It only drives the blood pressure up, and in this heat that can be downright dangerous."

Jaime swallowed and pulled her arm away. "I wish you wouldn't call me *chérie*."

"Sorry." The grin spread to a twinkle in his eyes. "Now, put your schedule down, Miss New York City, and let me show you a part of New Orleans you couldn't see any other way."

Jaime did not have to be an expert judge of human nature to realize that Quaid Gerreau was not the type of man one could expect to argue with, with any success, and it was beginning to sound as though she didn't have much choice. She was far too uncertain of her position at the settlement house—and of her standing in the eyes of this man in particular—to feel she could afford to put up much of a fight, but she did feel some show of independence was in order. She inquired politely, "Do I have to take orders from you?"

"Only when I give them," he replied easily. "Which, fortunately for all concerned, is seldom." He touched her shoulder and gestured toward the door. Resigned, Jaime preceded him.

"Hey, you!"

Jaime turned back and saw Cara glaring at her from the curtained partition. "You don't forget my coupons, you hear?"

Jaime mustered a smile. "Right. And your check, too. I'll look into it."

Cara looked satisfied, and turned back to her grandmother's room. Quaid opened the door and gestured Jaime out.

"I'm not riding the motorcycle," Jaime said as they stepped out onto the cracked sidewalk. A couple of teenage boys who were lounging against a graffiti-covered utility pole looked up suspiciously when they came out, but relaxed when they recognized Quaid.

"Yo, dudes!" Quaid called out to them. "Watch my bike, will you? It's around back."

"Sure thing, man," one answered. "You takin' me for a ride?"

Quaid cocked his thumb at him. "You got it, my man."

He tossed his helmet to the nearest boy and rested his hand on Jaime's shoulder, guiding her to the left. "It's not far. We can walk."

"If you tell me we're going to see a witch doctor I'm not moving another step," Jaime muttered.

"Okay, I won't tell you."

He kept his hand on her shoulder—not around her shoulders, as a man would generally walk with a woman, but just lightly cupping the shoulder nearest to him in a companionable gesture. It was easy to walk with Quaid like that; his steps were strolling, not striding, and he was just close enough to guide her without inhibiting her own movements. Being only five foot three herself, Jaime usually found it awkward to walk with a man, but Quaid was several inches under six feet and she felt comfortable beside him.

Or perhaps comfortable was not precisely the right word. Men who looked like he did—a little reckless, carelessly confident, haphazardly groomed and prone to winking and calling women *chérie*—seemed to wear their sexuality like a second skin, and that sort of blatant maleness never made Jaime comfortable. Add to that the incident with the car this morning and the fact that, as much as she would have liked it to be otherwise, he was undeniably good-looking in a primitive, unstructured way, and she had more than cause to be ill at ease with him.

She glanced at him cautiously. "You should have told me who you were this morning."

"So should you. If I'd known it was the newest member of our junior staff who was trying so hard to make a nuisance of herself, I might've even let you have the parking space. Daphene likes us to make a good first impression."

Jaime choked on laughter. "I'll be sure to report that you went out of your way for me this morning."

His eyes crinkled as he looked down at her. "You look young when you smile."

Jaime held his eyes for just a moment, and then she looked away. Her smile felt awkward as it faded.

"I meant it as a compliment," Quaid went on, obviously not knowing when to let a good thing drop. "Most of the time you look so studious and righteous it's downright depressing. You need to lighten up. Don't you know this is the 'City that Care Forgot'?"

"I hardly think you've known me long enough to judge whether I need to lighten up or not, Dr. Gerreau," she said stiffly, and he laughed. Too late she realized he had been baiting her, and she frowned in annoyance.

They were walking toward Esplanade again, and after a while crossed Jackson Square into the colorful, narrow streets of the French Quarter. The atmosphere was definitely much better appreciated by foot than by car, and soon Jaime began to relax and enjoy the view. Except for the heat, and her shoes—which were very fashionable but unfortunately not very comfortable on the uneven cobbled streets—she couldn't have asked for a more pleasant way to spend her first morning on the job. Except, of course, for Quaid Gerreau, whom she still couldn't quite figure out, and who still made her nervous.

After a time she decided to make another attempt at conversation. "How did you know I was from New York?"

"Oh, I know everything about you. Victory House is like a family, you know. Few secrets."

Jaime made a smug face. "Well, you don't know everything about me. I'm not really from New York at all. I just did my graduate work there."

"Oh?" He glanced at her, touching her elbow to guide her down a narrow alleyway that emerged on Basin Street. "Where are you from?"

She shrugged. "No place in particular."

"Everyone is from somewhere."

"Not me. I was born in the back of a van on a desert road in either California or Nevada—no one is really sure which. I answer the 'place of birth' question on application forms with 'unknown.' A curious distinction, at best."

Quaid seemed to think that over. "I like it," he decided.

Nothing more than that. Just "I like it." But hearing him say it made Jaime feel irrationally pleased with herself.

They walked down Basin Street, the birthplace of jazz, and New Orleans's original red-light district, and found little more of interest than housing projects and a series of memorials and statues to Latin-American heroes. Most of the tourists had dropped off, either due to the heat or the location, and with little else to distract her, Jaime found herself growing more and more aware of the man who walked beside her.

Now that she had a closer look at him, Jaime could see that his youthful appearance was not so much due to his face, which was nonetheless well structured and unlined, but to his manner. His cheekbones were high and the skin over them was taut, but there were definite laugh wrinkles around his eyes. The curly brown hair, which he wore brushed away from his face and long in back, waving in tendrils over his collar, added to his overall haphazard look, but if the scruff of whiskers on his lower face had been dark instead of blond he would have doubtless looked closer to thirty than twenty. His nose was delicate and straight, and his lips were full, but his mouth, too, was bracketed by faint lines that deepened when he smiled.

But it was his stance that had at first so deceived Jaime, his lean-muscled, slow-moving grace that seemed to exude hidden power and lazy sensuality. Those were not characteristics that Jaime had learned to associate with men of responsibility and authority, and it discomfited her when things—or people—could not be easily categorized.

She asked, "Have you lived here all your life?"

"As the old man was heard to reply when asked that same question—not yet, I haven't." He grinned at her in apology, then added, "I grew up here, if that's what you mean. The entire Quarter is my old neighborhood. I went to medical school in Atlanta, but always knew I'd come back home to practice."

"How long have you been running the clinic?"

"About three years now."

Jaime started to say something, but then thought better of it. Quaid, however, was quick to pick up on her swallowed words.

"You look disapproving," he said.

"Oh no," she answered quickly, and meant it. "Just—confused, I guess. There aren't too many doctors who would devote their lives to running a free clinic. I mean, medical school is awfully expensive and—well, how do you live?"

"One day at a time," he answered cheerfully. "Besides, it's not as though we have no income at all, you know. We get a lot of Medicare and Medicaide, and there are always my prescription kickbacks."

She stopped in mid-step to stare at him, and he chuckled, his eyes dancing merrily. "You *are* gullible, aren't you?"

Jaime scowled and picked up the step. "Not necessarily. It's just that having already learned of some of the ways Victory House collects money, I'm not sure I'd put anything past the realm of possibility."

"Oh-ho," he murmured. "I take it you've met Armand."

"That's right."

"I also take it you don't approve."

Jaime decided it might be in her best interest to pass on that for the time being, and she walked faster.

"Whoa!" He caught her shoulder. "Slow down. You're about to walk right past it."

Jaime looked around, and then at him, and then, with a sinking feeling of dismay, around again. *"Here?"*

Quaid only smiled. "That's right."

Jaime looked left and right, and finally, with a frustrated breath of resignation, straight ahead again. There was no mistake, and she should have known better.

They were standing right in front of the St. Louis Cemetery.

Chapter Three

Jaime said flatly, "Very funny, Dr. Gerreau. You took me away from my job, brought me all the way out here—you even made it sound like an order—just to visit a cemetery?"

He replied blandly, "Where better to go in search of a voodoo cure?"

"Oh, for heaven's sake!" She started to turn away, but he caught her arm. His eyes were twinkling.

"Come on," he insisted. "I want to show you something."

"I've had enough of your macabre sense of humor," she said, pulling her arm away, "I'm going back to work."

"You *are* working," Quaid reminded her. "Didn't Daphene tell you that part of your job is to help out in the clinic whenever you're needed? We all pitch in."

"We are not in the clinic," Jaime replied coolly, "and I have other people who need me. *Living* people, I might add." She swept a disdainful glance around the cemetery, which spoke more eloquently than words about what she thought Quaid Gerreau's idea of a joke.

It looked like a miniature walled city, with tiny, round-roofed houses for crypts, and narrow paths winding throughout like streets. The air of something ancient and mysterious hung over it like a pall, despite the tourists who wandered through it, singularly or in groups. Jaime did not think it looked like a very inviting place at all, and she had no intention of spending her first morning on the job exploring it.

Quaid's eyes were dancing with laughter, but he made an effort to restrain himself. "All right, I'll stop teasing you," he promised. "But you've come this far, you may as well see one of our foremost tourist attractions." He took her elbow. "Not afraid, are you?"

Jaime scowled defensively. "Of course not."

And, having said that, she could hardly refuse to accompany him inside. She wasn't afraid, not really. But she knew the only reason she had been so sharp with him earlier was because she was—well, uncomfortable. She had never liked cemeteries. Or ghosts or séances or Ouija boards, either. Even in broad daylight the shadowed lanes seemed heavy with menace, the silent crypts poised for unpleasant surprises. She kept darting her eyes around to make sure the movements she saw were from natural causes. She didn't like this at all.

Quaid escorted her through the gates with a hand firmly on her elbow as though he expected her to bolt at any moment. "The cemeteries around here are called Cities of the Dead," he explained in a tourguide tone. "I suppose you can see why. You'd be surprised how many people, on one level or another, believe the dead really live here, though, going about their business of eating, drinking and being merry just like you and me. I suppose you know why all the burial grounds in New Orleans are aboveground?''

''Because the ground is too soggy to hold a casket,'' she replied impatiently, not wanting to encourage him.

Quaid Gerreau did not require much encouragement, a fact she should have discerned long before now. ''Most of the time the graves would fill with water even before they could get the casket in,'' he agreed. ''And come the first rain, those boxes would rise to the top and break open, flooding the streets with bones and human remains...somewhat to the dismay of early New Orleanians, I would imagine. With a history like that, is it any wonder there's so much superstition left over in the collective unconscious?''

All that talk of bones and human remains was, of course, exactly what Jaime needed to put her mind at ease. She glanced around nervously, but managed to keep her tone light as she replied, ''Is this a lesson in culture and philosophy?''

His eyes glinted with approval. ''More or less. You can't really serve the community until you know it, don't you agree?''

Jaime glanced uneasily at the swaying branches of a huge oak overhead. She hadn't felt a breeze. ''This is all very interesting, Dr. Gerreau, but if we have to do this could we do it quickly?''

''There you go, getting in a hurry again. I told you that was bad for you.''

Something about his easy, laconic tone made Jaime suspect that he knew exactly what her real reason for hurrying was, and embarrassment shortened her tone.

"I *do* have other things on my schedule, as you know very well."

The glance he slanted on her was mocking. "Are you always so organized?"

"Yes," she answered without qualm. "It makes life much easier."

He shook his head sadly. "You *do* have a lot to learn."

She sighed. "Dr. Gerreau, I've been around the world more times than you have been around the block. While I don't deny I may have a lot to learn, I *don't* think I necessarily need to learn it in a cemetery."

Some part of Jaime was appalled to hear herself speaking that way to a superior—and on such short acquaintance—but it was easy to forget that Quaid Gerreau was someone to whom she should defer. And he hardly seemed to notice.

"Funny thing about cemeteries," he mused, "most people, no matter how modern and practical they claim to be, are nervous about walking through them. Especially a cemetery as old as this. Imagine the tales if these vaults could talk."

Jaime said quickly, "I'm not nervous. Just—busy." But she did not object when he rested his hand on her shoulder again, and when he smiled at her she knew that further pretending was futile. "Well," she admitted uncomfortably, "not very nervous, anyway."

The gentle smile lines around his eyes deepened with approval, and he squeezed her shoulder. She felt better.

"Look." They were walking along the outer wall, and Quaid gestured to the rows of names inscribed upon it. "This is where some of the poor are buried. They're called ovens."

"They're buried inside the walls?" Despite herself, Jaime was fascinated.

He nodded. "Burial space is at a premium hereabouts, as you can imagine." His thumb made an unconscious stroking motion against the back of her neck, and Jaime's skin prickled. His fingers were strong, yet smooth on the surface, flowing gently over her perspiration-dampened skin.

To distract herself—and him—from what she was sure was a purely unintentional sensual gesture, she moved away a little, pretending to read some of the names. There was a long list on almost every one of the concrete slabs. "Are all these people buried in one tomb?"

"Not at the same time," he explained, with a touch of amusement in his tone. "We have a very efficient way of dealing with overpopulated cemeteries. After a few years the old remains are removed and new ones placed in the same oven. Some people even say Marie Laveau herself is buried in one of these ovens—not here, but at the St. Louis II, over on Conti. People keep coming back and painting red crosses on the wall where she's supposed to be, and that's become a tourist attraction, too."

Jaime straightened up. "Marie who?"

His eyebrow shot up. "My, your education has been neglected, hasn't it? Marie Laveau, only the most powerful voodoo queen who ever lived."

"I might have known," Jaime murmured.

He caught her hand. "Come on, I'll show you where she's really buried."

"But I don't—"

"It's on the way," he insisted, tugging on her hand.

Jaime did not ask "On the way to where?" because she felt the question would be futile. And she did not try to pull away from his hand because... well, because she liked the way it felt, wrapped around hers.

Aside from his other, more notable characteristics, Quaid Gerreau was one of the most spontaneous men Jaime had ever known. He made instant decisions, he spoke his mind, he touched without inhibition; he was in all ways natural, unrestrained and unaffected. Yet instead of finding these characteristics warm and endearing, Jaime was intimidated by them. She suspected it would be all too easy to take this man more seriously than he was meant to be taken, and she knew she would have to be on her guard around him if they were to spend much time working together.

He took her down twisting paths beneath moss-draped oaks, through landscaped gardens surrounding miniature mansions, along shadowed trails and past dark, silent monuments. There was no doubt about it, even in broad daylight, this place was spooky. Jaime was embarrassed to find herself clutching his hand, rather than the other way around.

He stopped at last in front of a simple tomb inscribed in French, which Jaime translated to mean, "Marie Laveau, deceased June 11, 1897." There was another couple before the crypt, apparently tourists, from the animated discussion they were having over whether or not this was the right crypt, and Quaid waited until they had moved on to step forward.

"Very nice," Jaime murmured politely, as some comment seemed to be expected from her. In fact, she felt no particular magical emanations from the tomb, and it looked very much like any other of the older

burial places. The only unusual thing she did notice
was a small artifact laid upon the ledge of the crypt,
which appeared to be a chicken bone with a string tied
around it.

She pointed it out to Quaid. "What's that?"

"Gris-gris," he replied. "Some people believe that
if you leave an artifact on Marie Leveau's tomb overnight, then place it on the doorstep of the person you
want to influence, it will absorb some of the magic and
work voodoo from the grave."

Jaime shivered.

Then she remembered the fingernail clippings and
hair he had taken from Pearlie Franklin. She looked
at him slowly, almost afraid to ask. "You're not going
to...?"

For a moment he seemed puzzled, and then he
laughed. "No, I don't have much faith in magic twice
removed. I have a much better plan." He caught her
hand again. "Come on."

They emerged on the opposite side of the cemetery
from which they had entered, on a narrow street that
was unfamiliar to Jaime. The houses were the small,
one-story shotgun type, built close together with
scrappy handkerchief lawns. Some of them were in an
appalling state of disrepair, some of them were
brightly painted and more or less well kept.

Jaime's legs were tired from so much walking, and
she wondered what Quaid considered too far to walk
if he thought this was an easy jaunt. She had done a
lot of walking in New York, but not in new shoes with
narrow heels that kept catching in the uneven pave-
ment. The second time she stumbled, Quaid caught
her elbow and suggested, "I would think a rich young

lady like you would own at least one good pair of Reeboks."

"I do," she admitted shortly, "but I thought I could pack them away forever when I left New York. Furthermore..." She fixed Quaid with a steady gaze. "I am not rich. I earn my own way. Or at least I try to," she had to add honestly, for although she never accepted money from her mother she did accept other things. "Life-style improvements," her mother called them, and they could range from a designer dress to a microwave oven to—a pair of Reeboks. Jaime had never felt self-conscious about that, until now.

But Quaid merely murmured, bland-faced, "Sorry." And Jaime felt as though she should be embarrassed for being too sensitive.

"Here we are." Quaid crossed a short patch of lawn to a bright yellow house with a red door.

All the curtains were drawn and the place looked deserted. A pair of cowbells was suspended from a hook on the top part of the door, surrounded by a wreath composed of what appeared to be weeds wound around a collection of small wooden dolls and miniature masks. Already Jaime knew she didn't want to know what lay behind that door.

The cowbells clattered loudly as Quaid pushed open the door, and when Jaime stepped inside, her dreads were confirmed.

The room was dim, and cloyingly hot, and thick with the incense of dried herbs and musty age. It was an attic smell, of crisp timber and yellowing papers, things preserved in cedar and things cast aside to decay. The place looked like an attic, as well, or perhaps a cave—a cave of horrors.

It was crowded with small, scarf-covered tables and low chests upon which were scattered multicolored vials and bottles containing ingredients Jaime dared not examine too closely. The walls were hung with painted masks that could well be called works of art— as well as some things that were not so aesthetically appealing, such as shrunken heads, mummified animals, and lengths of what appeared to be human hair. There was a veritable plethora of statuettes and totems, some animal, some human and some in between. The only light, save that which filtered through the thick curtains, was from a candle flickering on a brass stand. The light the candle cast was swaying and erratic, causing shadows to leap from nowhere and the eyes upon the walls to glint with malice. Despite the heat, gooseflesh appeared on Jaime's arms. This was almost too much for one day.

Quaid called out, "Miss Mame! Company in the front room!"

Given the surroundings, Jaime had reason to expect a suitably dramatic appearance from the person they had come to see. The woman who came through the beaded curtain at the back of the room with a whisper of silk fabric and a tinkling of jewelry did not disappoint her. She was dark-skinned, dark-haired and ageless. She was largely, almost ponderously, built, and exotic from head to foot.

She wore a long purple and gold caftan and a paisley shawl. Her arms were laden with bracelets—some ivory, some metal, and some of indefinable, almost organic-looking material—and her dangling earrings appeared to be made of small bones. Her generous bosom was draped over with row upon row of necklaces—tiny bells, woven fabric, copper, and other, less easily recognizable items. She stood for a moment framed by the gently swaying beaded curtain, her face severe and her gaze piercing, looking precisely like what anyone who had ever seen a late-night movie would expect a voodoo queen to look like.

But there the theatrics ended, and what she did next was not at all what Jaime expected. Her stern face creased with a smile, she opened her arms wide, and she exclaimed in the warm, mellifluous tones of a native Cajun, "Quaid, you naughty boy! You been away too long. You come here and give Mame a big hug!"

Quaid embraced the woman, laughing, and she patted him heartily on the back. When they parted, Mame looked at Jaime shrewdly. "You bring a stranger to me. You never do dat before, Quaid."

Quaid said, "Jaime Faber, this is Mame LeCaree. Jaime works with me," he explained to Mame.

"Work! Bah!" Mame made a curt dismissing gesture. "Your work is nonsense, and so be hers. No good at all."

Jaime said, determined not to let the woman intimidate her, "Quaid is a doctor, and I'm a social worker. We try to do a great deal of good, and I think we succeed."

Mame gave her a penetrating look. "Then why you come to Mame?" she demanded.

Jaime opened her mouth to reply, but Quaid interrupted smoothly, "Jaime just wanted to meet you. I came to ask your help."

Mame nodded imperiously, a glint of satisfaction in her eyes. "Ah, as I said. Your work is nothing without you ask Mame for help."

Jaime said firmly, "Really, Dr. Gerreau, this has gone far enough. A joke is a joke, but it's almost noon and I have a full day ahead of me. Ms LeCaree..." She stepped forward, her hand extended. "It's been a pleasure meeting you, and I'm very impressed by your..." She glanced uncertainly around the room. "Everything."

Mame looked at her with narrowed eyes, ignoring her hand. "Who is dis child?" she demanded of Quaid.

"You'll have to pardon her," Quaid explained gently. "She doesn't understand."

Jaime was getting tired of hearing him make excuses for her. And she was more anxious than ever to be back in a nice, safe, ordinary working environment. "I understand," she said, "all I need to. This is all very quaint and picturesque, but if you think for one moment you're going to convince me that—"

"This won't take a minute," Quaid said deliberately, and it seemed to Jaime there was a distinct warning in his eyes. It was enough to cause Jaime to bite back the rest of her sentence and retreat into a polite—though hard-fought—silence. She had taken enough liberties with Dr. Gerreau today as it was, and she was beginning to suspect this all might just be part of an elaborate test: how well she worked with deranged personalities, for example.

Quaid said, "What I wanted to see you about, Miss Mame, was a patient of mine..."

He slipped his arm around Mame LeCaree's shoulders and turned her away, speaking quietly to her. After a moment, with some obvious reluctance, Mame stopped glaring at Jaime and began to listen to Quaid.

Jaime busied herself by looking idly around the cluttered little room, until the characteristics of the various talismans and fetishes became a bit too gruesome for her. Her uneasiness mounted, and she began to fidget. What was she doing in this bizarre place with a doctor who wore faded jeans and rode a motorcycle, trying to be polite while he recited the medical symptoms of one of his patients to a witch doctor? This was not at all what she had had in mind through four years of college and two grueling years working nights in a New York hospital while she obtained her master's degree. This was definitely not what she had expected when she had applied for the job at one of the most highly recommended community centers in New Orleans. Once again, probably irrationally, she felt she had her mother to blame.

Mame LeCaree exclaimed disdainfully, *"Oui, chérie,* it is bad stuff, what happens when them that don't know go messin' wid ze voodoo.'' She cast a dark, purposeful look toward Jaime, which Jaime felt was underserved. Then she turned back to Quaid. "Don't you worry none, chile, I fix you up fine.'' She held out her hand. "Let me see what you got.''

Quaid obligingly reached into his satchel and brought out the bag containing Pearlie's hair and fingernail clippings.

Jaime moved closer, hardly able to believe her eyes, as Mame LeCaree took the bag from Quaid and busied herself pouring unpleasant looking concoctions from a variety of vials into a small clay pot on the table. Jaime stared at Quaid. "Don't tell me you're serious.''

He replied mildly, "Would I have brought you all the way out here if I weren't?''

"But—but this is ridiculous!''

She watched, wide-eyed, as Mame, with much jingling of jewelry and flamboyant gestures, sprinkled the hair and fingernail clippings over the potion in the bowl and began to stir it with her fingers, mumbling to herself. She turned back to Quaid.

"This—this is like something out of the Dark Ages!" she exclaimed. "I can't believe I'm seeing this!"

He smiled smugly. "I thought you'd be impressed."

"Impressed!" She almost choked on an incredulous breath. "I'm—I'm speechless!"

"Not so that you could tell," Quaid murmured.

"You can't really believe in this garbage," she demanded, trying hard to keep her voice under control. "Tell me you don't really think this—this witch doctor—"

"You hush!" Mame LeCaree said so sharply that Jaime jumped. "Stop you' chattering. You' messing up my spin."

Quaid took Jaime's arm and led her away from the worktable.

Jaime looked at him, uncertain whether she was more horrified or disappointed. Until now it had been a joke—a rather twisted one, to be sure, but she had been willing to go along with it to a point. Now she was terribly afraid he was serious, and despite whatever else Quaid Gerreau might be, Jaime had wanted to believe that he was at least a dedicated doctor.

"I can't believe you're doing this," she said lowly. "You're supposed to be an educated man, a *doctor* for heaven's sake! You can't really expect me to believe you're going to treat your patient with voodoo instead of antibiotics, that you'd walk out on a sick patient and come back with nothing more than a bottle full of mumbo jumbo and expect her to get well! I know you're a little strange, but this is going too far."

He merely murmured mildly, "There are more things in heaven and earth, my dear Miss Faber . . ."

"Here," pronounced Mame imperiously. She strained the mixture in the bowl through a piece of gauze, and poured it into a small blue bottle. She stoppered the bottle with a flourish and handed it to Quaid. "You sprinkle this over the sick woman three times, left to right. Then you burn the bedclothes to cinders. She be up and crowing in no time at all."

Quaid smiled at her as he tucked the vial into his bag. "Thank you, Miss Mame. What do I owe you?"

Jaime's mouth dropped open.

"Ah you don' owe me nothin', sweet thing," Mame beamed. "You know I help you out anytime."

"Then let me pay you with a kiss." Quaid took her shoulders and kissed one cheek, then the other. "That's a down payment on the next time."

Mame stroked his cheek affectionately. "You' kisses like sweet wine, Quaid Gerreau. You come back anytime."

"This is the craziest thing I've ever seen," Jaime murmured incredulously. "And I lived in New York!"

Mame turned a sharp glare on her. "You got a wicked mouth, young one. You need to learn respect for powers you don't know."

Jaime did not bother to reply to that. She turned to Quaid. "Can we go now?"

Quaid cast an apologetic glance toward Mame, and gestured Jaime to precede him.

Jaime was almost to the door when she caught a movement out of the corner of her eye. She turned sharply and saw Mame LeCaree sprinkling a fine blue powder over the floor behind Jaime. She was mumbling to herself as she waved her arm in an arc over the place Jaime had walked, letting the powder drift down.

Jaime looked at Quaid suspiciously. "What's she doing?"

Quaid gave a small grimace, which could have been construed as regretful or resigned, and quickly ushered Jaime out the door. Mame LeCaree followed her all the way to the street.

"What is she doing?" Jaime demanded again, twisting around to look at Mame. Quaid had a firm hold on her elbow and was walking very fast.

"She's cursing your footsteps."

"She's *what*?"

"Cursing your footsteps. That means that wherever you go, troubles will follow."

For a moment Jaime was nonplussed. No one had ever put a curse on her before. She didn't know whether to be honored or insulted.

"But," she managed at last, "that's absurd!"

Quaid slowed down a little as they turned the corner. "I wouldn't worry about it too much. Miss Mame is a wise woman, and she knows you don't mean any real harm. She just wants to teach you a lesson. I don't think she'll give you any big troubles."

Jaime looked at him, and then she couldn't help it. She burst out laughing.

Quaid seemed to enjoy her laughter. The small lines that radiated toward his temples deepened, and his eyes took on a light-refracting, bubbly hue. For the first time, Jaime felt relaxed with him.

"Thank you," she said, when the laughter had died to chuckles, "for introducing me to New Orleans."

"Why, *chérie*," he said lazily, "I haven't even started yet." A smile slid across his face as his arm slipped around her shoulders. "Before I'm done you'll know this town like a native."

His touch, and the suggestive, appreciative glint in his eyes successfully dampened the remnants of Jaime's amusement. Her throat grew tight with awareness of his nearness, and for a moment she had difficulty moving her eyes away from his and the gentle pleasure she saw there.

Then, to break the moment and disguise her confusion, she started walking again. "But do we have to do it all in one day?" she said brightly.

"Of course not. That would spoil the fun." His hand caressed her upper arm, and her skin was tingling where he touched. "New Orleans is an experience to be savored slowly, like a seven-course meal . . . or like the way you look when you smile."

Jaime thought, *Oh-oh*. She might be mistaken, but that sounded very much like a come-on to her. And though she was usually very adroit at fielding—or encouraging—such things, she simply hadn't expected it from Quaid Gerreau. She didn't know quite how to react.

But perhaps that was only wishful thinking, because when she glanced at him there was nothing on his face but the same easygoing friendliness that had been there all morning. When they crossed the street, Quaid dropped his arm from around her shoulders, and Jaime thought she was relieved. Secretly, and much to her annoyance, the relief was mitigated by a thread of disappointment.

But who was she kidding? The man was a nut. He was eccentric, unprofessional and possibly even a hazard both to the community he served and the medical profession at large. It didn't matter how sexy he was or how flustered his touch made her, he definitely was not her type. Worse yet, she had to work with the man, and she could hardly do that if her blood pressure shot up—either from outrage or excitement—every time he looked at her. As Quaid Gerreau had pointed out himself, such exertion in this heat could be detrimental to the health.

Thus resolved she took a breath and began, "Dr. Gerreau—"

"Quaid. Everybody calls me Quaid."

"Dr. Gerreau," she continued firmly, and he lifted an amused eyebrow, "I want to apologize if I was too... well, outspoken before. I don't want us to get off on the wrong foot. It's just that I take my work very seriously and I expect others to do the same. I didn't mean to insult your friend, or..." She glanced at him hesitantly. "You."

"Too late," he replied mildly. "The spin is cast, there's no taking it back now. The only hope I see for you at all is to stay as close to me as possible."

She looked at him, once again thrown into confusion. Here she was, trying to make a mature apology and do her very best to put their relationship on a professional, or at least semiprofessional, basis, and he was making jokes again. Or making a pass at her; she wasn't quite sure which.

She said cautiously, "What do you mean?"

"This." He reached into his T-shirt and pulled out a necklace. It was a twisted black cord from which was suspended a small wooden doll, painted black, with a fierce looking face like those often found on totem poles. The two jewels set into its eyes looked like emeralds. "It's a charm to ward off evil spirits and protect me from bad spins," he explained. "As long as you're around me, you should be protected, too."

"Oh, for goodness' sake!"

Frustrated beyond speech, she whirled to cross the street, only to feel Quaid's hand jerking her rudely back up on the curb as a car sped by with a gush of air and a blaring horn.

"See what I mean?" Quaid said innocently.

Shaken from the close call, Jaime took a moment to collect her breath and her thoughts. When she could speak calmly again, she said, "Will you do me a favor?"

"I just saved your life, what more could you want?"

She ignored that. "Let's just stop with the voodoo talk, all right? It was cute for a while, and I imagine you get a lot of kicks from impressing tourists and college kids that way, but I'm not either one and to tell the truth it's starting to get a little old."

Quaid took her arm, checked for traffic and crossed the street. "You don't have to be embarrassed," he said, when they reached the other side. "Most people are afraid of what they don't understand."

Jaime released a low, long-suffering sigh. "I am not afraid," she said clearly. "I'm simply not impressed."

"Then why are you so hostile?"

"I'm not hostile. I'm—disapproving."

"You seem to disapprove a lot."

Jaime frowned. She hadn't meant to appear that way, but she supposed from his point of view she had done nothing but disapprove from their first meeting.

He went on easily, "So why, exactly, do you disapprove?"

"Of the practice of voodoo?" Her voice rose on a note of incredulity. "I should think that would be fairly obvious!"

"Moral or religious objections aside—" he cocked his head toward her inquiringly, and she gave a dismissing scowl "—I can't think of a single reason why you would object to a harmless superstition that has been going on uninterrupted in this part of the country for over two hundred years. So enlighten me."

It should have been very easy to do so, but in fact his question was more complicated than it first appeared. "I'm not going out of my way to be narrow-minded," she said after a moment, wanting him to understand. "I realize that a certain amount of—cultural tolerance is necessary in my position. But this voodoo business is *not* harmless, and that's the whole point, don't you see? Part of my job is to help people take responsibility for their own lives, to take control and interact positively with whatever circumstances are given them, and as long as they continue to fall back on pointless superstitions they're just taking an easy out. We're talking education, here, motivation, a willingness to learn to live in an organized society.... None of that is possible as long as these people are encouraged to believe every misfortune can be traced back to somebody sticking pins into little dolls, and *that's* the harm in it. Do you understand that?"

He was listening to her intently, and his expression was sober and studious. In fact, he was looking at her so closely that Jaime felt a little uneasy, wondering if her impassioned speech might have sounded too naive and idealistic for a man like Quaid Gerreau.

But he only said quietly, after a moment, "Yes. I understand." Then he smiled. "Do *you* understand that my job is to heal the sick, and I don't care how I do it?"

It seemed a very personal moment as they stood on the corner of a busy street with people jostling and laughing and pushing by, looking into each other's eyes and trying to communicate to each other two very important and perfectly opposing points of view. It was a moment that asked as much as it received; a moment in which differences were respected as much as accentuated, and that could draw them closer as easily as push them apart. Jaime, drawn into the gentle smile in his eyes, would have agreed to anything he said just then.

She smiled, and nodded, and a peculiar kind of tentative pact was sealed between them just then.

He put his hand on her shoulder, and they walked across to Jackson Square.

IT WAS NOON and the crowd was beginning to thin out as wise people sought the shelter of cool indoor restaurants for one of the day's three most important meals. But the square was still well-populated by street artists and strolling musicians, as well as a good number of people on their way to or from, or pausing to take their lunch in the garden. The interlude was over, and despite the fact that the time spent away from her work had been more demanding—and far more stressful—than what she had actually been assigned, Jaime still had a list of calls to make. She had no intention of disappointing Daphene Campion on her first day at work.

Jaime said, "I suppose you'll be going back to the Franklin's apartment right away?"

"That's right. Are you hungry?"

"No, thanks." That was a lie, of course. Jaime was always hungry. She had long avowed that she could look like Jane Fonda with no effort at all if she weren't always so *hungry*. "As long as you're going to check on Mrs. Franklin again, I'll wait until tomorrow to go back."

He slanted an amused look at her. "So you trust me that much, do you?"

She sighed. "Look, I know I have a tendency to be little aggressive at times..."

He pretended disbelief. "Is that right?"

"But I don't mean to be hard to get along with. It's just that growing up the way I did, having strong opinions about things was almost a matter of self-defense."

He stopped by a vendor and ordered two hot dogs. "You were raised to be opinionated and narrow-minded?"

She laughed. "Just the opposite. My mother went with a very liberated crowd. No one had an opinion on *anything*. Everything was esoteric or existential, nothing was concrete. But children have to have *some* ground rules, so I made my own. And stuck to them... loudly, sometimes," she admitted wryly.

He paid for the hot dogs, and handed one to her. "Oh, no, really..." she protested.

"Eat," he insisted. "That's one of the few tenets of traditional medicine I adhere to. Man cannot live by stimulating conversation alone."

Jaime did not need much persuasion, and she bit into the mustard-covered hot dog gratefully.

"So," he commented as they started walking again, "the original rebel without a cause, are you?"

She was surprised. "Rebel? Me? My mother would kiss you for saying that—if she didn't die laughing first! No, believe me, a rebel is the last thing I ever wanted to be, much to Mother's disappointment, I'm sorry to say."

"I take it your mother had grander plans for her finest work of art than to see you working in an inner city slum."

Jaime shrugged. "It's not that so much. It's not that she has anything particularly against social work—although I must say she's always been more interested in saving the whales than the human race—it's just that she isn't fond of taking a traditional approach to solving any problem." Jaime glanced at him shrewdly. "Much like someone else I know."

He pretended astonishment. "Who, me?"

"Exactly."

"Your mother sounds like an interesting person." He finished off his hot dog and wiped his hands on a napkin. "I'd like to meet her."

"Why? Because I said she reminds me of you?"

"Partly," he admitted with a grin. "And partly..." He surprised her by reaching forward and touching the corner of her lips with his napkin, wiping away a small smudge of mustard. His eyes seemed to soften. "Because she gave birth to you."

Jaime felt color warm her cheeks and her heart beat a trifle faster. She couldn't hold his gaze and she looked away quickly. She was no longer very hungry at all.

She said brightly, for lack of anything better, "Well, I don't think you'll get a chance to meet her anytime soon. She's in South America somewhere, painting ruins."

"That's okay, I've got the next best thing. Her daughter."

He was still looking at her in that peculiarly warm, assessing way, and Jaime still couldn't meet his eyes for more than a shy second. She didn't know what to say. She didn't know what to make of Quaid Gerreau at all. Did he never do anything that was expected?

They passed a trash can and she tossed the remainder of her hot dog inside, busily wiping her mouth and her fingers with the napkin first. "Well," she said with forced enthusiasm, "I guess it's back to work."

Quaid draped his arm around her shoulders companionably. "You know, you're not at all like I expected."

She couldn't resist. She glanced up at him. "What did you expect?"

"A Radcliffe accent, for one. Givenchy suits. A discreet little Rolex."

She laughed. "Thank heavens I disappointed you."

"Well, not entirely," he disagreed mildly. "That outfit you're wearing might look like it came out of a rummage sale, but I'll bet my last button it's got a designer label inside. And you're just as stuffy and uptight as any New England boarding school could want, but you're also funny and mule stubborn and, all things considered, you don't complain very much. And do you know something else?"

Jaime was just about to pull away in irritation when he bent another one of his gentle, thoughtful looks on her. "I think I'm beginning to like you," he said.

Jaime drew a breath to say something but let it fall empty, because she didn't know what to say and her throat felt so odd she wasn't sure she could speak, anyway. She gave him a weak, uncertain little smile, and he smiled back easily. They continued walking toward the Franklin's apartment building in what some might have considered a comfortable silence.

But it wasn't comfortable at all, for Jaime's thoughts were filled with tension and conflicting emotions. The trouble was, she was afraid she was beginning to like him, too. And that wouldn't do. Not at all.

Chapter Four

It was six o'clock when Jaime finished making her calls and arrived back at the settlement house. Daphene was just coming out of the office when Jaime reached the top of the stairs, a little breathless from hurrying.

"Well," Daphene declared, "we were beginning to think we'd have to send a search party after you. It would be a pity to have you meet with misfortune on your first day on the job."

Jaime remembered Mame LeCaree's curse and smiled. "It seems to me I had most of my misfortune before I ever actually started my job. I'm sorry to take so long. I got sidetracked."

Daphene smiled as she locked the door. "So I hear. You met our Dr. Gerreau, did you?"

"Yes. He's—" she chose her words carefully "—quite a character."

Daphene's dark eyes twinkled. "So he is. And the best thing to happen to this neighborhood since Jean Lafitte. He was quite a hero around here, you know."

"Dr. Gerreau?"

"Jean Lafitte. Most people think of him as a ruthless pirate, but he helped us win the war of

1812...come to think of it, there is a parallel there. Between Quaid and Jean Lafitte, that is. Both rascals, both Robin Hoods under the skin. Come on, I'll walk you out."

Jaime would have liked to hear more about Dr. Gerreau, but she thought she had best stick to business. That particular man had distracted her enough for one day. "Well, actually, I still have these reports to type up..."

Daphene looked blank. "What reports?"

"On the calls I made. As a matter of fact, I did discover one or two things..."

Daphene laughed. "Quaid said you were a stickler for detail. Well, you never mind about that tonight, honey." She linked her arm through Jaime's companionably. "You've had a long day."

Jaime assumed Daphene simply did not want to open up the office again, and she made a mental note to get her paperwork done before six o'clock from now on. "I suppose it can wait until morning," she agreed. "I'll just write up my notes at home tonight. I don't know where the forms are anyway."

Daphene chuckled again. "Then you're not the only one. As I told you, we're pretty loose around here. I'm sorry you didn't get much of an orientation today; we'll try to take it easier tomorrow."

"I do have a lot of questions," Jaime admitted.

"Good," responded Daphene cheerfully. "I have a lot of answers. And I'd love to give them to you over dinner, but I have a date. Quaid!" she called as they reached the front hallway.

He was just pushing open the outside door as they rounded the corner, and he paused to hold the door for them. "Evening, ladies. Quitting time already?"

"I see you're not letting any moss grow under your feet," Daphene teased him.

"I've been here since ten o'clock," he retorted playfully. "What do you want from me?" Though he was speaking to Daphene, he was looking at Jaime. That uncertain, quivering sensation started inside her stomach again.

"I swear you keep the laziest hours of any doctor in New Orleans," Daphene told him. "And what I want from you now is to take this young lady out to dinner. She has some questions, and I have a date."

Jaime was too startled to protest as Daphene gave her a gentle push forward, and a slow grin spread over Quaid's face. "Why, my pleasure, Miz Campion."

"Don't take any smart talk from him," Daphene advised, "and if he gets fresh, just slap his hand. He responds very well to ordinary behavior modification techniques. Ta-ta, all!" With a wave of her hand, she swept through the door, leaving Jaime standing alone in the hall with Quaid Gerreau.

They both spoke at once.

"Shall we go?" said Quaid.

And Jaime said, "You really don't have to—"

She broke off with an embarrassed laugh, and he gestured her to finish. "I'm not going to hold you to dinner. I'm really too hot and tired to go out tonight, and I have work to do at home, and . . ."

"And you haven't quite made up your mind whether or not you approve of me," he finished for her.

Her startled eyes flew to his even as she felt her cheeks start to tingle. "Why—why, no! That's not—"

"Come on, Miss Faber, your honesty was one of the first things I admired about you."

Jaime murmured uncomfortably, "There's a difference between honesty and tact." And he laughed as he held open the door for her.

"How is Mrs. Franklin?" Jaime asked quickly as they walked outside.

"She was up baking cookies when I left her," Quaid responded cheerfully.

Jaime stared at him. "You mean she was faking?"

"How could she be faking?" he insisted. "You saw her. That was one sick woman."

"But—what happened?"

"Miss Mame's potion, that's what."

Jaime looked at him very closely, trying to discern the truth behind those mild green eyes. "Are you telling the truth?" she demanded at last.

"You're welcome to go see for yourself."

"You can bet I will," Jaime muttered.

She walked slowly toward her car, trying to absorb this. No matter how eccentric Quaid was, she didn't really think he'd lie about his patient's condition, or leave her without treatment. But if he was telling the truth...

"I never heard of a psychosomatic fever before," she murmured after a time.

"Happens all the time," Quaid assured her. "My mother, for example, goes to bed with a fever every time I miss Sunday dinner. Which of course assures that I'm there for Sunday supper and a miraculous recovery. Not of course," he added, "that I'm suggesting that was the case with Pearlie Franklin."

Jaime didn't even bother to ask what he was suggesting. She was also too tired to argue.

She took out her keys as she reached her car. "Well," she said, "it's certainly been an interesting— my car!"

The last was a gasp of dismay as she stared at her car. "Someone stole my hubcaps! In broad daylight, someone walked right up and stole my hubcaps!"

Quaid walked around the car thoughtfully, examining each wheel. "They certainly did," he pronounced at last. Then he smiled at her. "Looks like you just lost yourself a parking place."

"You knew this would happen!" she exclaimed. "You—"

"I," he reminded her, "tried to warn you."

She had no answer for that.

Jaime spotted a slip of paper underneath the windshield wiper and snatched it off. She could hardly believe what she read. "It's a parking ticket!" The words were choked with incredulity. "I got a parking ticket!"

He looked meaningfully at the way the back fender protruded into the street. "Well, what do you expect?"

"But you're the one—!" She let the sentence die in outrage and defeat. "Never mind," she muttered, twisting the key in the lock. "Just never mind."

"Are you sure you won't reconsider dinner and a chance to take your mind off your troubles?"

"No thanks. The way my luck is running today I'll probably get food poisoning."

Quaid lifted an innocent eyebrow. "Luck? Sounds more like a little old-fashioned voodoo to me."

Jaime wasn't even going to begin to get into that. She got into the car and inserted the key into the ignition. "I am going home," she said firmly. "I am going to pour myself a glass of wine, get into a bubble bath, and read a good book. I'll see you tomorrow, Dr. Gerreau."

She turned the ignition key, and nothing happened. She tried again, and again. There was no response except a feeble click. Alarmed, she pumped the gas pedal and tried again. Nothing.

"This can't be." Her voice was low and stunned, but it rose in adamance as she gripped the steering wheel and insisted, "This is a brand new car! It only has sixty-seven miles on it! How can this be?"

Quaid stood patiently beside her open door. "Maybe it's the battery," he suggested.

"Well, couldn't you check under the hood or something?"

"Me?" He feigned astonishment. "Honey, I'm a doctor. I don't know nothing about fixing no mechanical contraptions!"

She gave the steering wheel a frustrated thump, and then, resigned, she got out of the car. "Well, I guess I'll just have to call a tow truck."

"Or you could apologize to Miss Mame."

She glared at him, and started to stalk back into the building.

"Wait a minute. Let me give it a try."

She waited impatiently as he slid behind the wheel and turned the key. Instantly the engine ignited.

"How did you do that?" she exclaimed, delighted.

"Just turned the key." He climbed out and gestured her into the idling automobile.

"It must have been a short or something," Jaime said as she got inside. "Well, thanks." She closed the door and rolled down the window, so happy she wouldn't be spending the next hour waiting for a tow truck that she easily forgave him his cryptic remark about voodoo. She smiled warmly at him. "Good night."

"Drive safely."

She slipped the transmission into Drive and the car stalled. Frantic, she turned the key.

"Put it in Park," Quaid suggested, leaning on her window.

Feeling a little foolish, Jaime did so. Still nothing.

She looked helplessly at Quaid, and he opened the door. "Move over," he advised.

He got behind the wheel, and the car started on the first try. He smiled at her. "Do you want me to drive you home?"

Jaime scowled at him. As hard as she tried, she could think of no earthly way he could be doing this on purpose. But he had to be responsible, somehow.

She said shortly, "No. Thank you."

"Suit yourself."

He got out of the car, and Jaime started to crawl over the console to the driver's seat. She didn't even make it before the car shuddered again and stalled.

Very slowly, Jaime moved back into the passenger seat and fastened her seat belt. Stubbornness could be a virtue, but not to the point of impracticality, and Jaime knew when she was defeated. She looked straight ahead, she kept her face impassive and said to Quaid, "Get in."

Quaid started the car on the first try and pulled out into the street. "I'm no expert on such things," he commented after a moment, "but I would say fate seems to be throwing us together."

With great self-restraint, Jaime said nothing. She told herself that her agreeing to let Quaid drive her home had nothing whatsoever to do with his supposed magical properties over her car, but rather that she simply did not want to try to maneuver a malfunctioning automobile alone through New Orleans traffic. That could be dangerous.

Quaid made the turn off Esplanade and asked, "Where do you live?"

"Garden District." She gave him the address.

"Nice area."

"Nice area, cheap house."

He chuckled. "You're really sensitive about it, aren't you?"

"About what?"

"Being rich."

"Pastries are rich," she told him with exaggerated politeness, "young ladies are wealthy. And it just so happens, I'm neither. I told you before, I earn my own way."

"Why?"

She was surprised. "What do you mean, why? I just do, that's all."

"It just seems to me that growing up the way you did..."

Now it was Jaime's turn to laugh. "You mean rich and pampered? Until I was nine years old I had never lived in anything but a one room apartment—a succession of them, as a matter of fact, always looking for cheaper rent—and I thought macaroni and cheese was the height of elegance in dinner fare. The highest paying job my mother ever had was as a waitress in a diner and even then she had to take in typing at home for extra money. I learned the work ethic the hard way."

"Sounds rough."

"I know it does." She shrugged, her earlier annoyance with him over the car completely forgotten. "But it was also an exciting way. And inspirational, as corny as that sounds. My mother never gave up on herself, you see. And you have to remember that she was an unwed mother at seventeen with no money, not even a high school diploma, and no skills at all except painting. But she never took the easy way out, she never asked for help. She always did things her own way. She kept me with her, she educated herself—and to this day is one of the most well-read people I know—and she never doubted for one minute that one day she would be a successful artist. You can't help but admire a woman like that." Then she glanced at Quaid, embarrassed for her lapse into sentiment. "Why am I telling you all this?"

"Because I asked."

"All right then." She turned a little in her seat to look at him. "Now I want to ask you something."

"But I'm not finished yet."

"Tell me about Armand," she said.

The little line at the corner of his mouth deepened with a wry smile. "Well, now, that's a long story."

"I'll take the abbreviated version. Beginning with why Daphene accepts illegal money from him to keep the settlement house running."

She had expected to see signs of discomfort or reluctance on his face—even a little embarrassment would not have been inappropriate—but Quaid only looked thoughtful. "I first met Armand about two years ago," he began after a moment, "when he broke into the clinic looking for narcotics. He used to run a gang called the Black Tigers—still does as a matter of fact, only now it's more like a social club..." Again the line at the corner of his mouth deepened. "Anyway, we got him into a program and off the junk, and he and his boys started hanging around Victory House, sort of like a home away from home. Well, you can imagine what that did to Armand's reputation, not to mention the morale of his boys, whose idea of Saturday night's entertainment was cutting up people and shaking down old ladies. On the one hand, they liked what we had to offer—food, color TV, and—dare I say it?—the sense of self-respect we gave them. They were getting jobs on the outside by then, and they were all involved in one program or another at the settlement house—teaching self-defense classes, escorting the elderly to and from the store, that sort of thing."

Jaime could not disguise her wonder. "Sounds like you did quite a job."

"Well, it wasn't as though we were dealing with hardened criminals in the first place. Most of them were just kids getting by the best they could, and Armand...well, he'd never known any other kind of life. We showed him another alternative, and for some reason it worked. I'm sure you know it doesn't always."

Jaime thought he was being far too modest. She knew exactly what it took to achieve those kinds of results, and she knew the odds against success. Victory House inevitably rose a notch in her esteem—which only made the entire situation with Armand and the protection money more confusing.

"At any rate, it wasn't all easygoing. There were times when we thought we'd see everything they'd accomplished go straight down the tubes—the kind of life those kids were used to is sometimes a harder habit to break than dope. In a neighborhood like this a man without a bad reputation is no man and all, and it wasn't long before word got around that the Black Tigers had gone under. The final insult came from a man named Deke, who was running a protection racket in the neighborhood, via Victory House."

Jaime tried, she really tried, to see it all with the equanimity Quaid and Daphene did. "But—you're talking gang wars—"

He chuckled. "Not gang wars, sweetheart. More like a little bitty board meeting, that's all."

"And stealing from honest citizens under the threat of violence—"

"We don't do the stealing," Quaid pointed out patiently. "Armand doesn't even do the stealing. It's just a business arrangement."

She shook her head fiercely. "It's wrong and you know it's wrong. You're encouraging violence and criminality, you're turning a blind eye to broken laws and worse yet, you're actually using the proceeds from crime to your own profit!"

"What were we supposed to do, turn our backs on Armand and his boys and let them go back to the streets? Refuse the money, turn it back over to the pimps and the pushers?" The veneer of patience in his voice was showing a thin edge. "Get in the real world, honey, because that's where we have to live."

"There are ways of doing things," she insisted stubbornly.

"By the book?" He shook his head with a half laugh that wasn't entirely from amusement. "Sweetheart, the book doesn't even cover the questions we've got down here, much less the answers. And if it comes to a choice between doing it right and getting results, I'll take the results any day."

"Creative problems demand creative solutions," Jaime muttered.

"What?"

She sighed. "Nothing. Just something my mother used to say."

"Sounds like a smart lady."

"I wish you'd never told me this."

"You asked me," he pointed out.

She frowned. "I mean I wish I'd never found out about it in the first place. And I wish your explanation had been different. And I wish I knew how I felt about it."

He glanced at her. "Don't you ever break the rules, Jaime Faber? Even a little bit?"

"No," she said adamantly.

He shook his head a little, murmuring, "You're a hard lady to figure out."

"I just like things in black and white, that's all," she told him. "There's nothing hard to figure out about that at all. My life is a lot simpler, as a matter of fact, than yours with your voodoo and your gang wars and your—creative solutions. That's my house, up ahead."

He gave her an appreciative glance as he spotted the gracious antebellum mansion dripping in lacy grillwork, and she informed dryly, "It's the carriage house in back. Take a right and circle around."

He parked in the street before the garden gate, for the carriage house did not have its own driveway. "This is nice," he commented as he got out. "I didn't think there were any of these places left to rent."

"There are if you know the right people. Besides," she added, once again feeling as though she should apologize for her good fortune, "this place was a dump. It had never been rented before, and the only way I got it so cheap was by agreeing to renovate it as I went along. I think the last time anyone actually stayed here was around the turn of the century, and you should have seen the mess."

He opened the creaky iron gate for her. "So who lives in the big house?"

"At present, a caretaker and his wife. The owners are in Europe or someplace."

He followed her up the cracked flagstone path with its riotous, weed-choked borders of peonies and wild nasturtium, and Jaime glanced at him questioningly. "Do you mind if I call a cab?" he inquired politely.

"Oh, no of course not," Jaime replied, abashed that she had not given a single thought as to how he would get home. She took her keys from him and hastily unlocked the door. "Now that we're here, it seems kind of silly that you had to drive me all the way home. I'm sure there was nothing wrong with the car, just one of those new-car bugs . . ."

She stepped inside, and could not explain why she was so nervous about having Quaid Gerreau accompany her. Perhaps it was because, even though they had spent practically the entire day together, this was the first time they had really been alone. And with a man like Quaid, there was no mistaking the difference.

"Why," he said, looking around with genuine appreciation, "this is really nice."

Almost immediately, Jaime relaxed. She had worked hard on the carriage house—the first real home she had ever had—and anyone who could appreciate that fact had an instant entrée into her heart.

The carriage house was built like a barn, with cathedral ceilings and a narrow staircase leading to an open loft, which Jaime used for a sleeping area. The floors were heart of pine which, after almost a week of scrubbing, sanding and waxing, had taken on a warm yellow patina, and the windows were mullioned to match the facade of the big house. Taking as her theme the cozy look of dimity and chintz from an earlier era, Jaime had begun covering the walls with a pale blue fabric dotted with small yellow daisies— fabric was cheaper than wallpaper, and easier to hang—and she repeated the pattern in throw cushions on the sofa and in her bedcoverings and curtains upstairs. The camelback sofa, which she had brought from New York, was covered with a light blue afghan embroidered with daisies, which, however inappropriate it was for the climate of New Orleans, brought the room together with a homey touch.

Except for an oak dining set in the kitchen area and the brass bed upstairs—both gifts from her mother and painstakingly crated and transported from the New York apartment—the rest of the furniture had been scavenged from junk shops in New Orleans. Small tables, hurricane lamps, bookshelves, a lovely old bentwood rocker and even the ceiling fan that Jaime had completed installing only the day before— all had been lovingly repaired, painted and restored to take their place among all that was uniquely Jaime's.

Quaid fingered the afghan on the sofa. "Did you make this?"

"Umm-hmm. The winters got cold in New York."

He glanced around at the needlepoint prints on the walls and the hooked rugs on the floor. "My mother does that stuff," he commented, "but I never knew anyone else who did. Nice," he repeated, looking around again and nodding with satisfaction, "this is really nice."

Jaime tried not to glow with his praise. "Of course it's not finished yet," she said, gesturing toward two walls that were yet to be covered, light switch plates that were awaiting replacement, and kitchen cabinets that were in the process of being stripped to their original wood. "I'm going to put in a new formica kitchen counter, too, as soon as I can afford it. But look. This is my favorite part of the whole house."

"The bathroom?" questioned Quaid as he followed her across the room.

Jaime gave him a secretive smile and opened the door.

It was built in a day when bathrooms were more than just closets tucked away in a corner, with an old-fashioned claw-footed tub, a wooden pull-handle toilet, and marble pedestal sink. When Jaime had first moved in it had been big, water-stained, and spartan. She had covered the floors with a plush white carpeting and the walls with a gentle seascape mural. With plywood and two-by-fours she had built a platform to the left of the room, carpeted it, added a small vanity table and mirrors, and created a dressing room. But the highlight of the room was the tub, which she had painted a deep royal blue, surrounded on three sides by a ledge that held candles, lush green plants and a neat row of paperback books.

"You read in the bathtub," exclaimed Quaid. "A woman after my own heart!"

She had a sudden unpreventable vision of Quaid Gerreau naked in the bathtub, and she moved quickly away to straighten the cosmetics on her dressing table. She couldn't help but wonder if Quaid was picturing her the same way, and the tingling in her cheeks was reminding her why she had felt uncomfortable inviting him in in the first place. Things like that seemed to be almost inevitable with a man like Quaid . . . an awareness, always just below the surface, a curiosity, an excitement she had no business feeling . . .

But he did not seem to notice her discomfiture as he looked around the room with undisguised admiration. "You did all this?"

She nodded, venturing to look at him again. "The hardest part was reglazing the tub. It can be tricky if you don't know what you're doing."

"You're quite an accomplished lady," he murmured, and the smile in his eyes made her feel warm all over.

She shrugged and moved past him into the living room—perhaps a bit too hastily. "My greatest skills are homemaking," she answered lightly. "Unfortunately, there doesn't seem to be a big market for that."

"Oh, I don't know." His voice sounded very close, and when she turned she was startled to see him standing only inches from her. The light in his eyes was gentle and teasing, and he was so close she could see the tiny scar that faintly bisected one eyebrow, and almost count the individual lashes that fringed his eyes. "I've got an apartment that could definitely use the skills of a qualified homemaker. So if you ever run out of things to do . . ."

Her laugh was a little breathless, and not quite genuine. "Oh, I doubt that. You know what they say, you never really finish decorating." She moved past him toward the window and until the very moment she was out of reach she kept expecting to feel his hand closing around her arm or her waist or her shoulder, gently drawing her close again. "I really love this place," she went on, chattering busily as she tugged the window open, "but it has one big flaw—no air-conditioning. It's awfully warm in here isn't it?" She opened a second window. "Who would think it could still be this hot at this time of day?"

"It's always warm down here," he answered, and there seemed to be a note of lazy amusement in his tone.

She opened all the windows she could, and when there was nothing left to do she turned and smiled at him rather uncertainly. "Well," she said, "the telephone is in the kitchen."

"Wrong," he said, and she looked at him blankly. "The next thing you're supposed to say is, 'Would you like a drink?'"

"Oh. Well, I suppose it's the least I can offer after you've gone to the trouble of driving me home." She hurried toward the kitchen, on the one hand anxious for him to leave so that she could relax, on the other oddly pleased that he had decided to prolong his stay. And that of course was ridiculous. She was treating him like a date, and that was the last thing he could ever be.

"All I have is cheap wine," she warned him, thinking he might reconsider.

"The cheaper the better." He made himself comfortable on the sofa. "Are you sure you won't change your mind about dinner?"

I am not going to offer to make him dinner, Jaime told herself firmly, pouring the wine. *If I had wanted to spend the evening with him I would have let him take me out to dinner. This is not going to get out of hand.*

And, so resolved, she heard herself volunteering, "If you're hungry, I could fix some sandwiches or something."

"I knew it," he said with a grin. "With all your other talents, you can't cook a lick."

"Ha!" She tossed her head as she returned to the sofa with the wine. "It so happens that I'm an excellent cook. As a matter of fact, until age fifteen my only ambition was to be a *cordon bleu* chef."

"And why didn't you?"

She handed him his wineglass and sat beside him on the sofa, one leg tucked beneath her. "My mother."

"She didn't approve?"

"On the contrary. She was always very careful to encourage me in anything I wanted to do. She was so confident in me, in fact, that she even arranged for me to prepare an elegant sit-down dinner party—for twenty of her closest friends."

His eyebrows shot up. "At fifteen?"

"Oh, I did fine. The dinner was delicious. Everyone raved. I told you I could cook. But I worked on it for a week, and afterward I was so tired I could hardly get out of bed for another week, and when Mother gently pointed out that I could be doing that day in and day out for the rest of my life, I decided it might be a good idea to start exploring other career opportunities."

He leaned back and sipped his wine, listening to her as though there were nothing else in the world he would rather be doing. "Such as social work."

"Oh, no. That came much later. Next I decided I wanted to be a domestic engineer—you know, a housekeeper." She made a wry face. "You can imagine how a liberated woman like my mother felt about that. So she got me a summer job working in a resort hotel."

"Thus putting an end to that ambition."

"Exactly. Next I thought I might like to be a preschool teacher."

"Don't tell me—baby-sitting."

She nodded. "With four of the most destructive little monsters who ever walked the earth. I don't think they were human children at all. I think she had them transported from an alien planet."

He chuckled. "Your mother sounds like a woman who knows how to get exactly what she wants."

Jaime tasted her wine. "It's hard to complain when all she wanted was the best for me. You've got to understand how ambitious she was, and how hard she had to work to succeed. She was terrified that she wouldn't always be around to take care of me, which is something a lot of people don't realize about her. She always said the only thing she wanted was for me to be able to take care of myself in a man's world, but what she really wanted was for me to excel. To be extraordinary, like she is. The only trouble was, I'm just an ordinary person."

She felt Quaid's thoughtful gaze on her, and she lowered her eyes, afraid she had revealed too much about herself. She took another sip of her wine. What was it about him that made her want to blurt out her life's story every time she opened her mouth?

"I'm still not sure I understand how you got into social work," he said after a moment.

The evening was so muggy that condensation had already begun to form on the outside of the chilled wineglass. Jaime absently traced a pattern in it with her fingertip. "Actually, I'm not either. By the time I got into college, Mother relaxed a little, and it was pretty much up to me to explore my options. Social service seemed like a place I could be useful, a chance for me to do something better..." The words "than my mother" were almost out before she knew it, and she clamped down on them swiftly. She had never said that out loud before. She had barely even admitted it to herself.

She looked quickly at Quaid and she saw an understanding in his eyes that embarrassed her. After all she had told him about herself, why should it make her uncomfortable that he could read her unfinished sentences? But it did.

She shrugged lightly and went on, "Anyway, I like my work. I like the sense of structure and accomplishment that comes from being part of an organized effort. At least," she added wryly, "*most* of the time it's structured."

"And organized," he pointed out, amused. "Victory House must be playing hell with your career expectations."

"To say the least. But then, as you probably already know, it was my mother who recommended this position."

He smiled. "And I, for one, am glad she did."

The gentle light in his eyes caused her skin to start to tingle again, and that discomfited her because he sounded as though he really meant it... that he was glad she had come to Victory House. She returned his smile, although a little uncertainly, before turning her attention back to her wine again.

"So," he wanted to know, "what did your mother say when you finally decided on social work for a career?"

"She said..." Jaime slanted an amused glance at him. "With a long-suffering sigh, she said, 'Well at least you didn't decide to become a doctor.'"

Quaid laughed, and Jaime laughed with him. It was a warm, easy moment, and one of the best Jaime had felt in a long time. The laughter faded, but the warmth in his eyes did not, and this time Jaime did not look away.

"So, Jaime Faber," he said. "What is it *you* want to be?"

She should, of course, have given the standard reply about having worked long and hard for her degree and being a contented career woman, but something about the gentle, earnest way in which he was looking at her made evasions seem unnecessary. Or perhaps a hidden part of her felt he deserved a warning. So she held his gaze, and she told the truth.

"A housewife," she answered simply.

If she had expected to startle him, she did not quite succeed. His eyes crinkled slightly with a smile, and he merely commented, "Now there's something you don't hear every day."

"I mean it," she said. "Looking back, I see that's all I've ever wanted to be, and what I'm most qualified for. I want a house with a thirty-year mortgage, a husband to cook and clean for, four children and car pools and PTA meetings, the whole works.''

He surprised her by chuckling softly. His eyes, when he laughed like that, were alive with muted lights and dancing sparks that played over her like a caress. "You are," he said, "the most complicated woman I've ever met."

Her eyes widened with surprise. "Me? I'm not complicated at all."

"You're a bundle of contradictions." He had propped his elbow on the back of the sofa while they talked, and it was a natural motion for him to stretch his hand out and capture one of her curls, twisting it lightly around his finger. Jaime's breath grew short with his touch, and she could not move her eyes away from his.

"You pretend to be so convention-bound and straightlaced," he said, "but you dress with your own distinct style and drive that flashy little sports car of yours like you've trained on a Formula One track. Every other word you utter has something to do with rules or regulations, and you don't even realize you've spent most of your life trying to break every rule in the book. You're full of lofty ideals and noble principles, but you recover from disillusionment faster than anyone I've ever known. You're naive and you're sophisticated, you're cute and you're sensible, and on top of all that you can fix dinner for twenty and reglaze a bathtub. You don't call that complicated?''

"I call that silly." Her voice sounded a little breathless, and she kept thinking, *Cute. He called me cute.* Yet from him it did not sound like an insult. It sounded like an endearment. "I'm not smart enough to be that complex. Besides..." Valiantly she struggled to retain some of that sensibleness he had just credited her with. "You're wrong. I haven't spent my life trying to break rules; just the opposite. I told you I like my life simple."

His finger drifted down to trace her collarbone, and her skin prickled; her heartbeat quickened. He smiled as he watched her, and Jaime thought certainly he could see the fluttering of the pulse in her throat. He said softly, "A young lady of the eighties' who wants nothing more than to be a wife and mother is definitely breaking a rule or two. And now..." He set his wineglass on the end table, and then took hers and placed it beside his. "I think you are about to break another one."

He took both of her hands in his, and gently pulled them to his chest, moving closer. Jaime knew she should move away, she should say something light or funny to break the mood, she shouldn't let this happen. But she did nothing except sit there and listen to the quick loud beating of her heart and let the warmth of his hands on hers flow through her like honey.

He said, "I'll bet you have a rule about kissing a man you've known less than twelve hours."

Jaime swallowed hard. "Forty-eight, actually." Her voice sounded raspy and uneven, and she thought, *I'm not going to let this happen. This is not a good thing....*

He smiled, and his face moved closer, and her hands were trapped gently against his chest, and his mouth covered hers.

Surprised jolts of electricity skittered through her veins and caught in her chest, flooding heat to her face and dizziness through her head. It was sweet and warm, infusing her with a liquid, swimming sensation, yet robbing her of breath and roaring in her ears like distant thunder. She felt the coarseness of his beard against her face, the silky touch of his tongue on the underside of her lips. She tasted him, her senses were flooded with him. It wasn't a demanding kiss, or invasive, but it was overwhelming; gentle and open and enveloping. His hands closed more tightly about hers in fractions, drawing her against him. She felt the rhythm of his breathing, and his fast, powerful heartbeat against the back of her hand. There was a moment when she seemed to flow into him, and he into her, so simple, so intense and so unexpected was the power of their kiss.

When he lifted his face she could still feel the moisture and the heat of his lips upon hers, still taste the hint of wine and warmth and maleness that was him. There was a dazed, muted light in his eyes, and the flush of passion on his skin. She could feel the rise and fall of his chest against her fingers, and the whisper of his breath across her damp and heated cheek.

He lifted their entwined fingers and lightly traced the corner of her parted lips with his forefinger. He said huskily, "I had to do that, you know."

Jaime's heart was pounding so powerfully against her ribs that she could hardly make her voice work, and her muscles were shaky and uncertain. Her eyes moved over his face, drinking him in, wondering, memorizing. She hadn't expected this. She hadn't expected anything like this.

"Why?" she whispered.

He smiled. "Because . . ." He moved his face to her hair, and she felt his deep inhalation. "I *don't* like life simple."

He straightened up and brought both her hands to his lips, kissing them lightly one after the other. Then he stood and left without another word.

Chapter Five

"Good morning," Daphene said brightly. "How are you this morning?"

"I had a cold shower," Jaime replied absently.

Daphene lifted an eyebrow. "Does that mean your dinner with Dr. Gerreau was a success?"

For a moment Jaime was startled, certain that Daphene had suddenly developed telepathic powers—or that Jaime's thoughts were so clearly written on her face that anyone could read them. Then she remembered that it had been Daphene's idea for her and Quaid to have dinner together and she gave a nervous little laugh. "No," she answered. "It means the hot water handle broke off my faucet this morning."

"Well, this time of year that can be a blessing," Daphene replied philosophically.

Amazingly, Jaime was actually on time today— thanks to forethought and the public transportation system. Naturally, her car wouldn't start, and she had had to call the dealer and have it towed, but after yesterday's fiasco she had been prepared for the unexpected, and had allowed herself plenty of time. It was exactly nine o'clock, and the small administrative office was buzzing with men and women beginning their day's work. Daphene took Jaime's arm and began to introduce her around, and Jaime smiled and said all the polite things. As a matter of fact, she was not sure she would remember anyone's name. Her mind, as it had been since last night, was elsewhere.

Jaime was accustomed to rationalizing things, and she never felt comfortable with any situation until she could pin it down to absolute cause and effect. She had spent a sticky, restless night trying to explain to herself what had happened between Quaid and her and was no closer to understanding it now than she had been then.

She had known her share of men: interns at the hospital, fellow graduate students, the occasional friend or brother or cousin of a friend. She had learned to instantly sort them into categories: "Yes," "No" and "Maybe." Quaid Gerreau was a definite "No," but no man's kiss had ever moved her like his had done, and she could not get him off her mind.

It was impossible, of course, and she could not believe she had let it get as far as it had. She was not in the least interested in Dr. Gerreau as anything other than a co-worker; there was simply no chance for any kind of personal relationship between them at all. He made her nervous, he made her angry, his outrageous behavior and incredible notions frustrated her to no end. He was unpredictable, unreliable and unconventional. He was exactly everything she was not looking for in a man. But he was also the most exciting person she had ever known, and convincing herself to forget about him was not going to be an easy task.

Daphene had just finished showing her the filing system, and Jaime realized to her chagrin she had missed every word. She would have to find time later in the day to explore it on her own. "Not that we're great record keepers," Daphene added with a chuckle. "Most everything that comes through here is either filed in our heads or in File Thirteen." She nudged the trash can with her toe. "If we can't figure out where else to put it, it goes in the file cabinet. If you need a typewriter, we've got three and at least one of them is usually working. As for work space, just take what's available; no one has an assigned desk, nor much need of one—except of course, myself. And that's just because I need a place to look important while I drink my coffee."

She poured two cups of coffee and handed one to Jaime. "So. How was dinner with Quaid?"

There were at least a dozen subjects Jaime would rather talk about, and none of them had anything to do with Quaid Gerreau. "Actually, we didn't have dinner. Listen, I wanted to ask you about the Franklin case..."

Daphene waved a dismissing hand. "Please, no business before I've had my coffee." She sat down behind a rickety little desk and gestured Jaime to pull up a chair. "Let's relax a minute first. Why didn't you have dinner?"

"Oh, I had car trouble, and it got late..." she answered vaguely. She found a metal chair and nudged it near the corner of Daphene's desk, sitting down and pretending to relax. Since Daphene seemed to be determined to be sociable—and to forestall further questions about Quaid—Jaime asked, "How was your date?"

Daphene gave a mock shudder. "Lord, child, they get worse and worse. I do believe I have more bad luck with men than any woman in the continental United States."

Jaime smiled. "As beautiful as you are? I can't believe that."

Daphene's eyes twinkled. "I see you know just how to make your boss's day. I wish some of the men I dated had your style. Do you know I once dated a man whose idea of an evening's entertainment was to sit at home and play back tapes of his old girlfriends on his telephone answering machine?"

Jaime choked on laughter and a sip of coffee and Daphene insisted, "It's true. Then there was this other fellow who thought the best way to impress me was to describe in elaborate detail all his previous sexual conquests—he had gotten up to number three hundred before I finally dumped him, and only then because I was afraid of getting some disease. I don't know who's more pitiful, the jerks who are roaming the streets out there, or us for putting up with them."

Jaime chuckled. "I know what you mean. I once met a man who claimed that by reading my aura he could tell we would be perfect in bed together. That was the only line he knew. And this wasn't at a singles bar—we're talking a nice, ordinary guy who took six weeks to get up his courage to ask me out."

Daphene leaned back and sipped her coffee. "I tell you one thing," she sighed, "if a man like Quaid Gerreau would ever once give me a second glance I'd snap him up like a hungry turtle after a fly." She glanced at Jaime shrewdly over the brim of her cup. "I'll bet you think he's a runabout, don't you?"

"A what?"

"You know, a playboy, a woman chaser."

Jaime fiddled with the handle of her coffee cup. "I really hadn't given it much thought."

"Well, he's not." Daphene's voice was casual but her eyes were alive with much more than an informal interest. "In the three years he's been here I've never known him to go out of his way for any woman in this organization—and we get some gorgeous girls in from Tulane, as you may have noticed. But he spent practically the whole day with you."

A tight little smile tugged at Jaime's lips as she stared into her coffee. "He told you about that, did he?"

Daphene replied airily, "Nobody keeps secrets from me. It's part of my benign dictator image."

"Did he also tell you that we spent the entire time arguing?"

"Wonderful. Nothing like a few fireworks to get a relationship off to the right start."

Jaime laughed helplessly. "Well, I'm sorry to disappoint you, but there's no relationship to get started." But her cheeks were warm and there was a strange effervescent sensation inside her chest, and from nothing more than possibilities Daphene had suggested. That happened every time she even thought about Quaid, and she simply had to get hold of herself. She doubted Quaid—Dr. Gerreau, she corrected herself firmly—had given her a second thought since he left her the night before.

Daphene looked as though she might say something else, but was interrupted by a squeal from down the hall. Startled, both women put down their coffee cups and went to investigate.

One of the caseworkers was kneeling in a puddle of water in the bathroom, frantically trying to mop up the mess with paper towels while water spurted from the pipe Jaime had installed yesterday. Jaime waded in and grabbed a handful of towels, stuffing them around the leak. "I don't believe this!" she exclaimed. "It was working fine yesterday!"

"Maybe it just needs to be tightened," suggested Daphene.

"It's as tight as it can get," Jaime insisted, and demonstrated. "I just can't understand—"

"Well, you did your best, honey," Daphene said sympathetically. "We can only patch together things so many times, I guess, and then the whole system goes."

Jaime wanted to protest—it was a simple repair and there was no reason it shouldn't have held—but Daphene turned to the other caseworker. "Just put an Out of Order sign on the lavatory. As long as the toilet holds up, I guess we're still in pretty good shape."

The leak slowed down as most of the water drained out, and Jaime left it reluctantly. "I'll go down to the hardware store," she volunteered, "and get some pipe compound. That should—"

Daphene waved a dismissing hand. "Forget it. One thing you have to learn around here is when to accept defeat."

But that was easier said than done for Jaime, and as she followed Daphene back to her office her annoyance only mounted. First her car, then the handle on her hot water faucet, now this . . . this was not a very promising beginning to the day, and it was not yet ten o'clock.

"I thought you could spend the morning following up on your cases from yesterday," Daphene said as she took up her coffee cup again, "and then this afternoon help Jolene out with the after-school program. For the next week or so you'll be working a little while in every department, just kind of getting the feel of things, as well as keeping up with your own caseload. One thing I can promise you, you'll never be bored.''

Jaime was relieved to have a chance to get her mind on her work again. ''That's great,'' she said. ''I still have to type up my reports—''

''Oh, we don't do reports,'' Daphene said. ''I thought I told you that. It only takes time away from what's really important.''

''But . . .'' Jaime tried to be tactful. ''You've got to keep case records. How do you keep up with what's going on?''

Daphene laughed. ''Most of the time, we don't.''

This was all making Jaime very uneasy. ''You don't mind if I keep my own records, do you?''

Daphene shrugged. ''Whatever. Now, there was something you wanted to ask me about the Franklin case?''

''Yes.'' Jaime released a careful breath. She felt as though she had just stumbled over one hurdle and was about to face another. ''Well, there were two things actually. Cara hasn't received her check this month, but I can take care of that.'' Daphene nodded approvingly. ''What I wanted to know was—Cara said something about your delivering her food stamps to her. Is that right?''

''That's right, I should have told you about that. They're in the bottom drawer of that desk over there.''

Jaime stared at her. ''You're authorized to give out food stamps?''

Daphene smiled ruefully. ''Well, not exactly. But there are some special cases, and we make arrangements. Just take out a few coupons and type Cara's name in. She gets fifty dollars worth a week.''

Special cases, Jaime thought. *Arrangements.* Fraud was what it was. Fraud against the U.S. Government.

Still, on a compulsion, she sat down at the desk and pulled on the bottom drawer. She wasn't a bit surprised when the handle came off in her hand. ''I seem to be a jinx today,'' she murmured, staring at it.

Daphene laughed. ''A little glue will take care of that. I wish everything around here was so easy to fix.'' She glanced at her watch, and stood. ''Well, I'm teaching a mothering class downstairs in five minutes. I'll check back with you in an hour or so. Meanwhile, if you have any problems...'' She waved a dismissing hand. ''What am I saying? You know what to do.''

Jaime sat at the desk, absently turning the broken handle over in her hand. She definitely had a problem, and she was not at all sure she knew what to do. She knew what she couldn't do, though. She could not issue forged food stamps. She could not falsify government documents.

After a moment she dug her wallet out of her purse and counted the contents. Fifty-seven dollars. She checked the balance in her checkbook, then regarded the bills in her hand sadly. Any way she looked at it, it was going to be a tight month. But she didn't really see that she had much choice.

She found an envelope on the desk and put fifty dollars in cash inside it, then wrote Cara Franklin's name on the outside. Somehow she would have to get Cara to go through the proper channels, but until then this was the best she could do.

She spent the next hour typing up reports no one but she would ever read, and trying very hard not to think about Quaid Gerreau. She wondered if she would see him today, and then realized that would be hard to avoid since they both worked in the same place. She wondered why he had not already happened by to see her, and then reprimanded herself for being silly. Despite what Daphene said, Jaime knew his type and she was willing to bet he came on like that to every woman who crossed his path. The best thing she could do was to chalk last night up to experience, and stay as far away from Dr. Gerreau as possible—within, of course, the bonds of their professional relationship.

But she couldn't help wondering what he was doing and if he was thinking about her and whether he had meant any of the things he had said last night at all.

At ten forty-five the *E* and the *A* keys broke off her typewriter simultaneously. She sat there in dismay, feeling she somehow could have prevented the accident if she had been keeping her mind on her work, when a voice caused her to look up.

"Well now, there you are. You're the little girl that come to visit me yesterday."

It was Pearlie Franklin, looking as fresh and healthy as any woman Jaime had ever seen. She was beaming a bright smile and carrying a shoe box in her hand, and she moved with a step that would have been sprightly for a woman half her age.

"Mrs. Franklin!" Jaime got to her feet slowly, unable to believe that this was the same woman who only yesterday had appeared to be on her death bed. "You look—why, you look just wonderful! How are you feeling?"

The woman's smile only broadened. "Just as right as rain, sweetheart, thanks to that nice Dr. Quaid." She set the shoe box on Jaime's desk. "I brung these cookies for you and him, 'cause you was both so nice to a poor old woman."

Jaime came around the desk, feeling that if she got a closer look she might be able to convince her mind what her eyes were seeing. "The doctor is in the clinic around back," she said. "I'm sure he'd love to see you."

"Lord, no, child, I got to get to my job. You just take some of them cookies to him, and tell him Pearlie says he can come see her anytime. Bye now."

She was almost to the door before Jaime recovered herself enough to call, "Mrs. Franklin!" She picked up the envelope from her desk and hurried across the room. "Will you give this to Cara, please? Tell her—tell her there was some problem with the food coupons, so I'm sending this instead."

Pearlie looked momentarily confused, then she took the envelope and tucked it into her purse. "Well, ain't you just the sweetest thing? My Cara said the folks down here was just as nice as they can be, and I reckon she was right. You come see us sometime, you hear?"

"I will," Jaime promised with a smile. "And—I'm so glad you're feeling better."

When she was gone, Jaime walked back to her desk, her hands clasped behind her back, her brow creased with a faint preoccupied frown. She circled the desk once and then twice, eyeing the shoe box thoughtfully. And then, on a sudden decision, she snatched up the shoe box and marched determinedly downstairs.

The clinic was housed in a cement block building—also painted pale yellow—which might once have been a garage. There were security bars on the windows, and on the door was a metal plaque that read, "Quaid W. Gerreau, M.D."—which answered Jaime's first question, whether he was a doctor of medicine or a doctor of some other weird, perhaps even metaphysical, discipline.

The waiting room was furnished with secondhand furniture, a small black-and-white television set, and a wooden toy box whose contents were being dropped to the floor one at a time by an inquisitive toddler. There were several people in the waiting room, their eyes glued to the TV, and when Jaime came in, the toddler's mother suddenly noticed what the child was doing and got up to swat her smartly on the bottom.

"You leave them things alone!" she scolded as the baby started to wail. "They ain't yours. You come over here and sit down." She jerked the child into a chair and began tossing the toys back in the box.

Jaime said, "But the doctor means for the children to play with the toys." She knelt beside the mother and smiled. "Hi. I'm Jaime Faber, from Victory House. It's okay for your daughter to have these, really." She picked up a battered Raggedy Ann doll and offered it to the child. "Here, honey, would you like to hold her?"

The sniffling child reached for the doll, but the mother snatched it out of her hand, tossing it into the box. "She's got to learn to keep her hands off what don't belong to her. And I didn't come here to see no social worker. I come for the doctor."

"Well you keep on hurting my feelings like that, Miz Shelby," said Quaid behind her, "and I just might put you at the bottom of my list."

Quaid was standing on the threshold, a diaper-clad little girl resting on his hip. Jaime's heart, totally without volition, skipped when she saw him. And his eyes, when he looked at her, were smiling.

He turned the smile back to Mrs. Shelby. "And after I spent all that money on toys just to keep these children quiet. Are you sure you won't let her play with just one?"

"Well, if you say so, doctor," the woman agreed reluctantly. "I reckon it's better than listening to her squawk." She retrieved the Raggedy Ann doll and took it over to her child. Her face softened as the little girl began to bounce the doll on her knee.

Jaime got to her feet and Quaid took his patient back to her mother. Jaime noticed the child had a gauze bandage over her right eye and forehead. "She's doing just fine," he told the woman as she stood anxiously. "I don't think we're going to have any problems with that eye at all. You be sure and bring her back on Friday to let me check that bandage. You won't forget, now?"

"No, sir, I won't forget. I'll bring her back." She reached for the child.

"Now wait just a minute little darlin'," Quaid said as the girl started to wriggle out of his arms. "How about some sugar?"

The child wrapped her arms around Quaid's neck and shyly kissed his jaw. Quaid laughed and returned a smacking kiss on the tip of her nose. Jaime felt a rush of tenderness so sweet it was almost physical at the picture he made, hugging the little girl and declaring, "I swear if you're not the sweetest thing God ever made. You take care of that pretty little face now, you hear me?"

The little girl nodded, and Quaid, smiling, returned her to her mother. He took a bottle of medicine from the pocket of his bright yellow lab coat and instructed, "You give her a teaspoon of this four times a day. Give her the whole bottle, do you understand? Use it up."

The woman nodded. "Yes sir, I will. The whole bottle."

Quaid patted the woman on the shoulder. "And bring her back next week. Don't make me come out to your house."

"No sir, I won't. Thank you, Dr. Quaid."

Jaime shook her head in slow wonder as Quaid, with a lift of his arm, indicated the way to his office. "You really are incredible," she murmured.

"Why, thank you," he replied smugly. "And if I recall correctly, I believe I tried to tell you that yesterday."

She chuckled. "I'm not sure I like it, either." She nodded toward Mrs. Shelby, who was once again watching television while her daughter played happily with the doll. "You're better at my job than I am."

"Oh, that." He shrugged. "That's just doctor worship." And he glanced at her with a twinkle. "An affliction from which I've noticed you don't suffer."

I wouldn't be too sure of that, Jaime thought, for when his dancing eyes captured hers she felt as helpless and enraptured as the child he had held in his arms only moments ago.

She said quickly, "I don't want to keep you from your patients."

He waved a dismissing hand. "Don't worry about it. My nurse will keep them happy for a while. This is one of my lucky days—I've got a volunteer from the hospital. Most of the time, I'm running this place by myself.'' He led the way down a narrow hallway off which two examining rooms and a small makeshift laboratory opened. "As a matter of fact," he added over his shoulder, "I have a couple of cases I'd like to talk to you about, when you have time. They need follow-up of a nonmedical nature."

"Sure," Jaime said, completely at ease now that the conversation had turned professional. "Anytime."

He stopped beside a small desk in the hallway to make a note on a file, and then tossed it on top of a rather large pile in a basket. He looked at her and smiled. "It's good to see you," he said softly.

Jaime swallowed hard. It was good to see him, too.

Somehow the misty images from last night had combined with the sparkling reality of the morning to make him even more powerful, more exciting and virile, than she remembered. He was clean shaven today, and his skin was smooth and lightly bronzed, delineating the lean shape of his jaw and neck. His hair, rumpled and trailing in that slightly rakish way over the back of his collar, was traced with blond highlights she had never noticed before. She wondered what it would feel like to the touch. The bright yellow lab coat he wore made him look young and energetic and as fresh as a new day, and the curve of his lips when he smiled reminded her of how those lips had felt, covering hers, and a shiver of pleasure started low in her abdomen, just remembering.

She thought he was remembering, too, for the smile deepened until a line bracketed one corner of his mouth and his eyes took on a muted glow. Jaime felt embarrassed color sting her cheeks, and she was annoyed with herself for blushing.

She said, "I only came by to bring you these." She thrust the shoe box into his hand. "Pearlie Franklin brought them over."

"She did?" He lifted an eyebrow. "I wish she'd stopped by. I would have liked to have checked her out."

"She looked just fine to me." Jaime looked at him closely. "Now tell the truth. You gave her a shot, right? One of those fast-working super powerful antibiotics?"

He chuckled. "No, I didn't. I told you what I did." He lifted the corner of the box and made an expression of delight. "Chocolate, my favorite. And not a moment too soon, I'm starved. Come on in my office. Time for a coffee break."

"Well, if you didn't give her antibiotics," Jaime insisted, following him, "and she was really as sick as she appeared to be yesterday, you should write this case up for the medical journals. You'd be famous."

"Honey, if I wrote up every strange thing I've seen since I've been practicing here I'd not only be famous—I'd be kicked out of the profession for a loon." He nudged open the door of a dim, windowless office and tossed over his shoulder, "Hit that light switch on the wall beside you, will you?"

Jaime found the switch and pressed it. The overhead light made such a snapping, sizzling sound that she jumped back in alarm, and Quaid turned to look at her, startled. The light flickered, flared, popped and died.

Jaime sighed in exasperation. "I don't get it. Everything I touch today seems to fall apart."

He lifted an amused eyebrow. "And this surprises you?"

"Don't start with me on the voodoo," she warned. "I think I'm having a stress reaction."

He placed the box of cookies on his desk and switched on a desk lamp. "Want a Valium?"

She frowned and sank into the chair in front of his desk. "No, thanks."

"How about a massage?"

She tried to keep a stern face, but it was impossible to do, looking into such a mischievously crooked grin, and she felt her own lips pull outward into a reluctant smile. It was amazing how easy it was to be with him . . . and how difficult.

"I'll settle for a cookie," she told him, and the warmth she felt inside had nothing to do with the temperature of the stuffy little office.

He pushed the box toward her and poured two cups of coffee from the machine behind his desk.

"I don't understand you Louisianians," she commented as she accepted the steaming mug. "Coffee, in this heat. Every time I turn around somebody's giving me a cup of coffee. It must be the state drink."

"When it really gets hot, we drink it iced. Long about August, generally, when we hit our first heat wave."

He sat down in the squeaky swivel chair and scooped up a couple of cookies, leaning back and regarding her with a marvelously relaxed, friendly air. No wonder it was easy to be with him. He always looked so comfortable. And he always made her feel welcome.

"So," he said. "Only two days on the job and already you're stressed out. This is not a good sign."

For once, Jaime did not want to talk about her job. She knew it would only lead to an argument, and she did not want to argue with Quaid this morning—not about anything serious. "All right," she said, biting into her cookie. "I can understand Pearlie Franklin. I mean, there has been a body of research indicating that people's states of mind can influence their health—even in things like cancer. She believed she would get well, so she got well. Conversely, that's how voodoo is supposed to work, isn't it? Not that I'm saying it *does* work, but if it did, it would be because the victims believed in it, right?"

Quaid nodded, an expression of great seriousness on his face, which she suspected was mostly mocking. "It's called sympathetic magic," he agreed.

"Right!" she exclaimed triumphantly, pointing her cookie at him. "But you see I *don't* believe in voodoo, so it can't possibly affect me."

He pretended to give that some thought while he munched on his cookie. "I don't believe in television," he said, after a moment.

"What?"

"I don't," he insisted. "I don't believe that a bunch of little dots can travel hundreds of miles across empty air and reform themselves into pictures and voices right before my very eyes. It's utterly ridiculous, when you think about it. There's no possible way it can work. But it does, every day."

"Bad example," Jaime said dismissingly, reaching for another cookie. "That's not the same thing at all."

"There are a lot of things in this world we don't have to believe in to be influenced by," he insisted.

"Name one. Besides television, that is."

"Love," he replied simply.

Jaime stopped with the cookie halfway to her mouth, caught by the smile in his eyes and the gentle way the word rolled off his lips. *This man,* she thought, somewhat hazily, *is really too much.* Just when she thought he could not possibly surprise her anymore, he did.

"Do you believe in love, Jaime?" His voice was casual, even academic, but the way he looked at her made her heart beat faster. Jaime thought she would have been safer had she kept the conversation to job-related matters after all.

She cleared her throat, she took a sip of the scalding coffee, she juggled the cookie awkwardly in her hand. "Well, of course," she replied eventually. "That is, if you mean the universal kind of love—well, naturally."

"I mean the very personal, knock-you-off-your-feet-drop-dead kind of love at first sight."

She wasn't comfortable with him any longer. Her throat was tight and her heart was going so fast that, as a doctor, he should have been alarmed. She could not understand how she had let the conversation slip away from her so quickly.

It was his method, she decided. Sneak up from behind, disarm, captivate. And he did it very well.

Still, she managed to answer firmly, "No. No one falls in love at first sight. People have to get to know one another, to explore common interests, to learn..." She saw the dancing light come into his eyes again and she knew she was fighting a losing battle. "Anyway," she said impatiently. "We were talking about magic. That's not the same thing at all."

"It's exactly the same thing," he told her. "And we're still talking about magic, don't you see?"

She met his gaze with a wry twist of her lips. "You were captain of your debating team at school, right?"

He chuckled and sipped his coffee. "I was about to say the same thing about you. There's nothing I like better than a woman who knows how to argue."

"Happy to be of service." She put her still-steaming coffee cup on his desk and stood. "But now I have to get back to work, and so do you. Thanks for the cookies."

"How about dinner tonight?" he asked, completely without warning.

And there it was, the moment she had been rehearsing for since he had left her last night. The time when she would turn to him with a polite smile and kindly explain all the reasons why any attempts to foster a personal relationship between them would be futile, why she didn't date colleagues, how they really had nothing in common, how there was no need to complicate their professional relationship with outside activities, how she was enormously flattered by his offer but he really wasn't her type at all.... And now that the moment was here all she could do was turn to him and say stupidly, "What?"

He smiled. "Those cases I wanted to discuss with you," he reminded her. "You said anytime, and dinner's the time I choose."

She began to stammer, "Well, I really don't think so, thanks anyway, but I'm not sure it's a good idea to...what I mean is, we shouldn't mix business and— That is to say, I think it's best that we keep things on a professional basis...."

He seemed amused. "But this is professional."

And when she looked dubious, he added patiently, "A doctor's time is not always his own, you know. I'm on call twenty-four hours a day and this place keeps me pretty busy. Sometimes the only time I have to talk business is over dinner. Ask Daphene, if you don't believe me. She and I have spent many a dinner hour together going over cases."

Jaime replied uncomfortably, "Daphene would say anything to get me to go out with you."

He grinned. "God bless her."

"Daphene also has terrible judgment in men," Jaime pointed out. "She told me so herself only this morning."

He merely shrugged.

Jaime looked at him, so casual and at ease leaning back in the chair with his coffee cup cradled against his chest, the light from the desk lamp glancing off his face and muting the highlights in his hair...looking comfortable, friendly and utterly harmless. And also more attractive to her than any man had ever been, God alone knew why.

Jaime said hesitantly, "Is this really a business dinner?"

He smiled enigmatically over his coffee mug. "What do you think?"

Jaime knew what she thought. She thought this could be the beginning of a string of complications she really didn't need. She thought the smartest thing she could do would be to refuse his invitation flatly and nip this thing in the bud. She thought he never should have kissed her last night, because that gave him an unfair advantage and had already confused her more than she wanted to be. And she knew if she said no now she would be wondering what might have happened for the rest of her life.

She said cautiously, "Maybe we do need to spend some time...discussing things."

"Great." He swiveled the chair forward and set his cup on the desk. "I'll pick you up at eight."

"I'm not riding that motorcycle."

His eyes twinkled. "You have absolutely no spirit of adventure. How is your car, by the way?"

"In the shop."

"Don't worry," he assured her. "I'm perfectly prepared to provide alternate transportation."

"Well." She smoothed her hands on her skirt, suddenly awkward. Already she was wishing she could find a way to back out without looking foolish. This was going to be a big mistake. She was certain of it. "I'll see you tonight then."

"Right."

He came around the desk toward her and she knew he was going to take her hand or touch her face or even do something utterly outrageous like kiss her, right there in his office in the middle of a business day. Her heart began a wild slamming rhythm that might have indicated anticipation or panic, and she looked at him anxiously.

But he only smiled, and opened the door for her. "Until tonight," he said politely.

She swallowed hard, managed a smile and replied, "Right."

She left the office as quickly as dignity would allow.

SHE SPENT THE REST OF THE DAY alternately trying to talk herself into breaking the date and trying to talk herself out of it. There was a card on the telephone listing frequently dialed numbers, and every time she picked up the receiver her eyes would fall on the listing for "Clinic." Once she even punched out the extension number, but lost her nerve before it could ring. The children in the after-school program did not get her full attention, and by the time she left Victory House for the sweltering bus ride home she was exhausted, irritable, and thoroughly disgusted with herself.

It was only one date, after all. She had gone out with less likely candidates than Quaid Gerreau before, and had never spent a fraction of this much energy worrying about it. But she had never gone out with anyone who made her feel so alternately comfortable and uneasy, who could arouse her to anger one moment and laughter the next, who frustrated her reason and assaulted her senses and who, in short, was perfectly wrong for her but who was as hard to resist as praline candy. She could think of a dozen reasons why she should not go out with him, and not one good reason why she should. But she never made the phone call.

The afternoon sun was hot and heavy, and she felt like a wilted pansy as she trudged up to the main house to get her mail before going inside the carriage house. The collection of bills made her moan as she remembered the seven dollars left in her purse, but a letter from New York cheered her up.

The letter was from her friend Marielle, who had lived across the hall from her in the Yorktown Towers. In many ways, Marielle, the traditional housewife, and her husband and children had been the closest thing to a real family unit Jaime had ever known. Some people might have looked with disdain on the choice Marielle had made as a professional wife and mother, but to Jaime she had the perfect life, and she had always envied her friend. She had spent as much time as possible in Marielle's neat, tastefully decorated apartment, trading recipes, playing with the children, absorbing the atmosphere of order, stability and nurturing she projected.

Marielle had lost her husband in April, leaving her a young widow with two preschool children, and Jaime had been worried about her. Her life had been so full before her husband's death: she hostessed elegant sit-down dinners, teas and cocktail parties for her husband's business associates, she did volunteer charity work, she filled her hours with all the occupations that went along with being a corporate wife. After her husband's unexpected death at such a young age, Jaime couldn't help being concerned—not with how Marielle would deal with grief, for she was a basically strong and resilient woman—but how she would adjust to the change in her life.

From her letter, at least, Marielle appeared to be adjusting well. She was concerned, of course, about the usual things—money, insurance, settling the estate—but for the most part she seemed to have everything well in hand. The letter was filled with chatty news about her children, their mutual friends Suzanne and Abbie, and myriad other details of life in New York City.

Reading the letter made Jaime nostalgic for all she had left behind in New York. Marielle with her playful personality and contented life; Abbie, with her sound advice and no-nonsense, levelheaded approach to problem-solving; even Suzanne, the glamorous soap opera star who lived next door and often intimidated Jaime with her beauty and confidence—she missed them all. Everything had been so simple then. Good friends, clear goals, order and security. She had known exactly what she wanted and had no doubt that she would find it. Nothing was ever unexpected, nothing was out of place, and all the challenges were ones she could easily handle.

And it never, ever, got this hot in New York City.

Wearily, Jaime inserted the key in her lock and was surprised when it didn't click. It wasn't like her to be so careless as to leave her door unlocked, and she pushed it open cautiously.

The first thing she noticed was that one entire wall of her apartment was painted red. The second thing she noticed was a woman on a ladder proceeding to do the same to the opposite wall.

The woman was wearing a pair of tiny denim shorts and an oversized white cotton shirt. Her feet were bare and her long slender legs were enough to make even the most self-confident woman sick with jealousy. Her waist-length red hair was pulled back at the nape of her neck and swung gracefully over her shoulder as she lifted the paint brush. She was tall, slim and exquisitely beautiful. She could have been a cover girl on any magazine in the country.

She was also Jaime's mother, and things had just gotten very complicated.

Chapter Six

"Mother!" Jaime exclaimed, dropping her purse on the sofa. "What—"

"Hi, sweetie." Leona Faber propped the paint-brush on the tray and climbed gracefully down from the ladder, her lovely face alight with sparkling welcome, and spread her arms. "Surprise, surprise, I'm back!"

Jaime laughed and ran toward her mother, hugging her hard. "God, I can't believe you!" she exclaimed at length, holding Leona's shoulders. "Look at that tan! You look fantastic!"

"I love your hair," Leona said at the same time, and they laughed and hugged again.

Leona pushed away and tried to look apologetic. "Are you terribly angry?"

"To have my favorite roommate back? You've got to be kidding! I can't wait to get into your wardrobe!"

"Good, because I've already unpacked."

"But..." Jaime looked over her mother's shoulder at the half-finished paint job. "What are you doing to my wall?"

"Do you like it?"

"It's . . . red," Jaime said.

"Oh, that's just the base coat. Wait until you see it finished. It's just what this room needs. I love this place, by the way. Didn't I tell you it would be great?"

"It's wonderful," Jaime said, still staring at the red wall. "Perfect. I've never had a place I liked better."

"I can't believe what you've done to the bathroom. God, I wish I had your knack for doing things like that." She clasped Jaime's hands with both of hers and pulled her toward the sofa, her face as animated as a child's. "Now tell me everything. How do you like New Orleans? How's your job?"

"No, I want to hear about South America."

Leona shrugged, sinking to the sofa with Jaime beside her. "Snakes, rebels, bad water, the usual. We'll get to that." She drew up her legs and clasped her arms around them. "I want to hear about *you*. Did you like the car?"

"Loved it. It's in the shop."

Leona made a face. "American workmanship in action."

Jaime laughed. "It was an import!"

"Well, I'll be damned. Must be catching. Now tell me." She squeezed Jaime's arm briefly. "How do you like my favorite city in the world? Isn't it great?"

"Who wouldn't love New Orleans? I've gained four pounds since I've been here!"

"What's four pounds?" she scoffed.

"On you, maybe. On me it's the difference between regular and queen-size panty hose."

"Well, I hope your panty hose budget can stand it because I did *not* come to New Orleans to eat yogurt and rabbit food. We're going to do this town up right and that means attacking the movable feast with both forks. But what about your job? Was it worth all those years sitting in a classroom? Do you like where you're working? What about the people?''

"Now there's an interesting subject." Jaime kicked off her shoes and tucked one foot beneath her, relaxing as always in her mother's easy company. "It's not exactly what I thought it would be, that's for sure. Victory House is great and the things they accomplish are incredible but…it's kind of weird." She looked at Leona closely. "What do you know about this place, anyway?"

"Just what my friends tell me. It sounds like a place that really knows how to get things done in the community. What do you mean, weird?"

"Bad choice of words." Considering the fact that Leona's friends, who ranged from street musicians to crazed artists to eccentric poets, could hardly be called anything other than weird, Jaime could hardly expect her mother to be sympathetic to her misgivings. In as neutral a tone as possible, Jaime described Daphene Campion and the policies of Victory House, up to and including her methods of alternative fund raising. When she finished, Leona laughed.

"She sounds like an incredible woman!" Leona said. "I have got to meet her."

"Daphene is incredible," agreed Jaime. "But don't you think what they're doing there is just the least bit on the illegal side?"

"Well," said Leona thoughtfully, "the purpose of the law is supposed to be to serve the citizens, and the law has to be measured against the standards of the community. So it seems to me the test question here is whether the police could have handled the gang situation any better than your Victory House is doing.

And from what I know about inner-city crime my guess is no. In desperate environments like the one you're dealing with, par law enforcement is about the best anyone could ask for, and if the police department knew about what this Armand character is doing—and I wouldn't be at all surprised if they do, by the way—they would probably applaud it."

Jaime nodded slowly. She had never thought about it like that before. And then she grinned. "You're a pretty smart lady, you know that?"

"Hey, that's why they pay me the mom money," Leona retorted and gave one of Jaime's curls a playful tug.

"Now, if only you could tell me what to do about the illegal food stamps."

"Oh, God you're such a little Republican," Leona groaned. "I say fleece them for all they've got and let Uncle Sam pay the bills. It's about damn time."

"Not another one of your lectures on the inefficiencies of the U.S. Government, please," Jaime laughed, going into the kitchen for the wine from last night. "Tell me about your trip."

They talked and laughed while the sun dropped lower to the sky and dusty shadows slanted longer and longer across the gleaming hardwood floor, and Jaime did not think about Quaid Gerreau and the confusion he had brought to her life once. That was one thing about Leona Faber—her energy and ebullience filled every corner, leaving no room for anything or anyone else. Just being with her was an adventure. Jaime had forgotten how much she missed that. Soon she would remember how exhausting it was.

"So," Jaime said when Leona had come to a stopping point in her tale about giant snakes and mystic ruins, "how long are you going to stay?"

"Well..." A peculiarly secretive look danced in her eyes. "I thought maybe forever." And then, at the expression on Jaime's face she laughed and slapped her hand affectionately. "Not with you, silly—I meant in New Orleans! You know—" she sipped her wine, lowering her eyes "—buy a house, settle down."

Jaime gaped at her. "You? Settle down? You've never owned a house in your life! Not even for investment purposes—you said it made you feel too tied down. You've never even talked about doing it before!"

"There are a lot of things I've never done before," Leona said, and she looked very odd—girlish and excited and almost shy. "As a matter of fact, I have another surprise.... Oh, damn! I almost forgot!" She gulped her wine and set the glass down, standing quickly. "I brought you a present."

Jaime had the definite impression the present was not the surprise Leona had been talking about, but when her mother hurried to the closet and removed a large wooden box she was too excited to question further. Her mother's presents were always cause for celebration.

Leona set the box on the floor and Jaime had to run to find a screwdriver to pry open the staples. When she removed the cover and pawed through the packing materials she sat back on her heels with a gasp of awe. "A mantel clock! Oh, Mother, it's beautiful!"

"I remember how you admired the one we saw in that little antique shop in Vermont that time. I always meant to get it for you, but when I went back it was gone."

"This one is even more beautiful." She admired the intricately carved, ancient oak cabinet and the etched glass cover, then she said, "But I don't have a mantel."

Leona shrugged. "So build one. You're good with your hands."

Jaime laughed and lifted the clock carefully from the box. "For now I think I'll put it on that table by the door. You got this in South America?"

"Actually, I was in London for a while," Leona answered. "As a matter of fact, that's part of the surprise..."

"Oh, look, Winchester chimes! I can't wait to get it set up." She attached the pendulum and opened the glass door. "What time is it?"

Leona glanced at her watch. "Seven-fifteen."

Jaime gasped. "Oh, no, I forgot! I have a date in forty-five minutes!" The dread word—date—slipped out before she was aware of it, and immediately sparked avaricious interest in her mother's eyes.

"A date! And you've only been here two weeks. I'm impressed. Do tell."

"Not a date, really," Jaime said hastily, stuffing the packing back into the box. "More like a business dinner..."

"What kind of business? Who is he?"

"You certainly do act like a mother sometimes."

Leona's eyes were sparkling. "Come on, now I'm really curious. Tell, tell. Who is he? What does he do?"

Jaime picked up the clock and took it to the table. "His name's Quaid Gerreau, and he's a doctor."

"A doctor!" Leona moaned dramatically. "Oh God, he's forty years old and drives a Mercedes, right? Wears Italian suits, gold pinky on his finger?"

Jaime couldn't help chuckling. "Hardly."

"But—a doctor!" Leona groaned again and buried her face in her hands. "That's almost as bad as a politician. Where did I go wrong?"

"He's not exactly your typical doctor, Mother. He runs the free clinic where I work. Anyway, I don't have time to talk about it now. I have to get ready."

Leona gave a martyred sigh. "Well, if you're determined to waste your charms on a cardboard cutout with a God complex and a golf handicap I suppose I have to let you make your own mistakes. Quaid Gerreau." Her eyes narrowed. "Did you ever notice how all doctors have crazy names, like Upton and Truman and Verne—and Quaid? I wonder if having to go through life with names like that turns them into such jerks, or if their parents recognize jerkdom from birth and give them a name to fit?"

Jaime lifted her eyebrows meaningfully. "This from a woman who named her only daughter Jaime?"

"Oh, all right." Leona got to her feet, searching for her shoes and purse. "I suppose as long as he's definitely taking you out and there's nothing I can do to prevent it, you may as well offer him a drink. And since we just finished the wine—" she lifted the empty bottle "—I'd better go out and get some more. And as long as I will be dining solitaire tonight, I think I'll pick up something more appetizing than tuna fish from the market. Have you had *beignets*, yet? God, just thinking about them makes my mouth water. That's exactly what I'm going to do—sit home alone and stuff myself on *beignets* and Irish coffee..."

Jaime smilingly waved her mother out the door, and once she was gone leaned against it for one brief moment of amused and weary relief before hurrying to get dressed.

Her day had been like being struck by one tidal wave after another, each one carrying her farther and farther out to sea until now she had completely lost her bearings and was too exhausted to do anything but try to keep her head above water. Yet the biggest challenge still lay ahead of her, and she had to rally herself to face the emotional turmoil Quaid Gerreau had brought into her life.

She could of course have used her mother's unexpected visit as an excuse to cancel her date with Quaid, and for a moment she was genuinely tempted. But that would not solve anything. They would see each other every day at work, and sooner or later one of them would have to define the terms of their relationship. The best thing to do was to get it over with now, to bring everything out in the open and lay down some ground rules. Both she and Quaid needed to know where the other one stood.

Jaime only hoped that she would be able to remember where she stood.

Jaime had time for a brief, cold shower, which, as Daphene had predicted and considering the state of her nerves, was a blessing. She even remembered to tape a note to the mirror informing her mother about the hot water faucet, and hastily began searching through her wardrobe for just the right dress. She wasn't sure exactly who she was dressing to please— Quaid, or her mother.

She had a gorgeous Gunny Sax dress that she had bought at a sale at Macy's in the spring and had not had a chance to wear yet. It was a soft lavender satin-et with a pale pink print, strapless and waltz length, with its own crinoline and a tiny wasp waist. The minute she had bought it she had thought the crinoline might be too much, and the skirt length reduced her legs to mere stubs, but the waist did make her look smaller and with the right heels she could achieve an air of almost-elegance. Besides, it was seven forty-five and she did not have time to be indecisive.

She piled her hair atop her head and fastened it with a pearl comb, and was just applying the finishing touches to her makeup when the doorbell rang. She grabbed a pink lace shawl and her evening purse and ran down the stairs, muttering as she went, "You wouldn't believe this one, Mother. A doctor who's actually on time."

She opened the door and Quaid stood there, smiling. He was wearing jeans and a soft chambray shirt open over a dark blue T-shirt. He looked wonderful, and Jaime felt foolish.

"I think I'm overdressed," she said.

The light in his eyes made her skin tingle as his gaze moved over her. "I think you look fantastic."

She stepped quickly away from the door and gestured him inside. "I think I'm going to change."

"In that case..." Before she knew what he was about to do, he caught her shoulders lightly and drew her to him. His kiss was gentle and warm and rushed through her like sunlight flooding a dim corridor, and her reaction to it was totally out of proportion. Her breath caught, her muscles weakened, her pores opened and ached with a sudden flare of awareness. The kiss was brief, tantalizing and far too potent.

He was smiling as he finished softly, "You don't mind if I muss your makeup a little, do you?"

Her eyes were caught by his and her heart was pumping in short, swollen beats against his chest. She no longer felt foolish; she felt helpless.

She said, somewhat unsteadily, "I take it this is not going to be a business dinner."

His fingers caressed her bare shoulders lingeringly as he released her. "You take it correctly."

Jaime took a deep, steadying breath, once again feeling the situation begin to veer out of her control. Wasn't it supposed to be she who was laying down the ground rules to him?

She opened her mouth to do so, but the only words that came out were, "I'll change."

She turned and went quickly up the stairs.

"I should have told you the place we were going to was casual," he called after her. "I'm sorry."

"No problem. It's too hot to dress up anyway."

"What happened to your walls? Redecorating already?"

"It's a long story." She grabbed a cotton skirt and T-shirt, selected accessories at random and hurried back down the stairs. "Make yourself at home," she said, not looking at him. "I'll be as quick as I can."

She closed the bathroom door.

Once inside she leaned against the dressing table, closed her eyes, and took another deep breath. *This is not going to work,* she told herself. *We can't even agree to have dinner together without getting our signals crossed.* But that wasn't what was really bothering her. It was the fact that she could still taste his kiss.

She opened her eyes slowly. The woman who looked back at her from the mirror was flushed, bright-eyed and a little out of breath. *All this from one kiss?* she thought incredulously. *This is serious.*

There was only one thing to do, she decided firmly as she began to take down her hair. In words of one syllable, and before this thing could go any further, she would explain to him exactly how she felt about him and what he could expect from her. Friends, colleagues, and co-workers—that was all they could afford to be to each other. And maybe not even friends.

With her new attack of nerves, her string of bad luck resurfaced, and what should have been a five-minute quick-change job took fifteen. The zipper stuck on her skirt and she broke a fingernail trying to unfasten it. She lost the back to her earring and spent more time than she should have looking for it before deciding to go bare-eared. The lace-up shoes with which she replaced her evening sandals had a stubborn knot in the laces, and as she was tying a decorative scarf around her waist she knocked over a bottle of bubble bath and shattered it. Small catastrophies in comparison to others she had endured that day, but nonetheless disconcerting—and time-consuming. She began to wonder whether Quaid was still waiting for her, and was ashamed of the small dart of relief she felt when she thought he might not be.

When she opened the door, however, her heart sank, and she saw that she need not have worried about Quaid after all.

He was sitting on the sofa with Leona, a glass of wine in his hand, chuckling while she told some story or another. There was Leona, leaning toward Quaid with one slim bare leg tucked beneath her, her elbow resting on the back of the sofa and a wineglass dangling from her fingers as she emphasized her words with graceful motions of her other hand; her long red hair cascading down her back and her face animated with her tale. And there was Quaid, as enchanted by Leona Faber as Jaime herself had been when she had sat in his place less than an hour ago.

It wasn't jealousy Jaime felt as she stood there, nor even hurt. It was more like resignation. She had played out this scene many, many times in her life. She brought a boyfriend home to watch television, and he ended up watching her mother instead. Her date came to pick her up and didn't want to leave. A girlfriend came over to study and ended up spending the afternoon talking fashion trends with her mother. Leona did not do it on purpose, and Jaime could not resent her for it. She had simply long ago learned that she did not have a chance when her mother was around.

But watching Leona with Quaid now made Jaime unaccountably sad. She did some rapid calculations and concluded that Quaid was actually closer to her mother's age than Jaime's. They even looked good together; he with his sexy nonchalance and she with her striking, careless style. And Lord only knew, they would have plenty to talk about....

"And you should try sitting through a magic show with her," Leona was saying. "It's the most frustrating thing. She always figures out how the illusions are done. My daughter has the most viciously linear mind of anyone I've ever known—it's positively heartbreaking."

Jaime painted a smile on her face and stepped into the room. "I'm ready," she said brightly.

Quaid was on his feet immediately, and Leona set her wineglass down, smiling. "I like your doctor, Jaime," she said.

Jaime pretended to be impressed. "Good for you," she told Quaid. "My mother thinks most doctors are sanctimonious do-littles with delusions of grandeur and calculators for hearts."

Quaid's eyes twinkled. "Yes, I believe she mentioned something to that effect."

"To which he pointed out how much the ghetto can do for a man's humility quotient, and that's when I decided I liked him," Leona replied. "Where are you going tonight?"

"Only the best restaurant in town," Quaid answered, resting his hand on Jaime's shoulder in a gesture that felt warm and affectionate and wonderfully natural.

Leona sighed. "Every restaurant in New Orleans is the best restaurant in town."

Jaime knew Leona didn't mean that to sound like a hint, but any other man would have picked up on it immediately and invited her to join them. She tensed for Quaid to do so.

And she felt the tension leave her body in a flood of wonder and surprise when Quaid merely replied with a chuckle, "A woman after my own heart. I hope your daughter has inherited your appreciation for the finer things in life."

"Don't worry, I've left it to her in my will." Leona gave them both a warm smile. "Now, good night, you two, and have a good time."

"I won't be late," Jaime promised.

"She'll be late," corrected Quaid. "Good night, Leona. It was good meeting you."

Leona winked at him. "I'm sure I'll see you again."

The tension was back as Jaime walked with Quaid out into the twilight. "Well, what did you think of my mother?"

"I liked her," he answered easily.

She gave him an astonished look. "You *liked* her?"

"I wasn't supposed to?"

"People don't just *like* my mother. They adore her, they're enchanted with her, they rave about her. They do *not* merely like her."

Quaid slanted her a peculiar look. "To tell the truth, she wasn't exactly like I expected."

"Oh?"

"No. From your description of her I expected her to be loud, domineering, manipulative and just a little bit shrewish."

Jaime had to stop, and look at him. "I said that?"

"You implied it."

Jaime was shocked. "But—my mother is wonderful. You saw that for yourself. She's beautiful and she's charming and she's without a doubt the coolest person I know. I don't see how you could possibly get the impression—"

He took her shoulders and gently turned her to face him. His smile was tender, and in the dying sunlight his eyes looked like two jewels on a background of rich velvet. "Your mother is wonderful," he told her simply. "I liked her a lot. But she's not nearly as beautiful or as charming as her daughter, and I don't like her even half as much as I like you."

Looking at him, listening to the soft note of sincerity in his voice, Jaime could almost believe he meant it. And whether he meant it or not, if it had been possible for Jaime to believe in instant love, she would have loved him at that moment just for saying it.

She smiled, a little shyly and very apologetically. "I guess I'm the one who's been acting shrewish. I'm sorry. It's just that—"

"It's not easy being her daughter," Quaid finished for her, and Jaime couldn't mask her surprise.

"You're awfully perceptive," she murmured.

He grinned. "I took a sensitivity course in med school." He grabbed her hand suddenly. "Now, come with me. I want to get something straightened out."

Before she could even remember that she was supposed to be the one to get things straightened out with him, he had pulled her before a brown Buick and stopped on the sidewalk, a few feet away from the car. "Look," he commanded.

She didn't understand. "Your car?"

"My brother's car," he corrected dismissively. "No, I mean look in the window. What do you see?"

She saw then what he meant. The setting sun behind them formed a mirror out of the window, in which her image was reflected perfectly. She replied, "I see a short, frumpy-looking girl who forgot to put on her lipstick."

"I see," he told her, "a strikingly unusual, completely fascinating, and incidentally very attractive, young woman who makes me wish I could know her better. A whole lot better. And..." He leaned forward, smiling, so that his face was between Jaime and her reflection. "That's the truth."

Jaime felt all her stern resolve begin to melt away like sugar in the rain. Every time she saw him, he became more difficult to resist, and how was she supposed to stand up against tactics like this?

Her lips curled into a wry smile and she gave a small shake of her head. "You're not going to make this easy, are you?" she murmured, almost to herself.

"Oh-oh." Quaid opened the door for her. "This is the part where you tell me all those very excellent reasons why we should keep our relationship on a professional basis."

"No," she protested automatically, getting into the car. "Not exactly. What I mean is . . . well, yes."

And, despite the teasing grin he flashed her as he got behind the wheel and started the ignition, Jaime could see she was not likely to get a better opening than this. Grasping for the shreds of her conviction, she plunged right in.

"It's not that I don't find you very attractive . . ." She had not meant to say that, and she did not dare glance at him to see what effect that announcement had produced. She hurried on, "And not that I don't think we should be able to keep up an—amiable—working relationship, but there's really no point in taking it any further, don't you see? I mean, we're totally different personalities from completely differing backgrounds, our values and opinions are polar opposites, we have nothing in common . . ."

"You never heard of complementary opposites?" Quaid interrupted mildly.

She went on determinedly, "I don't know why you would want to go out with me anyway. I'm not pretty, I'm not exciting, I'm not independently wealthy, and I've got fat thighs." He was laughing softly, but she did not let that stop her. "Furthermore, I'm not interested in casual romance, I don't go to bed with a man on the first date—"

"This is our second date," he reminded her.

She ignored him. "And if you would think about it, honestly, for even one minute, you would see that I'm not really your type, either. So there's really no point in either of us expecting something from this relationship that can't possibly happen."

He was silent for a minute, and Jaime cautiously flexed her tightly clasped hands. She thought she had done quite well. Reasonable, but not harsh. Honest, but not cruel. She didn't want to lose his friendship or hurt his feelings, but she had made her point.

And then he said, "What are you?"

"What?"

"You've told me all the things you're not; what are you?"

She looked at him calmly. "Wife material," she said simply.

He smiled, a slow, slightly crooked, utterly delightful smile that had less to do with amusement than with sheer pleasure. He said, "Sold!"

At her startled look, he chuckled. "Honey," he said, "don't you know those are the words every man longs to hear?"

She made an impatient face, certain he was teasing her.

"I'm serious," he insisted. "Deep within the id of every male lies a secret longing to return to the cradle, you know that. A woman to feed him, nurture him, structure his environment, direct his ambitions, stroke his ego. The only trouble is, finding a woman willing to do that is not as easy as it sounds—which makes you one of the most valuable commodities on the market today. I say again, sold!"

She frowned at him. "You're making fun of me."

"Not really. At least not much. And I don't mean to." He reached over and clasped her hand, and his smile was unexpectedly gentle. "I just don't want you to sell yourself short."

Jaime knew she should pull her hand away to add emphasis to her words. But her hand felt so right, nestled in his, warm and affectionate and natural, that she selfishly wanted to savor the sensation a moment longer. She said, "You sound like my mother. Anyway, I'm not selling myself short. I'm being very careful about the kind of man I choose to—nurture."

"And it's not a man like me."

There was a slight clutch in her throat, and she glanced at him quickly. His expression was bland, and matter-of-fact. She slid her hand out of his, pretending to adjust a strand of hair that was tickling her face, and she kept her tone light, "I don't think so."

"How do you know?"

He sounded serious, and that disturbed her. She forced a strained laugh. "I just do, that's all."

"Sounds like a snap judgment to me."

She was growing nervous again. "I don't make snap judgments. I gather the evidence, examine the facts and draw my conclusions carefully. Impulsiveness is one of your vices, not mine."

He appeared to consider this. "I think we're more alike than you realize."

"I disagree."

There was a challenging spark in his eye as he glanced at her. "Well then, we'll just have to see about that, won't we?"

He spotted a parking space up ahead and swung into it with a series of swift, reckless motions that had Jaime holding her breath and clutching the armrest.

He looked at her as he turned off the ignition, and he laughed softly.

"What's so funny?" Jaime demanded, unwinding her fingers from the upholstery.

"You." His eyes were dancing. "Having the gall to ask me why I wanted to go out with you. This is the most stimulating fifteen minutes I've ever spent. And..." He got out of the car and walked around to open the door for her. "The evening has just begun."

Chapter Seven

The name of the restaurant to which Quaid escorted her was called Lagniappe, pronounced Lan-yap and meaning, Quaid informed her, a little something extra, or a surprise bonus. Jaime wasn't sure about the something extra, but it was definitely a surprise. And she saw immediately what he had meant when he said casual.

It was located between Bourbon and Conti streets, in an area in which elegant dining establishments competed with flashy strip shows and neon-lighted porn parlors for the all-American dollar—and which were sometimes hard to tell apart unless one read the signs very carefully. Quaid opened the door beneath a blue-striped awning and a virtual cacophony of sensory impressions rushed to greet her.

It was more of a café than a restaurant, small, crowded and brightly lit. Definitely not for tourists, the clientele was an eclectic mixture of working-class singles, couples and families, all enjoying their meals with enthusiasm and verve. The air was rich with mouth-watering cooking smells and slightly tainted with cigarette smoke; glasses clinked, silverware clattered, voices mingled with bursts of gusty laughter. It was not the kind of place anyone would choose for a romantic rendezvous, and Jaime loved it immediately.

People looked up and called Quaid by name as he took Jaime's arm and escorted her slowly through the crowd of people at the door who were waiting to be seated. He responded with grins and waves and an occasional shout of greeting, and even those who were waiting for seats didn't seem to mind that Quaid was moving ahead of them. But it bothered Jaime.

"This is a great place," she said, "but it looks kind of busy. Are you sure we'll be able to get a table?"

He winked at her. "Don't worry. I know the maître d'."

"Well, will you look who just walked in the door! If it ain't the famous Dr. Quaid Gerreau!"

A short, rotund man dressed in navy whites and a cook's apron stood with arms akimbo in front of them, grinning a welcome. His head was completely bald, and he wore a gold hoop in his ear; his right arm was tattooed from wrist to biceps with a colorful dragon. He reminded Jaime of a genial pirate.

"And look at this," he went on, pretending amazement, "We're a party of two tonight. Well, well, well. Not bad." His grin widened as he looked Jaime up and down. "Better than what you usually bring in here. Got a little something up here." He made a cupping gesture with both hands in the area of his chest, and Jaime blushed.

"Do you want to give us a table," Quaid retorted, slipping a protective arm around Jaime's shoulders, "or do you want us to find someplace else to eat?"

"Oh, it's a table the good doctor wants! Well, it's a table he'll have." The little man hurried off, tossing over his shoulder, "Of course if you want a clean table you got to pay extra!"

He laughed heartily at his own joke and slapped Quaid on the shoulder as he gestured them to a small booth. Quaid said, "Just bring us some wine and stop trying to be a comedian. And make it the good stuff— not what you serve the customers."

The man shook his finger at Quaid. "One day you'll go too far."

Quaid grinned as he slid into the booth opposite Jaime. "Don't mind him; his idea of personal service is to insult the customers personally."

Jaime looked around as she unwrapped her napkin from around her silver. The tablecloth was blue-checked vinyl, the napkins were dark blue linen, and the silver was mismatched. "They must not mind," she commented. "It seems to be a popular place."

"I told you, the best restaurant in town. And the best thing about it is..." He winked at her. "It's free."

Jaime cocked an appreciative eyebrow. "A little bit of charm goes a long way for you, doesn't it?"

"I do try," he admitted modestly.

Jaime smiled across the table at him. "Thanks," she said.

"For what?"

"For not taking me to some place dark and romantic."

Quaid chuckled, glancing around the room. "It would be hard to get a good seduction going in a place like this, wouldn't it?"

There was that, of course, but what Jaime was grateful for was even more, and it was not something she could put into words. Most men, upon learning of her background, would immediately think in terms of

Arnaud's or Antoine's, with their elegant interiors and world-class cuisine and waiters who pretended, more times than not, to be unable to speak a language as bourgeois as English. Most men would never dream that Jaime would be more comfortable in a place like this; that trying to remember which fork to use spoiled her digestion and that the only French she knew came from a high school class ten years ago.

Most men, upon learning of her background, were either intimidated by her or went out of their way to impress her; Quaid did neither. He was perhaps the only man she had ever met who instantly looked beyond where she had come from to see who she was. There was something very valuable in that, and rare.

And scary. Because as many times as she tried to convince herself that the two of them did not belong together, even for so much as a simple dinner date, it all came back to one irrefutable point: she enjoyed being with him.

She said, "Have you been coming here long?"

He stretched his arm comfortably across the back of the booth. "All my life." He was watching her with a relaxed, almost intimate air, his eyes warm and absorbing, as though there were nothing he would rather do than simply look at her.

Jaime kept her eyes moving; there was plenty to see and hold the interest in a place as busy as this, but every time she glanced back at Quaid his eyes were on nothing but her. Such directness, such open appreciation, embarrassed her, and she murmured, "Don't."

"Don't what?"

Nervously, she toyed with the button on her T-shirt. His eyes, of course, followed the movement. "Look at me like that," she said.

"I like looking at you. You're pretty."

"Well, I like looking at you, too, but I don't do it all the time," she said, and the minute the words were out she felt her cheeks go scarlet.

He laughed. "Do you know what else I like about you? You're totally incapable of telling a lie." His voice softened and the merry lights in his eyes faded to a warm glow. He reached across the table and took her hand. "That gives us quite an advantage, you know."

She cleared her throat a little. Everything within her was tight and tingling, simply because he was holding her hand. "What kind of advantage?"

"Getting to know each other." His thumb stroked the back of her hand. "Getting to like each other. Getting rid of the games. And you can look at me all you want, by the way."

She did look at him then, quickly and shyly, and then nervously pulled her fingers away. "Public displays of affection embarrass me."

"Good." He sat back, still smiling, still watching her. "Because I like to see you blush, too."

She sighed. "That's nice. Because I do it a lot. Especially..." And she met his gaze again. "With men who move as fast as you do."

His eyes twinkled. "And who don't know how to take no for an answer?"

"Right." Struggling to regain a hold on the trend of the evening—which was once again veering down forbidden paths—her eyes moved around the restaurant, searching for a change of subject. "It must have been nice," she said, "to have grown up in one place, and to have lived there all your life."

"It was."

"And I'll bet you had a nice, ordinary nuclear family. Mother and father, brothers and sisters ..."

"A few," he admitted.

"You lived in the same house all your life," she went on, warming to the subject, "went to the same school until you graduated, everybody was together for dinner every night, your mother baked cakes for everyone's birthday..."

"Of course."

"And you had Little League games and sandlot baseball—"

He was chuckling. "This is beginning to sound like a fifties' TV show."

She shrugged. "Well, it's everything I didn't have and always wanted. A real home, an ordinary way of life, a nice, stable *normal* family...."

"Well, we're normal all right," Quaid agreed, and his eyes were dancing with delighted mirth Jaime did not understand. "We're so normal it could drive you right out of your mind." The pirate had returned with the wine, and Quaid surprised Jaime by reaching up and grabbing him in an affectionate hammerlock around the neck. "Isn't that right, Pop?"

Jaime watched the affectionate horseplay between father and son in mute astonishment, and had a moment to reflect once again how deceptive appearances could be and to wonder why she was in the least surprised that Quaid's father should wear a gold earring and have a dragon tattooed on his arm. Quaid introduced his father, who owned the Lagniappe, and then his mother, who bustled in from the kitchen on cue, squeezed her comfortably plump frame into the booth beside Jaime and immediately began to bombard her with questions.

Over the next three hours Jaime met five of Quaid's seven brothers and sisters; two of whom worked full-time at the restaurant, two who were students at Tulane and one who was pregnant with her fourth child. Another brother, Jaime learned, was a clown with a large circus, and a sister was a agronomist at a Midwestern university.

Quaid's father pushed dish after dish of the most scrumptious Creole cooking Jaime had ever tasted upon her; his mother beamed how good it was to see Quaid with a *nice* girl and never lost an opportunity to question her about her domestic accomplishments and whether or not she planned to have a large family; one of the younger brothers, who was majoring in sociology, wanted to discuss the socioeconomic implications of AIDS on economically depressed areas with her, which almost resulted in his having his ears boxed by his father for bringing up such a subject before a nice young lady like Jaime.

The family crowded around, pushing into the booth, drawing up chairs, passing around bottles of wine, all talking at once and about five different subjects, and Jaime was taken back to her early years when she was dwarfed among Leona's eclectic collection of friends and overwhelmed by the chaos they provided. The conversation was loud and animated, energy flared between them like lightning bolts, and the enthusiasm was nonstop. When she had pictured Quaid as a product of a nice normal nuclear family she had not imagined anything like this. Jaime was beginning to understand what Quaid had meant when he suggested they had more in common than she knew. With a family like that, his childhood could have been no calmer than hers—yet there was a difference. Just being with them was exhausting, demanding, and stimulating, but Jaime had never felt surrounded by so much love in her life.

When Quaid suggested it was time for them to leave—and with a look directed toward his mother that said he meant it and would listen to no protests to the contrary—Jaime was the recipient of so many enthusiastic hugs and kisses she felt like a well-squeezed rag doll. Quaid's father pinched her cheek and told her sternly, "Don't you take no smart stuff from that boy of mine. You're a good girl; you stay that way."

His mother boxed up a pecan pie and forced it into her hands, insisting, "That'll go good with coffee when you get home, and there's nothing Quaid likes better than pecan pie."

Then Quaid's brother punched him on the arm and said lewdly, "Well, I bet there's *something* he likes better." To which his mother slapped his hand so hard he yelped and told him to keep a civil tongue in his mouth.

There followed another round of hugs and kisses and admonitions to Jaime to come back soon and to Quaid not to let a girl like that get away. By the time they made their escape into the humid night air Jaime's head was reeling and she was laughing from sheer residual energy.

"Do you feel like you've been through a war zone?" Quaid grinned, drawing her to him with an arm around her shoulders.

Automatically, Jaime's arm went around his waist, returning his light embrace. "This is not exactly what I expected when you asked me out to dinner."

"It's not exactly what anyone expects when they go out to dinner."

She laughed. "You could have at least warned me!"

"Now I ask you, how could I prepare anyone for my family? Besides," he added, caressing her shoulder with his fingers, "if I had told you, you probably wouldn't have come, and that would have been a shame. You're more relaxed now than I've ever seen you."

Jaime realized then that she was walking with her arm around his waist, and it was such a natural, comfortable position that she hadn't even noticed before. The lingering effects of the easy, enthusiastic affection that flowed from Quaid's family were still with her, and it felt good.

"They approve of you, you know," he said casually, as they walked toward the car. "You're one of the few people I've ever known who's been able to hold her own with them."

"I had plenty of practice with crowds as a kid." She glanced up at him. "Was that a test?"

He chuckled. "More like a case of the punishment fitting the crime. You told me you wanted to get married, and my mother did everything but welcome you into the family. Be careful what you wish for."

Jaime didn't know quite how to respond to that, and she was glad when they reached the car. She carefully placed the pie in the back seat and reminded Quaid, when he got in, not to forget it.

He glanced at her before he started the ignition. "Does that mean you're not inviting me home for coffee?"

She smiled. "Afraid so."

"Well, Mom," he sighed, "you did your best."

Jaime chuckled and leaned her head back as he pulled out into the street. The evening had left her exhilarated and drained, and Quaid was right—she had never felt so relaxed with him before. For a time she wanted to simply be still and enjoy it.

It was a while before she noticed he was not driving toward her house. She sat up and looked around. "Where are we going?"

"What's the matter? Had enough surprises for one evening?"

"It's late, and I'm tired," she began to protest feebly.

In the flash of a passing streetlight she saw the cleft of wry amusement appear at the corner of his mouth. "And the unexpected always makes you insecure."

"You know me pretty well, don't you?" she murmured.

"Yes," he replied simply, and his tone sounded serious. "Which was exactly what I was trying to tell you when you said we had nothing in common."

A tightness formed low in her chest, like anticipation or nervousness, a fluttering sensation that spread hesitantly to her abdomen and seemed to hint of something important about to happen. It was always like that with Quaid. Always unpredictable, always on the edge of promise, always ready with some new challenge. She never knew what he would do, or say, next. And just when she thought it was safe to relax with him, something would happen to make her guard her emotions again.

"Where are we going?" she repeated, trying for a casual tone of voice.

"Well, since I promised your mother I would have you home late, and since it's barely midnight . . ."

"That's late enough!"

"You have two choices," he continued intrepidly. "Either a stop at my apartment for pie and coffee and..." The glance he tossed at her was blatantly teasing. "Whatever else might develop, or a nice romantic stroll along Lake Pontchartrain for some fresh air, quiet conversation, and...whatever else might develop."

Her lips tightened dryly. "What about just taking me home?"

"Not on my list."

She was trying very hard not to smile, and she realized with very little surprise that she was not ready to end the evening, either. She had had one of the longest, most demanding days of her life, and she should have been exhausted. In fact, a part of her was both emotionally and physically drained. But there was another part, the part that ran on sheer adrenaline, probably, that did not want to say good-night to Quaid yet. It was the part of her that was like a child who refused to go to sleep for fear she might miss something. Every moment with him was a celebration, and she just couldn't resist seeing what Quaid had in store for her next.

Her voice was a mixture of resignation and delight as she replied, "Lake Pontchartrain sounds nice."

He chuckled. "Now how did I know that would be your choice?"

They left the car near the closed amusement park and walked along the lakeshore, and Quaid surprised her again with an easy, comfortable silence. He held her hand, and Jaime let herself be mesmerized by the sparkle of lights of the dark water, the fluttering whisper of a breeze, the somnolent quiet...and Quaid's presence.

"Lagniappe," she said softly, after a while. "That's what this evening has been. A little something extra."

His arm went around her shoulders in a light, affectionate embrace. "I'm glad. That's what I wanted it to be. I have a feeling you're not used to getting much lagniappe from life."

She laughed a little. "Well, I generally like my life a little...calmer, if that's what you mean."

"Just as I thought," he mused, letting his fingers drift down over the bare portion of her arm, stroking the skin. "My family was too much for one evening, weren't they? I should have stuck to my original plan and jetted you to Paris on the Concorde for dinner. There's only so much excitement a girl can take, after all."

She laughed, uncomfortably aware of the gentle, caressing movements his fingers made as they slid around her waist. "I loved your family," she protested. "I'd rather spend the evening with them than on the Concorde anytime."

"But?" he prompted, and bent a look on her that was only half-teasing.

The touch of his fingers on her ribs was spreading awareness in thin, fluttering waves from her abdomen to her throat. Gentle strokes that were repetitive and soothing, soft circular touches that were exploratory and arousing. Innocent, yet sensual. And impossible to ignore.

She tried to recapture the train of her thought, and her smile was a little weak. "But they made me nervous," she admitted. "So much enthusiasm...and excitement..." His fingers were moving up now, still absently stroking, toward her breast. Her throat tightened. "Surprises—always make me nervous." She stepped away from him. "You make me nervous."

He smiled. "But that's good." The muted light in his eyes was warm and too knowing. "The stomach tightens, the pulse speeds, the adrenaline flows... That just means you're alive, and aware. You make me nervous, too." He took her hand, and drew it upward to his throat, pressing her fingers to the pulse that beat there. "See?" he said softly.

His skin was warm and slightly damp with perspiration, smooth to the touch. She could feel the throb of his pulse, rapid and strong against her fingertips, and it matched her own. Her eyes were caught in the soft low glow of his and she did not want to move away. She wanted to stay just where she was, close to the circle of his warmth, with the lake breeze tickling her cheek and the water lapping gently in the background; she wanted to let her fingers slide across his skin, around his neck and beneath his hair; she wanted to lean closer until her breasts touched his chest and pressed into him. She wanted to feel his arms around her, first tenderly, then tightly, crushing her, and she wanted to taste him....

It's a spell, she thought somewhat dizzily. A spell he had cast on her, and it was becoming harder and harder to break away. It made no sense, it had no reason, and it was impossible to fight.

She let her hand drift down over his throat, touching the soft material of his T-shirt, downward over the dip of his shoulder and the slight swell of a lean breast muscle. She felt his chest expand with a breath as her fingers fell lower, across his ribs and toward his abdomen. The light in his eyes was intense, suspended. She curled her fingers into a fist and turned away.

"You're very bad for me," she said quietly.

It was a moment before he spoke. "Yes," he agreed soberly. "I suppose I am."

She walked a few steps away. "I know what I want, Quaid." She spoke firmly, with her back to him. "All my life I've known what I wanted and I'm not going to change now."

"A house in the suburbs, a car pool and a husband with a nine-to-five job." There was no censure in his voice, just a mild statement of fact.

She clasped her hands tightly before her and turned to face him, feeling defensive and vulnerable and foolish and desperate for him to understand. "It's more than that," she said steadily. "Peace, order, security. I've had enough chaos in my life, enough unpredictability. Enough excitement. I want routine, and—and normalcy. Things that follow a nice, safe, predictable pattern. Meeting someone, falling in love—"

He smiled. "Falling in love. One of the two things I do best."

She didn't ask what the other one was. She knew what the answer would be.

"I don't do things that are bad for me," she said firmly. "And you're not a very orderly person, Quaid."

He took a step toward her. It was a casual movement, not purposeful or in any way intimidating. But it brought him closer, and Jaime felt intimidated. "And why do you suppose you're telling me all this?" he asked.

It might have been mistaken for a light question, or even a mocking one. It wasn't as though, after all, he had asked her to marry him, or live with him, or even go to bed with him. This was barely even their first date—perhaps second, if one counted the night before. She had known him for less than forty-eight hours. She was making a big production out of nothing, and it would have been well within his rights to tease her.

But he wasn't teasing. And he knew why she was telling him this, just as well as she knew.

Her voice sounded a little tight as she replied, "Because I'm careful. Because I can't afford to get involved with you. Because you confuse me."

He stood there in the faint misty glow of reflected lights and distant street lamps, watching her thoughtfully, smiling faintly. He was less than two steps away from her, and her muscles tensed, hoping he would not come any closer. She wanted more than anything in the world for him to come closer.

He came closer. He lifted his arm and lightly stroked her hair, letting his fingers curl against her neck, lightly tracing the lobe of her ear. Warm shivers emanated from his touch, and her throat felt dry. He said softly, "And maybe it's because you do believe in magic. And you felt it, just like I did, the first time we kissed."

"No," she whispered. Her eyes were helplessly locked onto his, almost pleading for him to let her go. But he wasn't holding her.

He rested both hands against her neck, his fingers spreading lightly across her cheeks. He was very close. His scent was warm and herbal, and his thighs brushed her skirt. Jaime felt weak inside, breathless and static. Her heart was racing, but nothing else about her moved. He murmured, "Lead us not into temptation."

Somehow she managed to lift her hands, and close them around his arms. She meant to push him away. She meant to be strong in her resolve, firm in her tone. But all that came out was a whispered, "Yes." And then her hands were sliding up his arms, around his shoulders, and her mouth was opening for his.

Her limbs melted and fever swarmed over her skin. She felt the warm musky pressure of his tongue filling her mouth, blending into her, and colors swirled behind her eyes. He gathered her close, filling her with his scent and his taste and his heat. She felt the beat of his heart against her engorged breasts and it was a thunder that shook her whole body.

She wound her arms around his neck; she touched the smooth damp skin at the edge of his collar and felt the tendrils of his hair brush the backs of her hands. She slid her fingers into his hair and traced the shape of his skull, the sensitive area behind his ear. Her hands moved lower, exploring his shoulders and his back and his waist, pressing him to her, blind with sensation, and drinking in all of him fully, desperately, and without inhibition. She opened herself to him, savoring him. She kissed him as though it was for the last time, for in her mind it was the last time. This would not go any further between them. It could not. But for now... For now, all she wanted was that the moment should last.

His dropped his lips to her neck and she arched backward to receive the quick electrical darts of sensation that were his kisses. Her skin was moist from the humidity of the night and the touch of his tongue. His hands moved over her body in long, slow gathering strokes, from shoulder to buttock to thigh, exploring her shape and reverencing it, with each touch making that part of her his own. She was liquid with the sensations he created, she was feverish and at the mercy of her body's desires, and she knew if he did not stop soon she would drop to the grass and make love with him in a public park with no thought and no hesitation and no regard for the consequences.

"Tell me," he whispered against her mouth. "Tell me you don't feel the magic."

So easy, she thought dizzily. So easy to let go and let it be, so easy to believe it was right, so easy to be swept up by his mesmeric incantations; if not forever, then for a little while.... For it felt so right. It felt like magic.

Her trembling fingers touched his face, memorizing by touch alone the arch of his cheek, the dip of his chin, the heated porous flesh that stretched over his throat. And then, with a force of will she did not know she possessed, she tightened her hands against his shoulders, and she stepped away. "I don't want this, Quaid," she said hoarsely.

His face was flushed and damp and hazy with passion. For a moment he did not seem to focus on her words, or understand them, and then his eyes searched hers with such low and thorough absorption that she wanted to hide. He smiled slowly, and faintly. "Liar," he said softly.

Jaime turned away, and he let her go.

She walked over to a nearby bench and sat down, smoothing her skirt over her trembling knees, trying to still the frantic pace of her breathing and calm the pounding of her heart. She ached all over, as though the emotional onslaught had been a physical battle.

She said, when she was reasonably sure of being able to speak normally, "I suppose you think I'm being silly."

He didn't answer at once, and she was afraid he was angry with her. She glanced toward him quickly in the darkness, but could see nothing of his expression. And then he answered gently, "No. I think you're very wise. If you're not sure, don't let me push you into anything. I don't want to be unhappy any more than you do, and I would be, if I convinced you of something that was wrong for you."

And then he came over and sat beside her. He smiled and lightly smoothed back her hair. "I make quick decisions," he said simply. "You don't. I can live with that, and I'll try to go slower. But I'm not going to let you convince me of something that's wrong for me, either. And forgetting about you would be very, very wrong."

Jaime's throat was so tight it hurt to speak. She made herself look away from him, because his eyes were going straight to her heart. "And do you ever...regret your quick decisions?"

"No," he replied without hesitation. "They're part of me, and regrets wouldn't change anything. Sometimes I make mistakes, and sometimes I wish I had chosen differently. But that doesn't happen very often, and you are not one of my mistakes."

She wished, with all her heart, that she could be as sure of herself as he was. Once she thought she was. Once she thought she knew exactly where she was going and how to get there. But that was before New Orleans, and Victory House...and Quaid.

His hand caressed her cheek affectionately and moved away. She thought he would take her home then, but to her surprise he made no move to go. After a moment he took something from his pocket and began toying with it against the side of the bench.

"Do you know what I want?" he said.

She made herself smile. "An ice-cream sundae?"

His laugh was short and muffled. "No. To be a carpenter."

She looked at him.

"It's true," he insisted. "I always wanted to build things. Working outside with simple tools, seeing your labor take concrete shape, packing up at the end of the day and going home with no worries and no responsibilities...that's what I want. And the best thing about construction work is that you don't have to do it when it rains. It rains a lot in New Orleans. The ideal job for a lazy man."

He made her laugh. She would have thought it was impossible at this point, but he did it. She said, "But you're a doctor!"

"Exactly," he agreed soberly. He did not look at her, still busy with whatever he was doing on his side of the bench. "And I hate being a doctor. I never get enough sleep, never have a vacation, always taking work home from the office. The responsibility, the suffering, the helplessness sometimes...no one in his right mind would go into medicine if he could help it."

Now she was beginning to suspect he was serious. She looked at him closely. "But you had a choice," she pointed out.

He shook his head. "Being born into the family I was born into, being raised the way I was, being who I am...I never had a choice. Some things you can't change, and life doesn't always deliver what it promises. Just like you. You want order and predictability, so you end up in a job that takes the whole of society's turmoil and dumps it in your lap. And maybe all you want is a quiet home and a normal family, but I'm willing to bet what you get is a whole lot different from what you imagine."

"Heredity and environment," she murmured. She was having difficulty absorbing what he was saying, and she wasn't at all sure she believed it. "It sounds depressing. Hopeless."

"Not really. It's just that what we think we want and what we really want are sometimes two different things. But there's a part of us that always knows what's right, and gravitates toward it. Which is why I'm now a doctor instead of a carpenter, and why you're trying to make order out of the junk pile of the inner city, and..." He looked at her, his eyes soft and absorbing. "Maybe why we're here together, tonight."

His eyes held her, and something inside her was pulled toward him, a piece of her heart yearning to take flight and mate with his. With the soft echo of his mellifluous voice still lingering in her ears, with the gentle, thoughtful planes and shadows of his face imprinting themselves on her soul, with his nearness, his simplicity, his quiet sincerity... it did not seem wrong at all. The only right thing she had ever done in her life seemed to be that she was here, with him, tonight. And she thought, simply and unexpectedly, *I could love you, Quaid Gerreau. I really could.*

The realization, soft and hazy as it was, startled her and frightened her a little. And because she was afraid to examine it too closely, and she did not want him to read it in her eyes, she said quickly, "What are you doing over there, anyway?"

"Defacing city property." He showed her the blade of his penknife, then clicked it closed and slid it into his pocket. "Want to see?"

At first she hesitated, suspecting mischief, but then curiosity overcame her. She had to get up and walk around him to see the edge of the bench, and a soft melting warmth started in her chest and spread like honey through her veins. In the soft green wood of the bench he had carved a heart, and inside it the initials "JF and QG." A prick of sentimental tears embarrassed her, and she blinked them away in surprise. No one had ever done that for her before. No one.

She said a little huskily, "You are incorrigible."

"Do you think God will get me?"

"No. But the city police might."

He slipped his arms around her waist and drew her with an easy, natural movement onto his lap. "It will be worth it."

Jaime linked her arms around his neck, smiling because she couldn't prevent it, because she was purely and simply happy. "You know how to have more fun with less effort than anyone I've ever known," she said softly.

"We could have fun together, Jaime." His hand, resting lightly on her knee, made soft, caressing motions against the fabric of her skirt. "And be serious together. Even sad together, sometimes."

His fingertips absently brushed away the lace edging of her skirt and slipped beneath, gently whispering over the smooth flesh of her calf. His eyes were as deep and as green as the bottom of a clear-water lake. "We could be good together," he said, "if you would let it be."

How wonderful it sounded when he said it. How easy to believe.

She brought her forehead down slowly to rest against his, filling her vision with his face and her senses with his presence. She thought she could stay like that forever, looking at him, reveling in him, glowing with the warmth of his touch and drinking in the peace of his quiet smile.

"You smell like an English garden," he whispered.

His hand drifted over her knee, and upward to the sensitive flesh of her inner thigh. She closed her eyes and drew in her breath with the sensation, a tightening and a melting as, sheltered by the fall of her skirt, his delicate fingers stroked and teased. Her heartbeat speeded and her flesh heated; she tried to stiffen her muscles but she had no will. He could do this to her, without even trying.

She said, somewhat breathlessly, "You promised— you wouldn't push."

She sensed, rather than felt his smile. His nose brushed lightly against hers. "I'm incorrigible, remember?"

Yes, she thought helplessly as his hand moved upward, over her thigh, toying with her panty line. *Ah, yes...* There was heat inside her, a pounding anticipation, a tight yearning that flooded her skin with dampness and fever. His fingers skated over the thin fabric of her panties and caressed her bare waist. Every nerve ending in her body flared and ached. And then he was still.

He said softly, "Open your eyes."

She did, hazily. His face came slowly into focus, through a mist of sluggish reason and flooded senses. His expression was quiet, and his eyes, beneath the glow of passion there, were earnest. He said huskily, "I've had sex before. That's not all I want from you. Do you understand that?"

She thought she nodded. She knew she understood, and that was what frightened her so.

"And if I make love to you tonight, I might not ever let you go."

Or she might not be able to let him go. That could be bad. Very bad.

"Do you want me to stop?" he asked softly.

Yes, she thought. "No," she whispered.

"Then..." His lips brushed hers lightly. His hand was warm on her waist and his eyes touched and probed and caressed, drawing from the depths of her soul. "Will you come home with me?"

No, she thought. *No...* "Yes," she whispered.

Her lips touched his; his clasped hers, and she was lost in their kiss. No thought, no caution, no reason or careful planning, just letting go. It was that easy, and that right.

Passion flared and dizziness swirled as his hand caressed her bare flesh, pressing her to him, opening his mouth beneath hers, giving of himself and taking from her. There was no restraint and no hesitance, just simple need and unvarnished urgency. She felt the whole world opening up before her at that moment, vast and free, and the world began and ended with Quaid. It was madness, it was weakness, it was dangerous. And it was wonderful.

Distantly she heard a sound, but she did not really recognize it until Quaid broke away. Even then it was misty and unsure, and she was confused.

He rested his head against her shoulder. She could feel the thundering of his heart and the uneven sound of his breathing. He whispered, "Damn."

She looked at him dazedly, trying to focus, and gradually the sound became clear. A high, shrill, intermittent beep, very close.

Slowly and somewhat clumsily he disentangled his hand from her skirt. His face was flushed and damp, and his expression grim. He fumbled with something on the side of his belt, and the sound stopped. He fastened his hands around her waist and shifted her weight onto the bench beside him. "My pager," he explained briefly, standing. He patted his pockets. "Do you have a quarter?"

Chapter Eight

The lights were on in the clinic when they arrived, and Armand met them at the door. He gave Jaime one brief, contemptuous glance, then spoke to Quaid.

"It's Luther Johnson," he said, "and he's a mess. I put him in the back."

"Thanks, man." Quaid touched Armand's arm and started toward the examining room. Jaime could not help noticing splatters of blood on the gray tile floor that marked the path Quaid took. She swallowed hard and steeled herself to follow.

Quaid hesitated, and glanced over his shoulder toward Jaime. "You'd better wait here," he said. "This isn't going to be something for weak stomachs."

Jaime looked at Armand, and decided that whatever she had to face in the back room would be better than waiting here with him. She strengthened her muscles. "I've seen blood before," she said. "Maybe I can be of some help."

His eyes sparked with brief admiration as he squeezed her hand. "Good for you."

"Does he sleep here?" Jaime asked in a low tone as they hurried down the hallway.

"Armand? Usually. He kind of keeps an eye on the place for us. Not a bad idea, in this neighborhood. And it comes in handy in emergencies, as you can see."

The moans of pain were audible long before they reached the examining room. "Luther Johnson," Quaid said loudly as he strode into the room. "I thought I told you to stay out of trouble the last time I saw you."

The man on the table was gray-faced and covered with perspiration. His face was twisted in agony and a bloody towel was wrapped around one leg. "Dr. Quaid, I try, I swear I do."

"You know this establishment only operates from nine to six. I'm going to start charging you for overtime." Quaid unwrapped the bloody towel and Jaime quickly averted her eyes. "How do you like my pretty new assistant?" he went on. "Something, isn't she? I had to bring her along so you could see just what you interrupted by barging in here in the middle of the night."

Luther's face contorted with pain. "My leg's on fire, Doc. I ain't never hurt so much. Can't you do something?"

Jaime went to the sink and dampened a paper towel, returning quickly to sponge Luther's forehead. She smiled at him. "Hi, Luther. I'm Jaime Faber. You're going to be all right. Do you want me to hold your hand?"

"Best offer I've ever heard," Quaid commented as he unlocked the medicine cabinet.

Luther's eyes were big with pain and pleading, but he mumbled, "I don't mean to be no trouble, Miss."

Jaime took his hand and he gripped it hard. "You're no trouble at all. That's what we're here for."

Quaid filled a hypodermic and swabbed Luther's upper arm. Jaime kept her smile in place and her eyes on Luther's face as Quaid gave him the injection then tossed the needle into the trash. He unwrapped a sterile tray and arranged it at the foot of the table.

"Who shot you, Luther?" he asked casually.

Jaime's eyes flew to Quaid's.

"It was a fight, down at Jake's place," Luther said hoarsely. His hand clamped down with a crushing force on Jaime's as Quaid began working on his leg. "The cops came. I didn't see nothing, and I didn't shoot nobody. They was chasing me, but I didn't shoot nobody!" His voice became frantic, and he half lifted himself off the table. "You know I couldn't shoot nobody, Dr. Quaid!"

Quaid's eyes went sharply to Jaime, and she murmured quickly, "It's all right, Luther, lie back down." She pressed his shoulders gently, her heart pounding. "Let the doctor do his job. You're going to be all right."

"They're gonna send me back to jail!" he moaned, and tears mingled with the perspiration that soaked his face. "I didn't do nothing, but if they catch up with me—"

"You're not going to jail," Quaid said calmly. "We know you didn't shoot anybody. You just take it easy."

Jaime looked at Quaid with urgency and concern, but he was busy, and this was not the time to speak.

"You're a lucky man, Luther," Quaid said half an hour later. He put the last piece of tape on the bandage around his leg. "The bullet went clean through and there's no bone damage. You got a place you can lay low for a while?''

The injection Quaid had given him had taken effect, and Luther nodded fuzzily as Jaime helped him sit up.

''Then you'd better go there, and rest up for a couple of weeks.''

Jaime couldn't keep silent any longer. "Shouldn't—shouldn't he be in the hospital?"

Quaid ignored her, going back to the medicine cabinet. He returned with two bottles. "These are for infection," he said, handing one bottle to Luther. "You take one three times a day. If that leg gets infected I'm going to have to cut it off, do you understand that? So you take these pills."

Luther nodded. "Don't want my leg cut off," he said.

Quaid gave him the other bottle. "These are pain killers. Don't sell them, because I'm not giving you any more. You couldn't get much for them on the street, anyway. They're not even enough to give you a good high. And you stay away from Jake's Place, you hear me?"

Luther staggered down from the table, clutching the pills. Jaime supported his arm until he was steady. "Don't need no more trouble, Doc. You can believe that."

Quaid shouted, "Armand!"

The big man appeared instantly, scowling and fierce.

Quaid nodded toward Luther. "Get him out of here, will you?"

Luther groped for Quaid's hand. "You a good man, Doc. A real good man." He turned to Jaime. "You too, Miss. Ole Luther don't forget a good turn."

Jaime watched in stunned silence as he limped out of the room with Armand.

Quaid went to the sink and washed his hands. "He'll sell those damn pills," he muttered. "God, I hate this job."

Jaime said hesitantly, "You're going to call the police, aren't you?"

"No." He dried his hands on a wad of paper towels and tossed them into the trash.

Jaime stared at him as he moved past her toward the hall, and it was a moment before she could even recover herself fully enough to follow him.

"Why not?" she insisted.

Quaid flicked on the light in his office and went over to a filing cabinet. His movements were tense and his voice was short. "Because he didn't shoot anybody."

"How do you know that?" Jaime cried incredulously. "You can't just—"

Quaid removed a file and slammed the drawer closed with a clatter that drowned out her words. "Luther Johnson," he said deliberately, sitting down at his desk, "is blind in one eye and only has thirty percent vision in the other. He couldn't hit a target two feet in front of him with a baseball bat."

"But that doesn't mean—" She caught herself on the verge of another foolish argument and drew a calming breath. "All right," she said. "Then you can testify to that. But you have to report this. You can't just ignore—"

"Luther is on parole," Quaid said briefly. His pen made harsh scratching noises against the paper and he did not look up. His jaw was very tight. "Just being in Jake's Place is a one-way ticket back to jail. Jail is where he lost his eye in the first place. I'm not sending him back there."

Jaime looked at him, and it was as if she was seeing a stranger. The gentle, tender lover of an hour ago was gone and in his place was a harsh, tight-lipped man whose casual disregard for the law made her feel cold inside. He would not even meet her eyes. It was as though the world had shifted just slightly on its axis within the past hour without her even noticing it, and now everything was just slightly out of focus, not quite what it once had been, and pieces that once had fit together smoothly were now jagged and out of place. She felt disoriented and a little dazed, struggling to keep up with the change. And she was fighting hard to keep from believing what her eyes and ears told her.

She had to grip the edge of his desk to steady her shaking voice. "This is not exactly like defacing public property, Quaid," she said lowly. "This is serious. All gunshot wounds have to be reported, it's the law. You know that."

He snapped the folder closed and stood abruptly, striding back to the filing cabinet. "The police have their job, I have mine."

Jaime turned to him helplessly, knowing she was fighting a losing battle, and worse, that she was no longer sure who the enemy was. Her voice was urgent. "Look, I'll talk to his parole officer, I'll—"

"Go through channels!" He spat it out like an oath and slammed the file drawer shut. He whirled on her, his eyes blazing. "Let your precious system take over! Well, let me tell you something, sweetheart, it was the *system* that put Luther Johnson in this mess in the first place and I'll be damned if I'm going to contribute to it further.''

His voice was harsh and his muscles radiated tension, and Jaime all but shrank back from the cold anger she saw in his eyes. "He was brought in for panhandling and agreed to stand in a lineup because he was too stupid and too scared to know better. A witness identified him on an armed robbery charge and he was sent up for five years. Well, six months later they discovered they had the wrong man, but by that time Luther had already been beaten, raped and charged with knifing a guard—in self-defense, as it happened. So he served more time on that rap and now he's back on the streets and what do you think he knows but what he learned in prison? He's got one chance and he's doing the best he can and I'm not going to let him be swallowed up by your blessed system again, do you understand that?''

Jaime took a breath, and another, but she couldn't seem to ease the tightness in her chest. His words were like a physical battering, and the anger in his eyes hurt her though she knew it was not directed at her. She had never known such intensity from him, nor suspected he was capable of it. She felt defenseless and out of her depth. Yet still she fought valiantly.

"I know," she said steadily. "I know the system doesn't always work. Luther's story is only one tragic example and I'm sorry, I'm more sorry than you can know. He and people like him are the reason I'm here, trying to help. But the rules were made for a reason, Quaid—''

"We are living in a goddamn war zone down here," he spat venomously. "Your rules and regulations mean nothing to the people who are fighting just to stay alive.''

Helplessness and frustration bubbled up within her and she was angry—angry with Quaid for being right, and with herself for being right and for caring so much yet being so impotent. Her control snapped, her cheeks flamed and her fists bunched as she cried, "You could lose your license over this! Don't you care? Don't you care at all?''

The shrillness of her voice echoed between them for what seemed like forever. The anger faded from his eyes and was replaced with a soft regret that gradually deepened to a sort of pain. And Jaime, trembling with residual emotion and cringing with shame for her outburst, met his eyes bravely. Something had changed between them in the past few minutes and it was not necessarily for the better; it left her shaken and confused and hurting.

She had never known him like this before, but then she had known him hardly at all. An hour ago she had been willing—no, anxious—to make love with this man, to commit herself to him in ways that were more than physical, yet she did not know him at all. It wasn't a stranger who had looked at her with such coldness in his eyes and spoken with such anger in his tone, only another part of Quaid. The warrior and the lover, two sides of the same coin, yet both of them strangers to her. The knowledge disoriented her and shook her deeply.

After a moment he sighed heavily and ran his fingers through his hair. "Look," he said quietly, "let's start over, okay?" He made a feeble attempt at a smile, but his eyes were intense upon her face. "I'm sorry. I shouldn't have been short with you. You're one of the best little assistants I've ever had, and I appreciate the help."

She said nothing. She didn't know what to say.

He took a breath and looked briefly away. "I was mad, okay? Not at you—at the system, at Luther, at myself for being so damn helpless. It gets to me sometimes. And I knew how you were going to react, and that only made me madder because I couldn't do anything to stop it."

He came toward her, but stopped a few feet before reaching her. His face was sad and open and defenseless. "Jaime," he said gently, "we're all just doing the best we can. Sometimes it seems like we're fighting a losing battle, sometimes our best isn't good enough. But we're all on the same side here. When the rules don't work, we improvise, because what we've got to lose is too important not to give it our best shot, don't you understand that?"

"Yes," she said quietly, after a time. "I do understand. I'm just—not sure I can do it, Quaid."

He came toward her, and he took her shoulders lightly. "Jaime..."

She pulled away from him, and it was an instinctive gesture of self-protection—not because she was afraid of him, but because she was afraid of herself.

He let his hands drop slowly. His smile was strained, and his tone hollow. "I take it the mood is completely broken."

She didn't know what to say to him. She wanted to say a dozen things, a hundred... but none of them made sense, and none of them, at that moment, would make a difference. "I think," she managed at last, "you'd better take me home."

He looked at her for a long time, and she did not know what he was thinking. There was sadness in his eyes, and regret, and longing. But there were other things, too. One of them was disappointment.

And then he said, very quietly, "I think you're right." Without touching her, he gestured her to the door.

THE FOLLOWING TWO WEEKS were the busiest, the hottest, and the most miserable of Jaime's life.

Her car was returned with the diagnosis of a short in the ignition switch. The first day she drove it, she had a flat tire in the middle of Pontchartrain Boulevard. The second day she ran out of gas with the indicator pointing toward full. There were other incidents—the windshield wipers locked on high when she signaled a right turn, the hazard lights came on whenever the transmission was engaged, the radio suddenly refused to receive anything but a Spanish broadcast from Miami. Leona, outraged, wanted to return the automobile for a full refund, but Jaime persevered. She saw no reason to inflict the Mazda people with the consequences of her own cursed footsteps.

Within the space of a week, she blew six fuses, her telephone stopped working, and her washing machine flooded the entire first floor. At work things were not much better. Calculators wouldn't work for her, light bulbs exploded at her touch, telephone calls were flooded with static. Her co-workers began to laughingly call her a jinx, and even Daphene began to look at her askance.

And she did not see or speak to Quaid alone even once.

The two red walls in Jaime's apartment gradually began to transform themselves into a brilliant sunset framing twin trompe l'oeil columned doors, wreathed with ivy and opening onto a field of cornflowers. The scene was striking and unquestionably valuable—how many people, after all, could boast a Leona Faber original painted *on* their walls—but it reminded Jaime of Dante's inferno. She did not complain, however. At least the painting kept her mother busy.

And that was another thing. Leona Faber was acting very strangely. For the first time in Jaime's memory, Leona's appearance in her life was not accompanied by fanfare, glamor and nonstop activity. In New Orleans, the party capital of the world, Leona Faber was content to sit home most nights and watch television with her daughter.

She had been out of the country for three months, but she had let no one know she was back. She spent her days shopping, puttering around, and looking for that mythological house she kept insisting she was going to buy. The evenings she devoted exclusively to Jaime. They went out to dinner, or to jazz clubs, or stayed at home making a mess of the kitchen like two teenagers. On the weekends Leona planned excursions to the country and picnics at the lake, always with just the two of them. It was as though she were trying to cram twenty-five years of mother-daughter relationship into two scant weeks, and that puzzled Jaime because as far as she was concerned nothing had been missing in their relationship before. They always had fun together.

Not that she wasn't grateful for her mother's companionship. Leona's carefree, exuberant presence was exactly what she needed to take her mind off her own troubles, and it would have worked if Leona hadn't *been* one of her problems.

Watching her mother change the shelf paper in her kitchen cabinets one evening—after having protested to no avail that the old shelf paper was hardly used— Jaime commented, "You're certainly getting domestic in your old age."

Leona only laughed. "It's about time, don't you think?"

"Menopause?" suggested Jaime.

"At forty-one? Are you kidding?" Leona tossed her head girlishly. "Why, I'm young enough to have another baby, if I wanted to."

That shocked Jaime and disturbed her beyond words. She half thought her mother might be serious, and the only conclusion she could possibly draw was mid-life crisis. She changed the subject and never brought it up again.

Leona, however, was not so sensitive toward the subjects Jaime did not want to discuss. She asked constantly about Quaid and ignored Jaime's efforts to evade her. It didn't take her long to figure out that Jaime and Quaid had had an argument of some sort, and she pressed relentlessly for details. This, too, was very unlike Leona. She had never insinuated herself into her daughter's life nor invited confidence when none was forthcoming. It was only another example of what Jaime had begun to secretly refer to as Leona's "motherhood phase."

There were times when Jaime was tempted to tell her mother the whole story, to seek impartial advice, to simply relieve her mind by speaking her uncertainties and her self-recriminations out loud. But she had never been able to talk to her mother about anything serious, and she could not begin now. Philosophy, religion, aesthetics, politics—these were all subjects for easy and lively debate between Jaime and her mother. But this was personal, and she did not know where to begin.

The trouble was, she needed to talk to someone, badly. And the only person she could think of who would understand was Quaid.

Sometimes, sweltering at night in her bedroom loft, with the covers tossed back and her nightgown pulled up above the knees in the vain hope of catching an errant breeze, Jaime would give up on sleep, turn on the bedside lamp and try to put her thoughts on paper.

Dear Marielle,
I miss New York. I miss you and the kids and the traffic on Fifth Avenue and the sound of garbage trucks at 5:00 A.M. I miss the temperamental plumbing and *air-conditioning*. I even miss the ghetto and the muggers in the park.... At least in New York you always know what to expect.

People are crazy down here. Drag queens wandering in and out of perfectly respectable shops, jazz music twenty-four hours a day, voodoo witches running around putting curses on people...

I met the most interesting man...

Or:

Dear Abbie,
First of all, it's hot. I know I wanted a change of climate, but no one told me I'd be moving to the

subtropics. Remember how I whined and complained about the blizzard last year? I didn't know when I was well off.

You were right when you said New Orleans was one of the crime capitals of the world. You wouldn't believe some of the things I've seen since I've been here. Even the people I work with act as though the law was invented for someone else. There's this doctor at the settlement house...

AND THAT WAS WHERE she always stopped.

For the first two days she concentrated on convincing herself it was for the best. Simple, straightforward, levelheaded Jaime Faber had come dangerously close to letting herself be swept away by that unpredictable and completely irrational thing called passion. And fate in the form of Luther Johnson had brought her back to her senses just in time. Nothing had happened at the clinic that night, after all, except that she had been reminded, rather graphically, of how ill-suited she and Quaid were for each other, and she had known that all along. If she had gone home with him that night she would have regretted it before he even unlocked the door, and she would be even more miserable than she was now.

It was around the third day, when her relief at having successfully avoided Quaid began to turn into regret—and an unhappy suspicion that he was avoiding her as well—that a new and very unwelcome idea began to occur to her. Perhaps she had been wrong.

Not that she had been wrong in her opinion of Quaid's action, but that she had judged him too harshly and too quickly... and much, much too emotionally. There were shades of gray inherent in the situation, and she refused to recognize them because she wanted Quaid to be perfect. She wanted life to be perfect. One of the first things she had learned as a caseworker was the necessity of making allowances for human weakness. Couldn't she extend that same capacity to her personal life as well?

It did not take much effort to find out about Luther Johnson, and everything she heard only strengthened Quaid's position. It was a tragic story, and not the first example of hopeless injustice Jaime had come across, but this one had a chance for a happy ending. Thanks to Victory House, Luther was beginning to hold down a job and make a new life for himself. Thanks to friends like Quaid, he might just succeed.

Was there anything so wrong in a doctor putting the welfare of his patients before that of himself? Was what Quaid was doing here in the inner city any less noble, less humanitarian or less courageous than the missionaries who gave themselves to starving third-world countries or risked their lives in the jungles of Guatemala or Nicaragua? And was Jaime so small, so rigid and self-righteous that she could not make allowances for a few bent rules?

She might never be able to approve of what Quaid had done, but couldn't she overlook it, just this once?

It was a big step for Jaime, and not one she was sure she could take. Separating professional ethics from personal needs was not an easy thing, and more than her moral code was at risk. Quaid Gerreau threatened her very heart.

Eventually, their paths began to cross at work, but their contact was always distant and polite: "Good morning, Miss Faber." "Busy today, isn't it, Dr. Gerreau?" Occasionally she would refer a case to him or he to her, but it was always over the telephone. He lifted his hand to her across the room or opened a door for her, or she would nod at him in passing, and there was never, ever anything in his voice or smile that was not present when he dealt with any other member of the staff. After a while she found herself going out of her way in hopes of catching a glimpse of him, but it hardly ever worked. And when it did, it only made her stomach ache and her throat tight.

Her chance came when Quaid casually invited everyone at the settlement house to the annual Fourth of July bash his parents were having, but at the last minute she lost her courage and did not go. Perhaps because he had not singled her out for an invitation, perhaps because she could not bear the thought of being so close to him in a crowd, perhaps because she was afraid that sometime during the day they might find themselves alone and she would have to face her feelings... but she knew she couldn't do it. When Daphene asked her if she planned to attend, Jaime told her she had other plans. As a matter of fact, she spent the Fourth setting the shrubbery on fire while barbecuing steaks with her mother, and when the holiday was over Quaid did not even remark on her absence at his party.

She could not believe how large a part of her life he had come to occupy in such a short time. As the nights grew longer and hotter and sleep became more elusive, she began to fantasize. A phone call in the middle of the night; one of her cases was in trouble and

Quaid needed her help. She rushed to his side, together they battled death and disaster; he took her into his arms and his eyes were aflame with adoration and admiration while passion swept them away.…

Or she was stricken by a mysterious fever and Quaid stayed by her side day and night, plumbing the very depths of his medical skills to save her and forging a bond between them that could never be broken. Or she was brought injured and bleeding into Quaid's office, and as he labored over her there was soul-striking terror in his eyes and he declared what a fool he was to ever let her go and she weakly forgave him.… At that point her health seemed a very small sacrifice to make in order to bring Quaid Gerreau back into her life.

The simplest fantasy of all was the one in which she arrived at work and Daphene informed her she was assigned to help Quaid in the clinic that day. But it never happened. All the other staff members rotated through the clinic, but she was never scheduled. She began to wonder if Quaid had requested that she not be.

Then there were other fantasies. These were the ones that came while she tossed and turned on her perspiration-dampened sheets in the sultry, fragrant night, and they were the ones that were the most persistently difficult to shake. Quaid's hands sliding over her body, his mouth infusing her with his taste, his heat inflaming her. Her limbs entwined with his, his heart pounding against hers. Touching, caressing, aching, loving.…

Fantasies. She had never indulged them before. She felt foolish and embarrassed and immature. This was not the way a determined, self-sufficient, competent young woman conducted her life. Jaime Faber did not wile away time with absurd daydreams, she did not arrange her life around alternately avoiding and desperately seeking glimpses of one of her colleagues. She did not let personal feelings impair her professional judgment or fall victim to voodoo spells, and she most definitely did not fall in love with a man who was completely wrong for her.

But that was unmistakably what Jaime had done. And she had never been so miserable in her life.

Chapter Nine

On the fifteenth day of Quaid's absence, Jaime shorted out her hair drier, broke the heel of her shoe and two juice glasses, and the handle came off the refrigerator door. This was all before breakfast. When she lifted the coffee carafe to pour cold water into the coffee maker the handle broke off and the carafe crashed to the floor.

Leona leaned against the door of the kitchen, fresh from her shower. Leona had called a certified plumber to repair the hot water faucet, and never had trouble getting a warm shower. All Jaime could ever obtain was a tepid trickle.

She was elegant even in a floor-length terry robe with a towel wrapped around her hair, and she looked at Jaime oddly. "Did you walk under a ladder or something?"

Jaime went to get the broom. "No. Somebody put a curse on me."

Leona nodded thoughtfully. "We're all in control of our own lives, you know. We attract what we need to shape our destinies."

"Thank you, Shirley MacLaine."

"What I mean is..." Leona picked her way carefully around the broken glass, toward the refrigerator. "Sometimes when you're under stress you can actually make accidents happen...or what appear to be accidents. Of course Freud—or was it Jung?—said there is no such thing as an accident, so what we have here is nothing more than your subconscious trying to tell you something."

"So what is my subconscious trying to tell me? Stay away from breakable objects?"

Leona pried open the refrigerator door with her fingers and took out the orange juice, glancing at Jaime shrewdly. "Like your heart?"

"Oh, Mother!" Jaime swept up the last of the glass and dumped it into the trash. "You and your amateur psychology. Don't you ever read anything useful—like the financial page?"

Leona made a face. "Too depressing. Do you want to use my hair drier?"

"No, if I touched it it would probably explode and we need at least one appliance in this house that's actually working."

"You're going to work with your hair wet?"

Jaime popped two pieces of bread in the toaster. "It's going to rain. No one will notice."

Leona sat down at the table and sipped her orange juice. "I saw Quaid yesterday," she said.

Jaime, half buried inside the refrigerator as she searched for her cologne, straightened up slowly, staring at her mother.

"Just out and about," Leona went on easily, her face a perfect mask of innocence. "We had lunch at Café du Monde."

Jaime struggled to keep her tone neutral. "Is that a fact? And what were you doing 'out and about' in Quaid's territory?"

Leona gave her an amused look over the rim of her glass. "I was interfering in my daughter's life, of course." Then, a trifle impatiently, "All sorts of people walk through Jackson Square, and the meeting was accidental, I promise."

Jaime found her cologne and spritzed the cool mist over her neck and arms, and then, for good measure, she lifted her skirt and sprayed behind her knees. Leona had taught her the trick of keeping her cologne in the refrigerator for a refreshing pick-me-up on muggy days, but on this particular morning it did little to ease Jaime's discomfort. Last night, even her ceiling fan had stopped working.

Jaime poured herself a glass of orange juice and sat down at the table. Still, she managed to keep her expression, and her tone, disinterested. "So. What did you talk about?"

Leona shrugged. "This and that. Art, history, religion. He's a fascinating man. Very bright, very eclectic. But I suppose you know that."

She murmured noncommittally, "Sounds like you had a very in-depth conversation."

"Not really. He's just one of those people who's easy to talk to."

Yes, Jaime thought bleakly. She knew.

Leona looked at her. "We didn't talk about you," she said, "since you're obviously not going to ask. Quaid's too much of a gentleman, and far be it from me to get involved in your personal life."

That much Jaime could believe. Leona Faber had always made it a policy not to get involved in other people's affairs. But even this much of a show of interest in Jaime's personal life was far out of character for her, and Jaime couldn't help being uneasy.

"However," Leona went on, "if either one of you at any time would care to drop just the smallest hint about what is going on between you two..."

Jaime sighed, uncomfortably and impatiently. "Nothing is going on." She drained her orange juice as the clock chimed the half hour. "Nothing at all."

"That's just what I mean," Leona persisted. "Listen, I've been thinking, I've been in your hair for almost three weeks now, and if some privacy would help..."

Jaime shook her head in amused frustration. "You've got to be the only mother in the world who would offer to move out so that her daughter could have a healthy sex life."

"Healthy being the key word," Leona pointed out. "And the way you've been behaving lately is not healthy at all. The toast is burning."

Jaime sprang to her feet just in time to see the top of the toaster pouf with small flames. She jerked out the cord, smothered the flames with a pot holder, and gazed with bleak resignation on the mess that once had been her breakfast.

"Why am I surprised?" she muttered. Glancing at her watch she groaned. "I've got to get to work. Will you take care of—" she gestured distastefully toward the charred toaster and the blackened crumbs that littered the counter "—that?"

Leona made a pained face. "Drudgery is my life."

"You're a sweetheart." Jaime kissed her quickly on her way to the door.

"A healthy breakfast is the cornerstone of well-being!" Leona sang out.

Jaime snatched up her purse and umbrella. "Have a good day," she chanted back.

"Jaime—"

Jaime turned impatiently, halfway out the door.

"There's just one thing." Leona looked flushed and uncertain and unaccountably shy. "Sort of a favor, really."

"Sure." Jaime hesitated at the threshold, curious. "What?"

"I'd like to have a . . . well, a sort of special dinner Friday night. At Antoine's. Will you come?"

Jaime laughed. "That's your favor? You've got it!"

"It's kind of a celebration. A surprise." Leona's color was high and her eyes were bright, and Jaime was more than curious.

"A celebration? What are we celebrating?"

"That's the surprise. Let's make it for eight and . . . will you bring Quaid?"

Jaime closed her eyes slowly. "Mother . . ."

"It would be better if you had a date," Leona insisted. "You'll see why, I promise."

"Mother, I can't—"

"Just ask him. Please."

The clock struck the quarter hour. "I've got to go."

"Ask him," Leona called after her.

Jaime knew she wouldn't ask him, and she was already trying to think of some excuse to tell her mother as she hurried down the walk. Perhaps that was the main thing that separated daydreams from reality: courage.

"WHEN I WAS IN graduate school," Jaime said, "I worked the evening shift in the social services department of a local hospital, to help with expenses, you know, and also to get some field experience."

"Better than being a call girl." Daphene peered at Jaime over the rim of her reading glasses, and when she got no reaction, explained, "As far as paying the expenses goes, that is . . . and getting experience."

"Oh. Yes."

Daphene cocked a slightly curious eyebrow at Jaime's uncustomary lack of humor, but Jaime barely noticed. For the past two weeks she had immersed herself completely in this project, and now that the moment of presentation had come she was too anxious, and concentrating too intensely, to be distracted.

Daphene said, "Go on."

They were sharing a soggy egg-salad sandwich in the Learning Center, sitting at a preschooler-size table in bright red and green chairs, and though Jaime could have wished for a more comfortable environment she had to take her chances where she found them, and this was the only quiet moment she had had with Daphene in a week. She went on quickly, "Anyway, one evening the police brought in an abandoned baby for a routine checkup before turning her over to Family Services. Apparently the child had been left alone in the apartment while the mother worked, and there had been a minor fire in the building. We were brought in as liaisons about the same time Michelle Dobbs, the mother, came flying into the emergency room, hysterical over her missing child.

"Michelle was barely more than a child herself— sixteen or seventeen—and she was living alone, trying to hold down a night job at a fast-food restaurant and raise this baby. As you know, it's not often we see somebody in those circumstances making that kind of effort, and here she was faced with losing her baby and going to jail for abandonment and endangerment.... The thing was, she was *trying*, and I've always felt that the reason we're here is to help people who are willing to try.

"To make a long story short, I met with the prosecutor from the D.A.'s office—Abbie Jarvis, I told you about her—and eventually talked her out of pressing charges, which was no easy task, let me tell you. She always was, and still is, a tough lady to manipulate. But she came around, eventually, and we even got to be friends when she found me an apartment in her building. Meanwhile I intervened with Family Services—and with Abbie's help, got temporary custody of Michelle's baby and let Michelle and the baby stay with me for a while. I found her a job working days as a cook in a preschool, where she could keep her baby with her. The last I heard they were both doing great.

"The point is," Jaime insisted earnestly, "that was the first time I knew, I mean I really *knew* that the system could work, that we could do something to help those who are willing to help themselves. Whenever I get discouraged, I think about Michelle Dobbs, and realize that no matter how many times I fail to make a difference, there is at least one little girl in this world who'll have a chance because of me. And if that sounds self-gratifying, I suppose it is."

Daphene smiled. "We all have our Michelle Dobbses to look back on. We have to have something to keep us going."

Jaime nodded, encouraged. "And if it can start with the children, the fight is more than halfway won. Michelle has been on my mind a lot lately—since the first day, really, when I met Cara Franklin and all she could talk about was how she couldn't leave the house for her three children and her sick grandmother. She was using the kids as an excuse. What you have here in this community is a mostly matriarchal family structure trapped by poverty and the traditional mother roles. Those women who are willing to go out and get work—even if it's just hooking on the streets—are leaving their kids unsupervised, which leads to juvenile crime and all those cases of child abuse that have been referred here over the past year. A day-care center wouldn't solve all the problems, but it would be a start."

Daphene nodded thoughtfully as she glanced once again through the stack of reports Jaime had prepared for her. "Well, you've certainly done your homework, I'll give you that. I've never seen so many charts and graphs and budgetary analyses."

Jaime's spirits fell. That did not sound very encouraging.

Daphene took off her glasses and looked at her directly. "The best thing," she said, "about getting somebody fresh out of college is that they don't know how to accept defeat yet. God willing, that enthusiasm of yours will last another year or two, and by that time I wouldn't be a bit surprised if you hadn't made quite a difference around here."

She stacked the papers and handed them back to Jaime. "You've got it all worked out; I say go for it. You can start this afternoon. There's a well-baby class meeting this afternoon; go down there and see what kind of interest you can generate. You might even be able to recruit some volunteers to man the program from the seniors group next door. Just get everybody together that you can and make your spiel. Word of mouth will do the rest."

Jaime could barely keep from beaming her satisfaction as she took the papers. "Thanks, Daphene," she said sincerely. "I can make this work, I know I can."

Daphene chuckled. "I don't have a doubt in the world."

Jaime was halfway to the door when she hesitated, and turned back. "Could I ask you something?"

Daphene spread her hands obligingly. "Sure."

"What is our relationship with the police?"

Daphene looked thoughtful, then shrugged. "Okay. Good. We don't make their job any harder, and they do us the same courtesy. Why, do you need a traffic ticket fixed?"

Jaime laughed a little uncomfortably. "No, nothing like that. Just curious."

Daphene nodded, understanding. "Armand, right?"

Jaime couldn't meet her eyes. "Well, actually..."

Daphene smiled sympathetically. "It's an adjustment isn't it? It might help to remember that it's not our job to change the world; just to make living in it a little easier, and sometimes—if we're lucky—more productive. The more unique the problems, the more creative we have to be in dealing with them." And then she shrugged. "If it eases your mind, the local task force on gangs is unofficially aware of our role here, and is unofficially silent. And no one is going to come banging on your door and drag you off to jail for collusion in the middle of the night, if that's what's worrying you."

Jaime smiled, weakly and apologetically. That did ease her mind somewhat, but that was not really what she was worried about. Suddenly she found she could not bring up the subject of Luther Johnson, and that in itself was a major step toward reconciling the entire matter in her head. She realized slowly that it had never been the incident itself that was at the core of her problems, but something much deeper. Had she been using Luther Johnson as an excuse to deny her feelings for Quaid?

She said, somewhat absently, "I guess I've still got a lot of learning to do."

Daphene replied merely, "That's what life is all about, isn't it?"

FOR THE REMAINDER of the afternoon Jaime threw herself into her work, mostly as a method of avoiding having too much time to examine her own motivations too closely. She addressed every group that came into the center, and excitement built at the cautious response she received. This was what it was all about— examining the problem, developing a solution, making a difference. There was satisfaction in what she was doing, but beneath it all was another kind of excitement, as subtle as a low-voltage current of electricity, and it was generated every time she thought about Quaid. Something was changing inside her, cautiously and uncertainly, and she was no longer quite as frightened as she once had been to see the change coming.

It was late in the afternoon, and she was explaining the concept of the day-care center to Daphene's well-baby class. Other people had wandered in, mostly to find something to do on the dull, drizzling gray day, and quite a crowd had gathered. The classroom was humid and stifling, and perspiration dampened Jaime's face and dotted her T-shirt beneath her muslin jumper. Babies cried and mothers lethargically stirred the air with paper funeral-home fans. Jaime, undaunted, kept her voice enthusiastic and her movements energetic as she answered questions and recruited volunteers.

There was a stirring at the back of the room, a murmuring and shuffling in the crowd, and Jaime felt attention shift from her to the new arrival who was pushing forward. There was consternation and alarm in the faces of those gathered, and Jaime glanced at Daphene, who looked just as puzzled as she was.

When Jaime looked back over the room, Mame LeCaree was standing in the center of an aisle that had been formed for her, looking as regal and as exotic as an old-world queen deigning to visit her subjects. Complete in gold satin caftan, turquoise shawl and laden with jewelry and talismans, she swept a haughty glance over the room very slowly, until her eyes came to rest at last on Jaime.

"Ah, there you are, you foolish child," she said. "Mame LeCaree has come to visit you."

There were more murmurings in the crowd, and the gazes that returned to Jaime seemed to be tinged with a new respect—or perhaps it was fear.

Jaime swallowed back her amazement. She said with the utmost politeness, "You're welcome here, of course. What can we do for you?"

Mame chuckled. "But the question is what Mame can do for you. You are enjoying the effects of my small spin? You have come to learn respect for what you do not know?''

Jaime said coolly, ''I don't believe in voodoo and I'm not afraid of you. So if that's all you came here to say...''

Mame's eyes narrowed, but her voice was very soft. ''You have learned nothing, I see.''

The alarm on the faces of the people in the room had become more pronounced now, and several of them began to inch toward the door. Jaime knew that the only way to regain control over the gathering was in a display of strength, and she took a deliberate step toward Mame. ''You have no business here,'' she said clearly. ''You're disrupting this meeting and upsetting these people. I suggest—''

Mame LeCaree's dark face flared with anger. ''These are *my* people!'' she declared loudly. She swept her arm around the room and the jingling and tinkling of her jewelry was a dramatic echo to the force of her words. ''This is *my* place, and you will learn of my power!''

Her voice lowered and her dark eyes fixed on Jaime with a force that would have made a lesser person cringe. ''The next time, foolish child,'' she said deliberately, ''you will come to Mame. Until then—'' she turned with a dramatic ripple of gold and turquoise and a clinking of jewelry ''—may you remain cursed. So speaks Mame LeCaree!''

She strode out of the room, and Jaime, feeling some action on her part was called for, pushed through the horrified crowd to follow her. She reached the foyer just as Mame was pulling open the outer door. Jaime called, ''Wait just a—''

And the light fixture suddenly fell from the ceiling and crashed at her feet.

Mame turned back, swept her with a cool, satisfied glance and walked through the door.

Jaime was aware of the clamor of voices behind her, the swift, frightened eyes that darted her way, and a cautious exodus of bodies that began to edge past her on the way to the door. Jaime gritted her teeth and stared at the shattered glass on the floor. "Damn," she said. She knelt to start cleaning up the glass; some of the children were barefoot. Daphene called for a broom and dustpan and knelt beside her. "I really wish you hadn't gotten on her bad side," she said sadly.

Jaime stared at her. "That crazy old woman? You can't believe—"

Daphene nodded meaningfully toward the wide-eyed faces that were gathered around. "*They* do," she said. Then, "Leave that be, you're going to—"

"Ouch!" Jaime exclaimed as a gash appeared on her hand.

"Cut yourself," finished Daphene. She fished in her pocket and brought out a tissue as one of the staff members appeared with a broom. "This is not good," she said regretfully.

Jaime wrapped the tissue around her hand and stood. "It's just a scratch," she muttered. "Do you have a Band-Aid?"

"In the clinic," Daphene said. "And then..." She glanced ruefully toward the door, where people were pausing only to cross themselves and gaze on Jaime with superstitious awe before hurrying out. "You might as well go home. I think you've lost your audience."

"But I can't just—"

Daphene patted her arm reassuringly. "It's late," she said, "and tomorrow is another day. Go on home now—and stop by the clinic for that hand. We're not insured against voodoo curses, and if infection sets in you're out of luck."

Jaime knew that Daphene was right: the day had ended on a dramatic flourish that she could not hope to follow, and there was no point in trying to salvage anything from it. She picked up her purse and headed for the clinic with an uncomfortable sense of frustration and failure.

It started to rain as she hurried down the path toward the clinic, intent only upon getting a Band-Aid for her hand so that she could drive home without any more discomfort. So involved was she with her own anger and self-recriminations that she did not even realize the irony of what she was doing until she had opened the door of the clinic and it was too late. She was acting out one of her fantasies. It wasn't exactly yellow fever or a severed artery, but here she was, injured and bleeding and turning to Quaid for help. Maybe her mother was right. Maybe she *was* subconsciously doing this to herself.

The only difference between the fantasy and the reality was that when Jaime stepped inside the clinic, Quaid was not there. The waiting room was deserted, and the only lights came from behind the reception desk. Relieved that her first face-to-face meeting with Quaid would not come at the end of a trying day, Jaime hurried forward.

Jolene was manning the office, and she greeted Jaime cheerfully.

"I just need a Band-Aid," Jaime said, indicating her hand. "Got any handy?"

Jolene made a sound of sympathy as she searched in her drawer. "What happened?"

"Oh, I was cleaning up some glass..." Jaime's voice trailed off as she heard the sound of Quaid's.

He was coming down the hall with his arm around a young pregnant woman, speaking to her rapidly and easily in a language Jaime eventually recognized as some bastardized form of French. All it took was the sound of his voice, musical and sweet even when speaking a language she did not understand, and her heart went into a scattering, tripping rhythm. The curve of his profile, the fluid gait of his walk, the way his hair curled over his collar—Jaime absorbed and memorized the details the way a starving woman might inhale the aroma of a succulent meal. And then he noticed her.

There was the briefest flash of something in his eyes—surprise, definitely; welcome, maybe—and then he turned back to his patient. He smiled at her, said something that might have referred to two weeks, and patted her abdomen playfully. She thanked him profusely on her way out.

Quaid glanced at Jaime and then leaned against the desk to make a note on the chart. "Well, well," he said, "another industrial accident, I see."

"I just need a Band-Aid," she replied and nervously looked away from him.

Quaid finished the chart and tossed it on the pile atop Jolene's desk. "You may as well pack it in, hon," he said to her. "Maybe if we put the 'closed' sign on the door they'll stop coming."

"None too soon for me," Jolene said. "You work too hard around this place. Here you go, Jaime." She handed her a Band-Aid.

"Come on back," Quaid said to Jaime. "Let me take a look at that."

"No, really, it's just a scratch."

Quaid put his hand on her shoulder, gesturing her toward the examining room. "Good night, Jolene."

His touch triggered a brief surge of warmth inside Jaime, which did not dissipate when he dropped his hand. He was close beside her in the narrow hallway, and she could see the light film of perspiration on his neck, the mauve circles under his eyes. There was a faint stubble of beard on his cheeks, and his face was strained with fatigue. His nearness, his familiarity, even his vulnerability, centered like an ache just below Jaime's breastbone, for it was not until this moment that she fully realized how large a gap he had left in her life.

She said, perhaps a shade too brightly, "What was that language you were speaking a minute ago?"

"What?" He seemed distracted. "Oh. Acadian French."

She pretended to be impressed. "Multitalented, hmm?"

"No, just multilingual."

He took her over to the examining room sink and discarded the tissue she had wrapped around her hand. "What happened?"

His manner was distant and professional, though not unfriendly, and a small knot of tension formed in Jaime's stomach, which she fought valiantly to keep from spreading into a wave of disappointment and hurt. Briefly, she explained about Mame LeCaree and the broken light fixture, and did not even have the spirit to try to make the tale amusing.

Quaid nodded as he drew her hand under the gentle flow of warm water. "My fault, I guess. I suggested that she try to make peace with you." He glanced at her. "Does that hurt?"

She tried not to wince. "It doesn't feel good. Why did you do that?"

"Speak to Miss Mame? Have a seat on the table." He blotted her hand with a towel and turned to take a small basin from the counter. "I just figured your job would be a lot easier if you didn't have to worry about enemies in high places."

"Well, it didn't work. She's angrier at me than ever." Jaime eased herself onto the high examining table, then felt foolish. "This is silly. It's just a scratch."

Quaid switched on the examining light and opened her hand beneath it. "Doctors," he said thoughtfully, taking up a small instrument, "spend eight years in higher education, one year of grueling internship and two years of hospital residency—" he probed the wound with the instrument and Jaime flinched "—just so we can tell wise guys like you—" he held up the instrument briefly for her inspection and then dropped a small piece of glass in the basin "—to leave the diagnosis to us. Good thing you stopped by. That hand would have been giving you some trouble by tomorrow."

Now Jaime did feel foolish. She flexed her hand cautiously. "Thanks."

She watched him as he took the basin back to the counter and opened a cabinet. "You look tired," she ventured after a moment, uncertain how he would welcome such a personal remark.

"Must be all those wild parties and wicked women." He took her hand again and spread a thin layer of antibiotic cream over the cut, his touch light and gentle. "As a matter of fact," he said, "I don't believe I've had four good hours of sleep all week. It's the full moon, you know. Always like that."

Jaime decided not to debate that point.

He placed a light gauze bandage on her hand and taped it loosely. "I'm not going to put in any stitches. Just keep it covered for a couple of days, it should be all right." With his head still bent over his work and with no change of tone whatsoever, he added, "My folks missed you on the Fourth. And for Sunday dinner. And the Sunday before that. I'm beginning to run out of excuses."

Jaime's heart began to beat a little faster. "I thought you were avoiding me."

"I was. I thought you were mad at me."

He looked at her, questioning and waiting. Jaime held his gaze as long as she could, then said, a little hoarsely, "I was." She looked away, and shook her head. "I mean, I was...confused, and—I don't know what I was. It doesn't matter."

His eyes were gently searching as he took her arm to help her down from the table. "It matters a lot to me," he said and smiled coaxingly. "Are you still...confused?"

She felt warmth tingle her cheeks with a rush of pleasure and the sheer welcome of seeing his smile again, directed at her. She shook her head, dimpling shyly. "No."

"Good." His fingers caressed her waist, briefly, before leaving her. "Because my folks aren't the only ones who've missed you."

Rain was splattering against the window and the day was dark and thick, but inside she felt flooded with light. She felt for the first time in weeks as though things were right with the world and she was content. Why had she waited so long?

Silence fell, and though it was not an uncomfortable one, it was fraught with awareness and tinged with tension that was undeniably sexual. He was very close to her, and she could feel his eyes upon her. She had to remind herself to breathe, so suspended was she with his nearness, waiting for his touch.

She said after a moment, trying to distract herself, "Are you on your way home?"

He glanced at the window. "In this rain?" He shook his head. "I'd be drowned before I got there. I'll just wait it out. Maybe catch up on my reading or take a nap. How's your car?"

"Better." She smiled at him. "Would you like a ride home?"

He grinned and draped his arm around her shoulders. "I thought you'd never ask."

Chapter Ten

Quaid drove, and Jaime did not object. At least, when he was behind the wheel, the windshield wipers worked when they were supposed to, and the headlights did not operate with a mind of their own. His apartment building was less than fifteen minutes away, but traffic was crawling in the rain, and it took twice that long to reach. By the time he pulled into a parking space in front of the modern, Spanish-style complex, rain was sheeting against the car windows and pounding like thunder on the roof.

Quaid turned off the ignition and removed the keys, turning to her. "I don't like the idea of you driving home alone in this storm," he said. He had to speak loudly to be heard over the din. "Why don't you come in with me for a while?"

Jaime drew a breath to refuse, but something in his eyes stopped her. There was question, and there was patience, and there was a cautious testing of their new relationship. The defensive refusal that would have been so automatic two weeks ago was no longer what she wanted at all.

He grinned. "I might even make you dinner. I'm not a half-bad Creole chef myself, given a chance."

Jaime smiled and handed her umbrella to him. "You're on," she said. The decision was that simple.

Quaid's apartment was in many ways typical of a bachelor—nondescript and haphazardly furnished with a sofa, a couple of mismatched chairs, a television set and an array of tables scattered around not for decor but for usefulness. There were no paintings or other wall decorations, and his books—an eclectic mixture of classics and science fiction—were stacked randomly on their sides on end tables and beneath the television stand. It looked like the home of a man who did not spend very much time there.

There was one thing about his apartment that was not typical, however: it was very, very clean. The air smelled of lemon wax and pine cleaner, the tabletops were sparkling, the carpet had vacuum tracks in it. Magazines—mostly medical journals mixed in with a few copies of *Time*—were attractively fanned over the coffee table. And there was another thing that Jaime found of more immediate interest.

"Air-conditioning!" she exclaimed gratefully.

"All the conveniences of modern living," he assured her, and then he sniffed the air appreciatively. "I see the maid's been here." He grinned at her. "My mother. She comes through here like the board of health once a week and gives the place a shakedown whether it needs it or not."

He placed Jaime's dripping umbrella in the corner near the door and let his satchel slide off his shoulder to land beside it. Most of the meager protection afforded by the umbrella had been given to Jaime, and he was soaked. He blotted his face on his sleeve. "Listen, can you make yourself at home for a minute while I take a shower? There's wine on the kitchen counter, unless Mom hid it. It takes me a week to find things after she's been here, and by that time she's back again.''

Jaime had thought it would be awkward, being here with Quaid, but it was just the opposite. Left to her own devices while he showered, she found the wine, poured two glasses and had a brief tour of the kitchen and living area. She even took a moment to call her mother so that she wouldn't worry, and Leona was ecstatic when she finally pried out of Jaime the fact that she was with Quaid.

"No big deal," Jaime said, "I'm just waiting for the rain to stop."

"I won't wait up," Leona assured her. "Have a good time."

"As long as I have your permission," Jaime said dryly.

Leona laughed and hung up the phone.

Jaime settled back against the sofa and sipped her wine, amazed at how easy it all seemed now that she was here. But things were always that way with Quaid. Easy, natural . . . and insidiously dangerous.

Quaid came in from the bathroom wearing un-belted jeans and a soft gray sweatshirt. His hair was towel dried and dark with dampness, and his feet were bare. He looked surprised to see her curled up on the sofa sipping wine.

"You're still here," he said.

"Wasn't I supposed to be?"

"I knew I was taking a chance, leaving you alone," he admitted. "I never know when you're going to bolt. But then, you're always surprising me." He sat beside her and took up the glass of wine she had poured for him. He smelled like herbal soap and after-shave, and his smile drifted over her like sunshine. "Sometimes you're like a skittish colt, so shy and naive it breaks my heart. The next minute you're Joan of Arc on a white charger, ready to take on the world with a sword and a vision." With his finger he pushed back a curl that had tumbled over her forehead and smiled when it merely sprang back into place again. "And all of that combined with a streak of sophistication and that straightforward, literal-minded honesty of yours is enough to keep any man guessing what you're going to do or say next. I also like your hair."

"It's not natural," she said, and he laughed. "I mean," she corrected, "the color is, but not the curls."

"Do you see what I mean?" His eyes danced with delight as he ran his fingers playfully through her hair. "Never a dull moment. God, I've missed you." His eyes softened, and so did his tone. "It's no lie to say that I've thought about you every single day for the past two weeks, and not about much else."

She forced an uncertain smile. "You certainly hid it well."

He leaned back, cupping his wineglass with both hands. "I had to give you time, didn't I?" he said simply. "I did promise I wouldn't push. And I knew you had some important things to work out. Was I wrong?"

She shook her head, looking into her wine. "Quaid..." She looked at him hesitantly, but she knew it had to be said. "It wasn't...that I was angry with you, or disapproving of you, about what you did—even though I still think you were wrong," she had to add quickly. His smile reassured her, and she went on, "It was just that I was afraid, because everything was happening between us so fast, and...I was just afraid."

He said, "You scared me, too."

Her surprise showed in her face, and he nodded soberly. "A woman like you, so rare and fragile and earnest—that's quite a responsibility. Maybe I needed some time to think about it, too."

She wanted to know what he had decided. Then she didn't want to know. Perhaps, for once in her life, it would be best not to think so much, or analyze so much, or demand so much. Perhaps, just for tonight with Quaid, she could just relax and let it be.

He said gently, "Come here." He slipped his arm around her and drew her against his shoulder, and she felt his face brush against her hair. "It's nice, isn't it, to have company on a rainy night?"

"Yes," she murmured. Nothing had felt better in her whole life than Quaid's arm around her, the soft fabric of his sweatshirt against her skin, the lean strength of his shoulder beneath her head. The rain splashed and pattered outside as an early twilight fell, but inside she was warm and secure and perfectly at home. She could stay like that forever.

He bent his head a little to look at her, and his eyes crinkled with a teasing smile. "You're not nervous around me anymore."

"You just take a little getting used to." She saluted him with her glass. "Like this wine."

He tasted his wine and grimaced. "It does taste a little like vinegar doesn't it? Maybe we should save it for the salad."

She laughed. "It's not that bad yet. Give it a couple of more days."

He leaned forward to set his glass on the table. "At least you know I'm not an alcoholic. I can't even finish a bottle of wine before it goes bad."

She cocked her head to look at him thoughtfully. "What are you, Quaid?"

"Methodist," he replied promptly. "Underweight, slightly astigmatic, tone-deaf...and completely crazy about you."

The laughter of delight that bubbled up inside her throat was as delicate as champagne, and she could feel it sparkling in her eyes and warming her cheeks. How good it was to be with Quaid. The gulf of hurt and confusion that had separated them these past weeks was gone as though it had never been, and mere minutes, instead of days, seemed to have passed between their last meeting and this. Nothing had really changed, she knew. They still were polar opposites, they still had no real future together. But could anything that felt this natural and good really be so wrong?

"Crazy about me," she teased him, "or just crazy?"

"Both," he responded. "I'd have to be, to let you put me through what you have the past two weeks. And all without even once giving in to the urge to drag you by the hair into some private corner somewhere and shake some sense into you."

"The old caveman approach, huh?" Her eyes danced a glance at him as she set her wineglass on the end table and, slipping off her shoes, tucked her feet beneath her. "It wouldn't have worked."

"I suspected as much," he admitted. "My second choice was one of Miss Mame's black market love potions."

"Well, I'm certainly glad you decided against that."

"How do you know I did?" he teased her. "How do you know that's not what's making the wine taste so bitter?"

She glanced suspiciously at the wineglass, and he laughed. She laughed with him and impulsively entwined her arms around his neck, flooded with such sudden and simple joy that she could hardly contain it. "You're so much fun," she said.

Quaid clasped her laughing lips playfully with his own. "So are you." He kissed her again, still lightly, but the light in his eyes was deep and glowing, and Jaime's heart speeded with anticipation as his gaze moved over her face. "It's good to be with you," he said softly. "It's good to be together."

"Yes," she whispered, and his lips came down on hers again—just a touch, just a breath, tantalizing with restraint and delicately deepening until Jaime's breath was hardly more than a whisper in her throat and the slow, heavy muscle that was her heart seemed to swell until it filled her entire chest.

He moved away with a gentle, lingering reluctance, leaving her suspended in awareness and heavy with promise, and the soft sweeping glow of his gaze seemed to capture and caress. She looked at him, wanting and hesitant, aching and unsure, and she asked, "Are we going to make love tonight?"

He smiled, and tucked a wayward curl behind her ear. His finger lingered to trace the shape of her ear, slowly from skull to lobe, and even so simple a movement was erotic. "I think so," he answered softly. "I hope so. Does that make you nervous?"

She nodded, aware of the tightness of her throat and the sudden dart of what felt like anxiety deep within her abdomen. "Not making love with you," she said a little unsteadily, and she searched his face, needing him to understand. "But afterward."

His face sobered, and his eyes deepened with the understanding she sought. "I can't promise you afterward, Jaime," he said quietly. "I can only give you what I have. Is that enough?"

It shouldn't have been, but strangely, for this night, it was. She tightened her arms around his neck and brought her face slowly to rest against his chest. She felt his deep inhalation and the flutter of breath across her cheek as his arms went around her and she thought in dizzy contentment, *Yes. This is the way it should be.*

"Come here," he murmured. He slipped his arm beneath her knees and pulled her onto his lap. "Let me hold you. I can't get close enough to you."

He cradled her against him with one arm supporting her shoulders and the other across her thighs, and he seemed to be satisfied with just looking at her for the longest time. She lifted her hand and touched his face; it was smooth from his recent shave and responsive to her touch. She outlined his lips with her fingertip, and the touch of his tongue sent shivers down her arm.

She leaned forward and kissed his lips, and she watched as his eyes slowly closed, then his tongue sought the parting of her lips and her own eyes closed helplessly against the surge of fever his soft warm invasion incited. Her hands moved over the flat breadth of his shoulders and downward until she discovered a gap of flesh between his jeans and sweatshirt. She slipped her hands inside, flat-palmed, and discovered the sensitive flesh of his abdomen and the passion her touch evoked as his fingers tightened on her thigh and his kiss deepened. She pressed her hands upward, over sinew and bone and smooth, lean chest. She felt the heat and dampness of his skin and the flatness of his nipples and the powerful, anvillike pounding of his heart. She filled her senses with the sensation of his nakedness, dark and secret and heated.

His fingers were strong against the back of her neck as his lips left hers and dropped slow, drawing kisses upon her throat. Her breath was shallow, and fever spread from each place his lips touched until it seemed to consume her body from the inside out. It was not what Quaid did that aroused her so, but what he did not do.... The hand that cupped just beneath her swollen breast, not touching, not caressing, though she ached for him to do so. Fingers that moved across her ribs and her abdomen and stroked her thigh so lightly, creating a gentle abrasiveness with the material of her skirt against her aching skin, circling her knee then moving slowly up the inside of her thigh toward its apex, yet stopping just short. His tongue brushed her lips but did not enter. His breath heated the material that covered her breast, but his lips did not touch. His hand stretched low and captured her bare foot, massaging gently and moving slowly up the calf until she trembled with pleasure, pushing aside her long skirt to trace a maddening pattern along the tendons behind her knee.

He took her face in both hands and kissed her deeply, then lightly, on the lips. Her hands threaded through his hair and then drifted over his cheekbones and his chin and his throat. His face was flushed and his eyes a blur of light and dark, need and pleasure.

He unfastened the metal buttons at the shoulders of her jumper, first one, then the other, and let the gar-

ment fall to her waist. His hands caressed her arms,
moving inside the sleeve openings of her oversize T-
shirt, and he smiled. "Why do you wear so many
clothes?" he murmured.

She replied, a little breathlessly, "I never thought
I'd need to get out of them so quickly before."

He smothered a sound of laughter and pleasure
against her neck, embracing her tightly. Then with a
subtle movement he shifted her onto the sofa and,
taking both her hands, drew her to her feet. Her
jumper slid over her hips and she stepped out of it,
standing before him in her thigh-length T-shirt while
his eyes moved over her slowly, adoringly.

He stepped toward her until his body was full-length
against hers, his chest pressing her breasts, the rigid
strength of his desire hard against her abdomen. Still
holding her hands stretched out beside her thighs, he
kissed her, opening her mouth to the pressure of his
tongue, drawing on her and exploring her, slowly,
sensuously, deeply. And though she ached to draw him
close, to discover him by touch and feel, he held her
hands still, and with his kiss alone he opened her body
to a rush of liquid weakness and an ache of need more
powerful than any she had ever known.

When at last they parted there was no need for
words or questions. He took her hand and led her into
the bedroom.

Their clothes came off in random order as the flare
of passion, once kindled, refused to be quenched. His
hands traced the shape of her nakedness and hers discovered the sharp planes and harsh contours of his, as,
by touch and by taste, they absorbed and memorized
intimate knowledge of each other. The streetlight filtered through the rain-slick windowpane and cast ca-

pricious shadows over their bodies as they lay together
on the bed, entwined in still, poised moments of dis-
covery or moving in sweet desperate grasps of urgency. When Quaid slid inside her and was at last a
part of her, Jaime clutched him tightly to her and
arched against him, dazed with rapture and prolong-
ing the precious moment and knowing only that all her
life, all her needs and all her yearnings had been in
preparation for this moment, and him.

When the pinnacle of passion had been reached and
passed, the euphoria did not go away. Jaime lay within
the circle of his arms, listening to the rhythm of his
heart and letting her fingertips trace again the body
that she knew so intimately, discovering new wonder
in the texture of his perspiration-slick skin, the shape
of his collarbone, the curve of his jaw. *It's not supposed to be like this,* she thought somewhat dazedly.
Not the first time. The power of it confused her and
disturbed her greatly, but hadn't she always known it
would be like this? Wasn't that why she had fought it
so hard?

Making love with him was easy; it was explosive and
magical and all encompassing, just as she had known
it would be. But loving him . . . loving him could hurt.
Loving him meant confusion and dissonance and an
utter disruption of her carefully planned and orches-
trated life. That she had also known. And had she for
one moment believed she could separate the two?

Then what spell had led her into his arms, into his
bed? What mystical shield had he wrapped around her
to make her forget that a future was impossible between them? And why, even now, did she feel so
peaceful, so content, so *right*? She wanted to run from
him and never look back; she wanted to hold him

tightly and never let him go. She wanted to believe, with all her might, that she would never regret this moment.

She must have made some small sound or movement indicative of her inner turmoil, or perhaps Quaid was simply so tuned to her moods that he sensed the small thread of tension that was creeping through her. His arms tightened around her shoulders slightly, and he looked down at her. "Jaime?"

But she could not deal with it now. Not the doubts, the questions, the uncertainties. She laid a finger lightly across his lips, and she smiled up at him. She let her fingers trail down his throat, circling his collarbone. "Do you own a tie, by any chance?"

He relaxed with the playfulness of her tone, and pulled a pensive face in the dimness. "I might have one lying around here somewhere. But I'd look pretty silly wearing it now, wouldn't I? However—" he brushed her hair with a kiss "—if it will make you happy..."

She chuckled throatily. "Actually, I do need a favor, but that's not it. My mother has invited us to dinner at Antoine's Friday night. Will you come?"

A slow grin played with his lips as he wrapped one of her curls around his finger. "Why, darling, you didn't have to sleep with me just to get me to take you to your mother's dinner party. After you put up with my family for a whole evening, I would have done it for nothing."

She laughed and buried her face in his chest, hugging him hard, and suddenly she was overcome by a stab of longing so severe it hurt and the laughter turned into a muffled sob. "Oh, Quaid, don't let me fall in love with you!"

His arms held her tightly and she felt the deep expansion of his breath as he whispered, "Oh, Jaime. Don't be scared, sweetheart. Not anymore."

His hands slipped beneath her arms, edging her upward, and then he took her face in his hand and made her look at him. His smile was gentle and coaxing. "Don't you see," he said softly, "it's too late?" His fingers pushed aside her hair, and his eyes, beneath the tenderness, were intense and probing. "I was in love with you twenty-four hours after we met. It knocked me off my feet, what you did to me. I knew it was real, I knew it was meant to be, I knew there wasn't a thing I could do about it. I didn't want it to happen. Out of all the women in the world, do you think I would have picked a know-it-all yuppie who had one of the few mothers in history who did *not* teach her from birth that her highest calling was to grow up and marry a doctor?"

The playfulness of his tone coaxed a weak smile from her, but his own smile faded into sincerity as he finished simply, "I had no choice, Jaime. Life is like that sometimes. Turbulent, unpredictable, full of things you didn't plan for."

She shook her head tightly against his shoulder. "For you, maybe. Not for me. I *have* to know what to expect, Quaid. I have to know the rules, I—"

"I know that." Soothingly, he ran his hand along her spine from shoulder to hip. "I know it's too soon for you, and I know that having me in your life is the last thing you need...."

Quickly, she opened her mouth for a protest, because that sounded very much like a prologue to goodbye, and the thought panicked her. But his smile was reassuring, and he finished, "But if it will help, I'll tell you the rules."

He fastened his hands on either side of her and gently slid her weight on top of him, so that they were touching at all points. His hands stroked her hair, and his eyes were deep and soft and adoring. "For now," he said, and lifted his face to kiss her lightly, "Just love me, and let me love you. The rest will take care of itself."

It sounded so easy. And for a while, it was.

Chapter Eleven

Throughout her life Jaime had never handled changes well. Instability upset her, made her anxious and ill at ease. She could feel the subtle currents of change within her now, and perhaps that was why she felt so nervous as she walked into Antoine's on Quaid's arm that evening.

They had slept together until dawn, when Quaid received a medical call. Jaime, abruptly awakened from a euphoric dream, which was not much different from the reality which had just passed, was flustered and unaccountably embarrassed. She began to dress quickly, chattering all the while, until Quaid gently drew her back into his arms again.

"You're still expecting something bad to happen aren't you?" he had inquired.

She couldn't meet his eyes. "I don't know what you mean."

He smiled. "You broke the rules; you took a chance. Now you're waiting for the roof to cave in."

All Jaime could do was laugh, brightly and a little falsely. "The way my luck's been running lately it might just do it—literally."

He tweaked her nose affectionately. "You're starting to get superstitious. That's a good sign." He lifted the little wooden talisman that dangled from his necklace and brushed it across her lips. "Remember, I told you—as long as you're with me, you'll be okay." And his eyes sobered. "You keep that in mind while you go through the day making a list of all the reasons you and I are wrong for each other."

She went through the day, and she tried to make that list. But she couldn't. Because all she could see was the face of the man she could not afford to love, the gentle planes, the soft curves, the tender eyes. And all she could feel was his touch and all she could smell was his scent and all she could hear was his voice; he consumed her. She couldn't think at all. And that's when she knew things were changing, and that was when she began to be frightened.

Jaime's mother had made no comment about Jaime's night out—which was not particularly strange, except that after all the interest Leona had expressed previously in Jaime's relationship with Quaid, Jaime might have expected *something*. But Leona had seemed excited and distracted and concerned with very little except that Jaime be on time at Antoine's that night. And when Jaime returned from work to change for dinner, Leona had already left.

Pausing at the maître d's stand in the elegant interior of the restaurant, Jaime felt overwhelmed, ill at ease and uncomfortable. She was once again wearing her pink and lavender Gunny Sax dress, which was the dressiest outfit she owned, and she vacillated between feeling awkwardly overdressed and understyled. Quaid looked wonderful in a gray suit and peach shirt—so wonderful, in fact, he was almost a stranger. She liked him better in jeans. She liked him better *out* of jeans. That thought made her blush, and she wished they were spending a quiet evening at home. She wasn't sure their relationship was up to a dinner with her mother yet.

Jaime muttered, "I really hate places like this."

"Want to go home and order a pizza?" Quaid suggested.

Jaime caught his hand. "Let's go."

He laughed and drew her back. "No you don't. You're not cheating me out of a free meal at Antoine's."

She made an incredulous gesture around the room. "You really like all of this?"

"Love it."

She sighed. "Only another thing we don't have in common."

The maître d' returned to escort them to Leona's table and Jaime said, "I wish I knew what this celebration was about. Probably she's opening a new show; she still makes a big deal out of things like that after all this time. She said she was bringing a guest, and if it's one of those weird gallery owners she's always hanging around with I'll make some excuse and we'll leave early. I mean, she has some of the strangest friends. I suppose they're nice enough, but a little hard to take for a whole meal. The last person mother brought to dinner was a psychic healer who spent the whole time lecturing on the healing properties of asparagus. It was fairly disgusting."

She spotted her mother across the room, and Leona lifted a hand in happy greeting. Jaime smiled back.

Leona was striking tonight in a green satin gown with winged shoulders and a scooped neck. She wore a diamond choker and diamond clusters in her ears, and her upswept hair was dotted with a jeweled net. Her companion at the table was a young blond man in a white dinner jacket, and Jaime thought in passing that her mother's taste in gallery owners had improved. Sitting at the table, sipping champagne and laughing with the young man, she looked as glamorous as a movie star and as radiant as Jaime had ever seen her, and she was attracting more than her share of attention from the other diners. Jaime immediately felt dowdy.

"She looks beautiful, doesn't she?" Jaime said wistfully as they approached the table.

Quaid studied Leona thoughtfully from a distance. "A little bit overdone, I think," he decided.

Jaime laughed and squeezed his hand. "Have I told you lately that you're wonderful?"

"It bears repeating." His smile swept away her lingering discontent and warmed her to her very heart.

The evening suddenly did not seem so bleak anymore, and her smile was genuine as they reached Leona's table. The young blond man immediately got to his feet and Leona reached across the table to squeeze Jaime's hand. "Darling, Quaid...I'm so glad the two of you could come." Her eyes were sparkling and the becoming color that rouged her cheeks was not cosmetic. Jaime could not remember seeing her mother so excited, and she thought the new show—if that was what it was—must be a very important one.

"Jaime, I'd like you to meet someone." Leona glanced at the young man, and there might have been just the faintest trace of anxiety in her eyes. Automatically, Jaime turned to smile a greeting at him. "This is Richard Downs, from London. Richard, my daughter Jaime, and Dr. Quaid Gerreau." And then, with hardly a pause for breath or a change in inflection, Leona finished, "Richard is my fiancé."

The shock that went through Jaime was like a moment out of time, frozen and absurdly larger than life.

Every detail was sharp and clear, yet strangely distant. Richard's handshake was warm and firm, and his smile sincere as he said, "Jaime. It's such a pleasure to meet you at last." His accent was British, and his eyes incredibly blue. His face was smoothly handsome with a dimple when he smiled. His shirt was silk, his cologne expensive and elusive. He couldn't have been thirty years old.

He turned to Quaid. "Dr. Gerreau. So happy you could join us. Leona has been telling me something of your work at the clinic. Do let's sit down, shall we?"

Some time had passed before Jaime realized that the maître d' was still holding her chair for her, but she hadn't the presence of mind to be embarrassed. She sank into her chair, and she couldn't stop staring at Richard Downs. Quaid was saying something pleasant and casual to Richard, Richard was responding in kind and Jaime felt as though she had wandered into a French farce. She had the sudden hysterical urge to laugh. It was a joke; it had to be. She had never known her mother to go in for practical comedy, but with Leona anything was possible and this simply had to be a joke....

But one look at her mother's anxious, bravely smiling face assured Jaime it was no joke, and Jaime felt ill inside.

Quaid was saying, "So, how did the two of you meet?"

"In London, this spring," Richard answered.

"Richard is a stockbroker," Leona supplied. "We met when he took over my account."

A *stockbroker*? Leona Faber and an ultraconservative, British *stockbroker*? This grew more absurd by the minute. Yet Jaime found herself saying in an almost steady voice, "You met while you were in London, Mother? Three months ago?"

Leona smiled a little nervously. "That's right. A whirlwind romance, really. Richard accompanied me to South America—"

"And that was quite an experience, let me tell you." Richard chuckled, and he took Leona's hand across the table.

Jaime interrupted bluntly, staring at Richard, "How old are you?"

She saw her mother tense, and even Quaid looked somewhat disapproving. She was beyond caring.

Only Richard did not seem offended, and he turned to her with an easy smile and steady eyes. "I'm twenty-eight, Jaime," he answered gently.

The waiter filled Jaime's glass with champagne, and she snatched it up and drained half of it without tasting it. She felt cold inside, and her muscles were as hard as steel. She couldn't believe it, but she had to believe it. Her mother was serious.

"This was your surprise," she said flatly.

"Only part of it," Leona said. Her eyes were overbright and her voice a little too eager. "The other is— we've bought the Fullbright house. You know, the house behind yours. We're going to be your new landlords!"

The announcement hardly could have come out more clumsily, or more ill timed, and the stricken expression in Leona's eyes said that she knew it. Jaime set her glass down abruptly and stood. "Excuse me," she said.

Leona was two steps behind her as she entered the ladies' room. Jaime caught a glimpse of her own reflection in the mirror—her face pale except for two streaks of color high on her cheekbones, her eyes a dark glittering smear, and she hardly recognized herself. Nor did she care. She was shaking as she gripped the counter and turned to face her mother.

"You're serious," she said tonelessly.

Leona's face was torn with anxiety and apology. "Perhaps this wasn't the best way to tell you, Jaime, but I was afraid you'd react like this and I thought if you met him in person, and got a chance to know him—"

"He's a child!"

Leona flinched from the words as though stung, then pressed her hands tightly together. Her voice was filled with forced calm. "That doesn't make any difference to us—"

"Of course it doesn't!" Jaime's voice had taken on an edge of shrill, incredulous laughter. "You were never one to do things the ordinary way, were you? And a stockbroker! I mean, I might have believed it if he'd been some eccentric Italian poet or a crusader from the IRA or an animal-rights activist—but this! For heaven's sake mother, can't you see this is a setup?"

Leona said stiffly, "I don't know what you mean."

"All your life you've flouted the rules, sought out the unusual, gone for the shock value. You're still doing it, and he's taking advantage of it! Marriage is not something to joke about, Mother. It's not a way to make a statement or prove a point or—or to compete with your daughter! It's serious!"

Leona's eyes went wide with hurt. "I'm not competing with you, Jaime," she said softly. "I never wanted you to think that—"

Jaime made a curt dismissing gesture. "You don't want to get married," she said sharply. "All my life you've done nothing but tell me how useless and outdated marriage is. Now all of a sudden at the age of forty-one you decide there's nothing more important than getting married—and to a man half your age. You still do it with style, I'll give you that!''

"You can't always control who you fall in love with," Leona said quietly. "I thought, after meeting Quaid, you'd understand that."

Jaime drew a breath, staring at her mother. "So," she said softly. "That's it. That's the reason for your sudden interest in my personal life, that's why you've been pushing me and Quaid together—"

Leona closed her eyes, slowly and tiredly. "I only wanted you to be happy, Jaime," she said. "Just like I am."

"Since when did you ever care about my happiness?" Jaime shot back. Her own words came at her from a distance, tumbling and rushing out before she had a chance to recall them, and she hated herself for it but she couldn't stop now. Twenty-five years of fear and resentment and insecurity came bursting out and she was helpless to control it. "Did you ever bother to give me a home, stability—a family? I'd been in eight schools before I was in third grade, Mother! Let's not even talk about all those nights I had to do my homework in the bathroom because my bedroom was filled with strangers, let's not talk about the meals I missed because you were busy painting or the times I didn't see you for days on end while you were locked in your studio.... How about the report cards I brought home you didn't even bother to look at, how about the essays I wrote that you rewrote behind my back, how about the fact that nothing I could do was ever, ever good enough for you? Do you think trips to Europe and Mazdas and designer dresses could make up for *that*?''

Leona's face was white and her eyes were dark with pain. She whispered, "I'm sorry...."

Jaime drew a shaky breath. She was in agony, she was horrified at herself, she was angry and helpless and achingly alone, but she couldn't stop it. It was too late. She said quietly, "My life with you has been one surprise after another. It's been a series of broken rules and disappointments and upheavals. I've tried to look the other way, I've pretended I approve.... Well, I *don't* approve of this, Mother, and I'm tired of pretending! I just can't deal with it anymore. This time you've gone too far."

She snatched up her purse and she strode out of the room, and her mother's tight, hurt face was only a blur on the way out.

SHE HAD A DIM IMPRESSION of Quaid and Richard chatting amiably at the table as she approached; she did not know what excuse, if any, she gave for asking Quaid to take her home. She did not remember the drive or unlocking the door or turning on the lights. Inside she was a twisted knot of shock and hurt and shame and regret. And anger—irrational, inexplicable. And the worst was she did not even know whom she was angry with, or why.

She tossed her purse on a chair and paced across the room. Quaid closed the door quietly and leaned against it. "I take it you don't approve of your mother's fiancé?" he said calmly.

She whirled on him incredulously. "And you do?"

He shrugged. "He seems like a nice enough fellow."

"He's twenty-eight years old!" she cried. "He looks and sounds like a rock star!"

Quaid's expression was mild and detached, yet his eyes were alert, watching and waiting. "And you find that offensive?"

She gave a high, shrill laugh. "Oh, no! I find him adorable! I might have fallen for him myself if Mother hadn't gotten there first!"

She drew in a sharp breath and clasped her arms tightly across her chest, turning away from Quaid. She wanted to be quiet, she wanted to be mature, she wanted the awful, hateful malice to stop bubbling out of her. She didn't want Quaid to see her like this. She wanted her life to stop spinning out of control.

She said, as steadily as she could, "She's been doing things like this to me all her life. The outrageous, the unexpected, the bizarre. But this—this is too personal. She wants him to be my stepfather, she wants to live next door to me with her gigolo lover and she wants me to *like* it! He's closer to my age than hers. All her life she's despised anybody who wore a suit, and she's marrying a stockbroker!" She tilted her head back with a helpless breath of despair. "This is crazy. *I* should be in love with Richard and *she* should be in love with you! It's all backward, it's depraved, it's... *sick*."

"Yes," Quaid said, rather coldly. "It is."

The tone of his voice made her turn, and the expression on his face momentarily shocked her out of her own self-involved turbulence. He took a step toward her, and his voice was bland and restrained, but beneath the surface there was anger. "First of all," he said, with deliberate control, "don't compare me with Richard. I don't appreciate it, and neither would he. Secondly, stop comparing yourself with your mother. Thirdly, grow up."

That, above all things, was not what she needed to hear from him at that moment. It hurt her like a slap, and even though she knew he was right, the gulf that opened up between them in that moment was wider than years, deeper even than opinions or values or lifestyles. It was a breach of understanding that could never be spanned.

Yet what more could she have expected from him? She knew Quaid, she knew their differences, she knew that no matter what the subject, if she said it was wrong, he would say it was right . . . just like her mother.

She said weakly, "You're—on her side, aren't you?"

A trace of impatience crossed his face. "Don't you see, that's just the point. I'm not on anybody's side. This is her business, it doesn't affect me—and it shouldn't affect you."

"How can it not?" she cried. "She's going to marry that man. She's my mother, and she's making a mockery out of everything I've ever believed in. . . ."

His expression softened, and for a moment she almost thought he did understand. "Jaime, life doesn't always follow your set of prescribed rules. People are different, and they don't always look for the same things in life. . . . Like us for instance."

His tone was careful, and his expression was sober, and Jaime held her breath against the pain she knew was about to start because she knew whatever he was about to say would not be good, and that she did not want to hear it.

"You want a husband, a home, a family and all the traditional trappings," he said quietly. "But I'm not a traditional man. I don't need a wife to take care of me. I can take care of myself. I'm not looking for a baby machine or a housekeeper or a cook or a mother. I want a lover and a partner and a friend. And you simply refuse to believe that we could ever be happy together, just like you refuse to give Leona and Richard a chance—because they refuse to follow your rules."

She looked at him through a flood of pain and helplessness, and her throat was so thick she could hardly speak. How had the subject turned from her mother to herself? Why was Quaid looking at her with such sadness in his eyes, and why had he picked now, of all times to say these things to her? She couldn't lose him, too, not now, not tonight....

She said hoarsely, "This is not about us—"

"The hell it's not." He came toward her swiftly, and his sudden grip on her shoulders startled a gasp from her as he turned her to face him. His face was stern and intense. "Do you think I don't know you by now, Jaime? Don't you think I can see what you're doing to yourself—what you've been doing all your life?"

"You don't know anything about me!" she cried. She tried to pull away, frightened and unsure, but he held her firmly. And a wave of defeat and anguish went through her; she let her shoulders sag beneath the weight of it. Why was she fighting with him? Why was she fighting at all? For a moment, a brief space out of time last night, she had almost convinced herself it would be all right, that she could change or he could change or that the differences didn't matter...but they did. No matter how hard she tried, she could not ignore the things that separated them, and neither could he.

"Oh, Quaid," she said helplessly, and her voice was tight with pain and fatigue. "I tried, I really did. But you're right. What you want and what I want are two different things. And it's not you—it's me. I just can't let go...of the way I think things should be, of the rules I've made for myself. And you—you're like my mother. You just can't stop flying in the face of convention and taking the radical approach to every situation and I just can't deal with that, not from you, not from her." She turned her head away tiredly, and she could barely bring her voice above a whisper. "I think you'd better go now."

"That would be easy, wouldn't it?" His voice was harsh, and he did not release his grip on her shoulders. Jaime looked at him, silent with pleading. Why must he make this so painful? Didn't he know she was breaking apart inside?

"All right," he said with a breath. "Maybe it's none of my business, and I've tried to stay out of it until now. Your problems with your mother are between you and her, but dammit, she's starting to take you away from me and I can't keep quiet any longer!"

Jaime was still, staring at him in surprise. "What are you talking about? My mother adores you!"

His hands relaxed on her shoulders fractionally, but he did not let her go. He released a long, tight sigh. "That's just it, Jaime, don't you see?"

His eyes brushed away from her momentarily, as though searching for words, and when he looked back, his expression was filled with frustration and a desperate need for her to understand. "You have a great mother. Beautiful, independent, successful, charming, adored by people all over the world. Thousands of kids would have envied you your childhood. And aside from everything else your mother is, she's impossible not to like. But she casts a long shadow, and it would have been unnatural if you had grown up any other way than thinking you had to compete with her.

"But she's impossible to compete with, don't you understand? Not just for you, but for *anyone*. She wouldn't be Leona Faber, she wouldn't be the best in her field, if it were otherwise. But a child couldn't be expected to understand that, and somewhere along the line you decided you weren't good enough for her. You couldn't compete with her, so you moved out of her field—in every respect. You couldn't stop loving her, so you stopped loving the things she did.

"She's liberal, so you're conservative. She's high fashion, so you're traditional. She's a free spirit and you're housebound, she's modern and you're old-fashioned, and she likes *me* so you're going to turn away from me and that's not *fair*, Jaime." His hands tightened on her shoulders again. "Now she's getting married to a man you would have approved of for yourself, and that's thrown your whole concept of the competitive field out of balance. You've spent your whole life trying to outrun your mother's shadow and now it's making you run from the only good thing you've ever had in your life.

"Jaime. Love." His hand moved up to caress her cheek, and his eyes were filled with helplessness and sorrow. "Don't let her do this to us."

Jaimé closed her eyes slowly against the brimming film of tears there. His words echoed and bounced inside her head and she did not understand them, nor even fully believe them, but she knew the essence. She wanted it to be different. *She* wanted to be different. Didn't he know how badly she needed him, ached for him inside? Didn't he know how badly she wished she had some magic words, some instant formula that would make everything right between them again? If only it could have lasted a little longer, the wonder, the conviction, the certainty she had felt in his arms. If only she could believe it would last forever. But it wasn't her mother's shadow she had been trying to escape last night, it had been herself. And she was tired of running.

She whispered shakily, "I can't, Quaid. I can't...deal with this tonight."

He slowly let her go, his hands falling lightly down her bare arms and lingering there for a final caress before he stepped away. Through a blur of tears she saw him reach up and remove the talisman necklace from around his neck; very gently he draped it over her head. "I think you'll be needing this more than I do for a while," he said quietly.

Jaime's hand closed tightly around the small statuette, still warm from his body, but she could not speak. Her throat was too heavy, aching with tears that wouldn't come.

He started for the door, and he turned back. His face was very sober. "Someday," he said, "you're going to have to start doing things because they're right for you, not because they're wrong for your mother. Someday you've got to realize that you're more than Leona's daughter. And I hope that day comes soon, because until it does...I don't think we have a chance, either."

Jaime locked the door behind him, then she sank to the chair and, still clutching the talisman in her hand, she cried.

Chapter Twelve

Things went from bad to worse. The voodoo charm might well have protected Jaime from life's little disasters, but it had no effect whatsoever on larger tragedies. Perhaps it was because Jaime brought those upon herself.

Leona packed a small bag while Jaime was at work and moved out of the carriage house, leaving only a note stating that she was staying with Richard at his hotel. Jaime had never fought with her mother before. They had always been best friends, girlish confidantes, happy roommates who swept in and out of each other's lives like playful birds. The ugliness that stood between them was like a black scar across Jaime's life, leaving her wretched and ashamed. But she made no move to phone Leona or to stop by the hotel. She wouldn't have known what to say.

At Victory House disaster was a mild term to apply. Word had gotten around like lightning about Mame LeCaree's visit, and superstition had the populace of the community by the throat. People stopped coming by for the recreational programs. Children, frightened into obeisance by their parents, cut a wide swath around Victory House on their way home from school. Attendance even dropped off at the AA Drug

Recovery programs, which were not even supervised by Victory House personnel. And interest in Jaime's day-care program was less than nil. When she went door to door people crossed themselves and slammed doors in her face; others shook their heads sadly and declared they could not afford to make an enemy as powerful as Miss Mame. Jaime would have laughed if it had not been so tragic; she would have been angry if she had not felt so impotent.

"I just don't understand it," she exclaimed in despair to Daphene after three days of rejection and frustration. "This is the nineteen eighties—television, computers, space flight! These people can't really believe this voodoo garbage."

Daphene perched on the edge of Jaime's desk, crossing her slender legs comfortably. "Some do," she answered seriously, "some just figure it's best not to take any chances. It's always very difficult to get the confidence of a community like this, Jaime, and that confidence will always remain a very precarious thing, ready to disappear at a moment's notice and without much of an excuse at all."

That made Jaime feel very guilty, as though the fate of the entire settlement house and everything they had worked so hard to achieve were in her hands. "But surely," she insisted, "this will blow over. Victory House has a lot to offer this community, everyone knows that. People will forget, they'll start coming back."

Daphene was thoughtful. "Probably so. After a time. But meanwhile our effectiveness is seriously diminished, and people who need our help out there aren't getting it. That's what we're all about, Jaime—getting help to those who need it. And it doesn't really matter how we do that, does it?"

Jaime shook her head in confusion, uncertain of what Daphene was trying to tell her. "But what can we do? That crazy old woman has these people scared to death. How can we fight that?"

Daphene smiled patiently. "We can't. Honey, Mame LeCaree and her predecessors have been ruling this city long before you or I showed up, and if you want to know the truth, will probably be going strong long after we're gone. But it's more than that. It's a whole way of thinking, a culture, a history that we can't just come in here and sweep away overnight, even if we wanted to. And I for one, don't want to. It's not for them to adjust to us, but for us to adjust to them."

"Then what can I do?" Jaime insisted.

Daphene said, "I think you know the answer to that."

"Do you mean—make peace with Mame LeCaree? Apologize to her?" The idea went against every tenet of personal integrity Jaime knew, and even as she spoke she was shaking her head.

Daphene said, "I mean work with her. Teach her to trust you—and learn to trust her. You'll never gain her confidence or the respect of this community, until you do."

Still Jaime was shaking her head, slowly yet with adamance. "My job is to fight ignorance and fear, to teach self-reliance and personal dignity. If I give in to one woman's superstitious threats I'll be going against everything I was taught, everything I stand for. That's *wrong*, Daphene."

"Jaime, honey." Daphene placed her hand over Jaime's kindly. "We're not missionaries in darkest Africa, you know. We're not here to save their souls; we're just trying to make living in a hard world a little easier, that's all. And you can't always do that by following the textbook. You have to compromise, improvise."

There it was again. Improvise. Ignore the rules. Whether it was Mame LeCaree or Leona Faber or...or Quaid, it always came down to the same thing. And all they demanded of Jaime was that she be someone she was not.

She said quietly, "I don't think I can do that."

A look of regret came over Daphene's face, and she withdrew her hand slowly. "Jaime," she began, and it was apparent from her expression that this was difficult for her to say, and she was trying to find a way to do it gently. "You are a bright, dedicated young woman, and we're lucky to have you. I know this is all very...new to you and strange, and, as I told you when you first came here, it's difficult for some people to adjust. You have a real talent for this kind of work, and you care genuinely, and those are traits that aren't easy to find.

"But I have to tell you this." Daphene's eyes were steady now, and they held no trace of compassion. "There's no room for dogmatism here. People's lives are at stake, and we must do whatever it takes to fulfill our function in this community. That means absorbing the culture, not fighting it. It means being flexible. And if you're not willing, or able, to set aside your own ideas for the sake of getting the job done— then I'm very much afraid your ability to serve this community will be severely limited. Please think about that."

Jaime thought about it. She thought about very little else. And the only conclusion she could come to was a bleak and unforgiving one: she was failing. Daphene was right; she had to learn to adjust to this life, to these people, and she wasn't at all sure she ever could. But if she did not, she was useless here.

She felt alone, lost and hurt. She needed her mother, but her mother was lost to her, perhaps forever. She needed Quaid, but Quaid was not hers.

He would call her every day, sometimes more than once, and she saw him now and then on her way in or out. He never said much, he just wanted to let her know he had not given up on her. He didn't pretend as though nothing was wrong; his voice, and his eyes, were sad. He was waiting for her, but he was waiting for something she did not know how to give.

One day, because her other functions at Victory House had been almost negated, Daphene assigned Jaime to the clinic. There was not a moment, between the constant stream of patients and charts to file and calls to make, for Jaime and Quaid to have a word alone; he did not even take time for lunch. For ten hours she watched him, ever patient, ever gentle, ever ready with cheerful advice or sensitive consolation for those who came to him and seeming never to tire, and Jaime realized then a fundamental difference between her work and his. These were Quaid's people; he spoke their language. He knew them, he cared for them, he belonged here. She did not.

She watched him, and her heart filled to bursting with love and loss. Lifting a laughing child above his head, bending to kiss an old women's brow, harshly scolding a young man who had been in a fight... That was Quaid, tender, impulsive, innovative, sensitive. Not always right, but always certain. He knew the secret to getting the best from life, and Jaime was too afraid to try.

At the end of the day he came to her. "I'd like to be with you tonight," he said simply.

Jaime wanted to be with him, too, for comfort, for strength, for reassurance. But another night of hope and promises, pretending everything was all right while hiding silent recriminations and wishing things could be different...that would change nothing. She shook her head slowly. "I don't think that would be a good idea."

He asked quietly, "Have you talked to your mother?"

She shook her head, unable to meet his eyes.

"I can't help you with this, Jaime." His voice was heavy. "I wish to God I could. I wish I could get inside your head and turn your thoughts around, I wish I could wave a magic wand and make you see how good we could be together.... I wish I could make you, for once in your life, take a chance."

She looked at him in despair. "I'm trying, Quaid. I really am. But I don't know what to do." She turned to go.

"Love me," he answered simply.

At the door she turned back, her eyes brimming with a quick hot film of tears, and she whispered helplessly, "How could I not?"

And she left quickly, before she gave into helpless need and forgot how much it would hurt later.

RICHARD CAME TO SEE HER.

She was alone in the office, feeling extraneous and hopeless, shuffling through paperwork that no one cared about but her, when he came in. He sat on the edge of her desk and placed a folded copy of the *New York Times* before her.

"Don't you Yanks have a saying," he inquired, "if you read it in the *Times* it must be true?"

Distractedly, she saw the article to which the paper was opened had to do with young financial wizards; it featured a small blurred picture of Richard Downs and devoted several paragraphs to his biography and accomplishments.

"I thought you might be reassured to know I am what I claim to be," he went on. "I'm not a gold digger or a gigolo or an opportunist. I've quite a fortune in my own right and have every expectation it will continue to grow. Further, my family is quite well established in England and abroad—not wealthy, mind you, but distinctly comfortable with a name and lands that go back to the first King George. Very old school, you know, what one might even call 'uppercrust.'" A self-mocking smile played with his lips, then faded into sincerity as he looked at her. "I just wanted you to know."

Jaime cleared her throat nervously and folded the paper. She couldn't quite meet his eyes. "This... wasn't necessary."

"It was to me." He looked around for a chair, and finding one, drew it up close to her desk. He sat down, his hands clasped lightly between his knees, and he leaned forward earnestly. "If it's of any comfort to you," he said quietly, "my family is not exactly wild about this match, either. Well, you can imagine. An older woman, and one as beautiful as your mother, quite aside from her reputation as a bohemian and the fact that she is an artist... As I told you, my family is very conservative. You might as well know they've threatened to disown me, and most likely will once we're married."

Jaime could not hide her shock, and it was underlined with more than a little outrage. "Why... why that's absurd! My mother is a wonderful woman.

Lovely, intelligent, gifted, extraordinarily successful—how dare they!''

He smiled gently. ''Perhaps you are aware that in
England a great deal more is dependent upon appearances than in this country. In my profession particularly, where one is called upon to deal with other
people's money, both one's public and private life is
scrutinized very carefully. You must believe me, I've
heard all the shocked protests and well-meaning advice and commonsense objections that man has ever
devised, and none of it has been able to sway my conviction in the least. I hope you won't take offense,
Jaime,'' he added gently, ''when I tell you that nothing you can do or say is likely to change my mind,
either.''

Jaime swallowed hard and glanced again at the
folded paper in her hand, deeply ashamed. ''I—be-
haved very badly at dinner the other night,'' she managed at last, and made herself look at him. ''I'm sorry.
It was childish and unforgivable, and I've regretted it
ever since. Please believe it has nothing to do with you
personally. I simply... don't understand,'' she had to
admit honestly.

He replied merely, ''Are these things ever ra-
tional?''

''The two of you are so...'' She struggled for the
right word. ''Different.''

''That we are. And we have everything imaginable
working against us. If life were predictable, we should
never have met, much less loved each other. But love
rarely ever conforms to our ideas of conventional behavior, does it?'' He smiled. ''Perhaps that is why it's
called the 'grand madness.' ''

Jaime said slowly, ''You risked a great deal to love
her.''

"I would walk through hell for that woman," he responded simply, and the quiet sincerity of his words twisted at Jaime's heart.

Richard leaned forward a fraction more in his chair. "Jaime," he said sincerely, "we love each other. Deeply, completely, and to the exclusion of all else. It's not a one-way street. I may have endured the disapproval of my family, public censure and professional uncertainty, but Leona has given up much more. She has had to rearrange an entire way of thinking, a system of beliefs that she's lived by all her life in order to let herself love me. She has sacrificed a portion of her life-style, her friends and her public image for my sake. I should not like to add the sacrifice of her only daughter to that list," he added soberly.

Jaime released a shaky breath. "Neither would I," she admitted softly.

She looked at him. "There are things—between my mother and me that have nothing to do with you. You...were simply the catalyst. I never meant to hurt you, or her."

Richard nodded. "I know that. So does she. But she wants desperately to make peace. Could you, for all our sakes, at least try?"

"I am trying, Richard," she said, and a wave of helplessness and anguish crept through her that was almost choking. "I'm...just not sure it's that simple."

He looked very sad through the smile that seemed at the same time both sympathetic and forced. "Nothing worthwhile ever is," he said, and he rose to go.

IT WAS NOT THAT SHE could not forgive her mother, Jaime realized bleakly as she made her way home at the end of the day. Leona had done nothing to be forgiven for. It was perhaps that Jaime could not forgive herself for the things she had said, the unhappiness she had caused, the restrictions and the fears she had built around herself, which refused to allow her to adjust to an ever-changing world or to accept the surprises life had to offer. Some of it was Leona's fault; most of it was Jaime's.

Perhaps Quaid was right. She had spent her life reacting to her mother rather than acting on her own behalf. She had taken Leona's standards and pushed herself as far away from them as possible, learning to hate what Leona loved and embrace what Leona despised, as a measure of self-defense. But those were deeply ingrained instincts that she could not reject now, no matter how badly she wanted to, nor how consciously she tried. How could she change, at this late date, what she was inside?

A letter from Abbie was waiting for her when Jaime got home. She took it to the sofa and opened it gladly, more than willing to lose herself in chatty news from New York, to travel back in her mind to a simpler time and an easier place, when life was straightforward and her actions direct, and every decision she made was the right one.

And the first two paragraphs brought back all the reassuring memories of home.

Dear Jaime,
I know I shouldn't be complaining—New Orleans must be even hotter than New York—but honestly, it is so muggy here I can hardly stand it. In honor of the heat and humidity, all the city buses' air conditioners decided to break. What-

ever it's like where you are, it can't possibly be worse than this.

I probably should have taken a week on Cape Cod in June, as I'd originally planned. But part of that plan was that I would go with Bob, and now that we're history I couldn't bring myself to go alone. It was stupid of me—I'm in dire need of some cool ocean air. But I've been to the Cape with Bob three summers in a row, and I just wouldn't feel right going back there without him.

There Jaime had to pause. The last thing she needed to hear right now was of Abbie's broken romance. Yet Abbie seemed to be taking the loss with her usual cool style, and she and Bob had been together for almost four years. Would Jaime ever be able to be so blasé about Quaid?

She had to tighten her lips against the knot of pain that thought caused, and she read on.

Everyone here is doing about the same, swelter-ing along with me. Marielle is having more fi-nancial problems than she anticipated, and she doesn't know how much longer she'll be able to stay here. And Suzanne—get this—has quit her job and is getting ready to drive her daughter, Mouse, to school in Colorado, but after that she has no plans whatsoever. I think you started a chain reaction when you left. Pretty soon there's going to be no one here but me. And I'm already starting to feel lonely.

Jaime was surprised. There was something discon-certing about realizing that the group she had left be-hind in New York was breaking up. Even though she knew she would probably never see them again, there had been comfort in imagining them all together, as she had left them. Strangely enough she began to feel lonely, too. She looked back to the letter.

So... here's a tidbit to make your hair stand on end: Remember Michelle Dobbs, your candidate for Mother of the Year? (How could you forget?) I thought you might be interested to know that your sweet, misunderstood client—whom you swore really loved her little baby even though she all but abandoned her—was arrested last week on charges of trying to *sell* the kid. My office got the tip, the police did an undercover and sure enough, Michelle had the girl on the market for five hundred dollars. Five hundred dollars! Believe me, I was tempted to write Michelle a check, just to get that poor child in my arms and hug her and assure her that someone in this world cares what happens to her.

Needless to say, I did not get to hug the child. Social Services has found her a foster home. I hope your buddy Michelle spends the rest of her life rotting in a jail cell somewhere. She won't, of course. She'll be convicted, get the standard slap on the wrist, and be sent to someone just like you for counseling. Why do I waste my time? Why do I care?

This letter is turning into a real downer, isn't it? God, I need a break.

Hope things are going better for you.

Love,
Abbie

Jaime read the last part of the letter twice and then

a third time. She leaned her head back against the sofa
and closed her eyes, waiting for the pain to come, the
sickness, the defeat. All she felt was a bleak resignation and an emptiness inside that went deeper than any
she had ever known.

God, she thought dully. *The one thing I did right.
The one thing . . .*

How pointless it all seemed. All her grand notions,
all her crusading ideals—for what? She could not
make the system work for her, and she was unable to
work against the system. Was there any hope at all?

She lay down on the sofa with Abbie's letter still
clutched in her hand and she let it all flow through
her . . . the defeat, the sorrow, the regrets, the recriminations. The shock and the pain in her mother's eyes,
the sadness and longing in Quaid's. The needs, the
uncertainties, the challenging faces and the decisions
made wrongly from all these past weeks marched
across the field of her emotions and she let them come,
tired of fighting, tired of questioning. And by the time
an exhausted and uneasy sleep overtook her, Jaime
knew, with a sorrow that twisted her soul, what she
had to do.

Chapter Thirteen

It was ten o'clock the next morning when Leona let herself quietly into Jaime's house with her own key. Jaime was sitting at the table, holding an untouched cup of coffee and gazing out the window at the muggy, overcast day, and Leona looked startled to see her.

"I'm sorry," Leona said. "I just came by for the rest of my things. I thought you'd already be at work."

Jaime got up from the table, her heart beating a little harder. "I'm not going to work today," she answered, watching her mother carefully.

Leona was wearing an apple-green Chanel suit and a peach blouse. Her hair was arranged in a braided coronet around her head and she looked stylish, elegant and cool. She also looked older.

Jaime came into the living room. "That is," she added somewhat hesitantly, "I'm going in late." She took a breath. "I've decided to leave New Orleans, Mother."

A look of alarm crossed Leona's face and Jaime added quickly, "Not because...I mean, it has nothing to do with you. It's just..." And she looked around the room with a hopeless shrug and a forced smile. "New Orleans isn't really my town, you know?

Things here are so different from what I'm used to. It's like Mardi Gras every day of the year—bizarre and frantic and happy-go-lucky and always unexpected." She shrugged again. "I'm just not comfortable in that kind of environment. What I need to do is find a nice safe little nine-to-five job in a government office somewhere, where I know the routine and no one expects me to take any risks. It's what I should have done in the first place."

Leona said quietly, "I'm sorry. And thank you for saying that you're not leaving because of me, although I suspect that's not entirely the truth."

Jaime hesitated. "Richard came to see me yesterday."

Leona looked surprised. "I didn't know that."

"He's a nice man, Mother," Jaime said, and it wasn't as difficult as she thought it would be. "I like him."

Leona smiled, faintly. "I'm glad. Because as much as it was tearing me apart inside, I couldn't give him up, Jaime. Not even for you."

"I don't want you to," Jaime said, and she meant it. "I want you to be happy."

Leona released a soft long breath, and the lines of tension in her face gradually relaxed. "I'm so glad," she whispered.

And then, as though embarrassed by the sudden emotion, Leona turned away, absently trailing a hand along the back of the sofa. "You know," she said in a rather strained voice, "you were not an easy child to raise. And I don't mean in all those cliché ways—a single mother, no money—those things never bothered me. It was just that you and I were so *different*. I never understood you."

Jaime said quietly, "I know I disappointed you a lot."

Leona turned, amazement genuine in her eyes. "Disappointed me? Jaime, I was so proud of you! I always admired you so, and wished I could be more like you."

Now it was Jaime's turn to be amazed.

"You were always so calm," Leona went on, "so logical and controlled. You could deal with anything, and you knew the right response for any situation. People were always coming to you for advice, even when you were a young girl, even when they were *my* grown up friends, don't you remember that? And you always knew just what to say. You had everything worked out in your head. Life made sense to you. Whereas for me, it's always been a come-as-you-are party."

She sighed. "Jaime, ever since you were born you've been the only thing in the world to me. The only constant, the thing I could depend on. You were all I had in the world. And every day of my life I had to face the fact that I was failing you. I never knew how to do the right things for you, I never knew what you needed. I wanted, more than anything in the world, to be a *mother* to you, but I didn't know how. So I had to settle for being your friend, instead."

She smiled wanly. "Maybe that's why I've been such a pain these past few weeks. I've learned a lot from Richard—a lot about you, believe it or not, and a lot about being a grown-up woman. A mother. I guess—" she spread her arms in a faint shrug "—I was trying to make it up to you, at this late date, all those years of not being a real mother. Only I still don't know how."

Jaime blinked away the sting of tears. "You don't have anything to make up to me," she said thickly. "You showed me things and taught me things, just by being you, that most girls never have a chance to know. The only trouble was, I was too stupid to see it."

Leona looked at her with pain and longing in her eyes. "Oh, Jaime, I can't stand for this thing to come between us. Everything used to be so open and easy between us. We could always be honest with each other. Please, can't it be that way again?"

Jaime swallowed the moisture in her throat and managed a smile. "I hate red," she said.

Leona looked confused, and Jaime gestured to her walls. "I love you, Mother, but I hate these red walls."

Leona laughed, though her eyes, too, were bright with tears. The two women came toward each other and embraced fiercely. "Well," said Leona, her voice muffled in Jaime's shoulder. "At least that can be fixed." And then she moved a little away, cupping Jaime's face with both of her hands, and tears of joy and sorrow trickled down her perfectly made-up cheek. "Oh, baby," she said, "if only the rest of your life was that simple."

Jaime released a shaky breath. "It never is."

Leona asked quietly, searching her face, "What about Quaid?"

But Jaime could only shake her head on a throat that was too tight to speak. "I guess..." She managed at last, shifting her brimming eyes to a far corner of the room. "It wasn't meant to be."

"I am so sorry," Leona whispered, and her lashes lowered. "I wish I knew what to tell you. There must be some right, motherly thing to say, some advice I could give, something I could do to make it all right.

But I don't know what it is. I'm afraid . . . this you'll have to deal with on your own."

Jaime tried to smile. "It's about time, isn't it?" She reached up and touched her mother's face, catching a tear on the back of her finger. "I think," she said brokenly, "it may be too late for you to be my mother . . . But I sure could use a friend right now."

Leona took her tightly in her arms, and Jaime let her own tears fall. Leona held her and comforted her, rocking her like a child, until the worst was past.

JAIME WENT TO THE CLINIC with a feeling of peace and despair. After all these years, she had begun to take the first cautious steps toward resolving her relationship with her mother, and that was a good thing, a solid thing. It would take time and lots of understanding on both their parts, but Jaime knew that today marked the beginning of a new closeness between mother and daughter. A new life, perhaps, for both of them.

It had taken a trial by fire for her to come this far, and she was grateful for what she had gained with her mother. But in the process she had gained and lost a love she would never forget, and the pain of that knowledge was almost more than she could bear.

She did not know what she was going to do, or where she was going to go. She only knew it was unfair of her to keep Quaid waiting like this any longer. She had a lot of thinking to do and a lot of growing to do, before she was mature enough to accept the kind of love he had to offer—or before she was daring enough to give him what he needed from her. She went to the clinic to return his necklace and to say goodbye.

The girl at the desk told Jaime, Quaid was in his office, and she gave her a furtive, almost frightened look as she did so. Jaime hardly noticed.

Her heart was pounding with dread and anticipation as she reached the office. His door was half open and, taking a deep breath, she pushed it open the rest of the way.

Two uniformed police officers were just getting to their feet. One was short and rotund, the other young and sandy-haired. Both looked grave.

"I'm sorry you feel that way, Quaid," the short one was saying. "I don't like doing this to you. But you leave us no choice except to come back with a search warrant."

Quaid said mildly, "I'm sorry you have to waste your time." He walked them to the door.

"You know," said the sandy-haired one, "if we find out you've been concealing evidence, there's going to be trouble."

"And if we find out you knew the man you were protecting was involved in a felony," said the short one heavily, "you're going to be in more trouble than even I can get you out of."

Quaid's face revealed absolutely nothing. He shook hands with both of them. "Goodbye Lyle, Ken. Come around again."

"We will," replied the man he had referred to as Lyle, and he did not look happy. "You can bet on that."

The two policemen nodded briefly to Jaime on their way past, and Jaime heard the front door clatter closed behind them.

She came slowly into the office. Her heart was going in a strong, heavy rhythm, and her cheeks felt cold.

She didn't know how she formed the words. "Luther Johnson?"

Quaid nodded. For all the front he had put on for the policemen, now he looked drained and very tired. "It seems the other man involved in that shooting was some bigwig movie producer out to check the local color. The mayor's office is putting the pressure on to get this one solved—bad publicity and all that. They don't have any leads except the officer's statement that he wounded the assailant. So they've been checking out all the local clinics and doctors for gunshot wounds they might have treated in the past month. They finally got to me."

Jaime's voice sounded hoarse. "What did you tell them?"

He lifted his shoulders lightly, and even managed a near smile. "Doctor-patient confidentiality."

Jaime's knees felt weak. Her fingers were still wrapped around the wooden figure on the necklace she had come to return to Quaid, but the reason she had come here was no longer in her mind. She tried to make herself think; she tried to hear above the pounding of her own heart the quiet, calm, orderly logic that usually came to her at such moments, but she couldn't. Even the question she asked next was foolish, pointless, and its answer far too obvious.

"What will happen to you?"

He took a folder from his desk and walked to the file cabinet. "They'll come back with a warrant and confiscate my records. I don't imagine having to go through all this hen scratching will improve their mood any, either. Eventually they'll find Luther's chart, and that will be that." He filed away the chart and turned to her, a wry, resigned smile on his face. "That's one rule even *I* can't ignore. Doctors write things down, they keep records. It's a curse."

She tried to take a deep breath, but found her chest constricted. The wooden statuette dug into her palm. "And then?"

He went back to his desk, absently straightening some papers scattered there. "Then I'll be charged with obstructing justice, or aiding and abetting. Depending on how big a deal the mayor wants to make out of this, I might do some jail time. Whatever, my license will be called up for review. And Luther Johnson will be convicted of a crime he didn't commit."

Jaime felt ill, and everything inside her was whispering, *No . . . no.* It was wrong, it couldn't happen. Quaid had done nothing wrong, this couldn't happen to him. . . .

She could not believe it was her own voice that uttered the next words. "You could destroy the record," she said. "No one would ever know. They wouldn't be able to trace Luther to the scene of the crime, or you to Luther. No one would ever know."

He looked at her, and his eyes were very sober. "Yes," he agreed slowly. "I could do that. I could get away with it, easily. You wouldn't even be surprised if I did."

She couldn't answer. She didn't know what he expected her to say. She didn't even know what he was trying to say . . . and suddenly she did.

"No, Jaime," he said quietly, "I'm not going to do that. Because even though it would be the easiest thing to do and maybe, in this case, even the right thing, and even though you might even understand why . . . you could never forget it. And because if I take the shortcut this time, it's going to cost me something I value more than my license to practice or my freedom or even my integrity. You."

The cord upon which the talisman was suspended snapped under the unconscious pressure of Jaime's fist. She wanted to cry out to him, she wanted to run to him, she wanted to take him by the arms and plead with him.... But she stood there, mute and swollen with confusion and fear and knowing that nothing she could say would save him now....

A voice behind her abruptly jolted her back to herself as the girl from the desk poked her head around the corner. "Doctor, room two."

Quaid nodded to her and then looked back to Jaime, torn. "I'm sorry," he said. "I've kept patients waiting. I know you came here to talk to me about something . . . wait for me, please. I won't be long."

Somehow Jaime managed to nod. She felt him squeeze her arm, lightly and affectionately as he passed, and everything inside her then seemed to crumple and die.

She did not know how long she stood there, clutching the broken talisman in her hand, aching and afraid and paralyzed with the consequences of what had just passed in this room.

Quaid could go to jail. He could lose his license. She had warned him, but he had risked it all for what he believed was right. And it *was* right. She saw that now. And now it was too late.

He had broken the law, he had taken his chances. And now, according to everything that was sane and orderly in a civilized society, he must pay the consequences. But he would lose his practice; all these people who depended on him would have nowhere else to turn. An innocent man would be convicted; Quaid, who was guilty of nothing but following his own conscience, might even go to jail; hundreds of people would suffer...because it was the law. How could that be right?

How could this happen to him? How could she stand by and let this happen?

As though in slow motion, she walked over to the desk and she placed the talisman there. And then, because she simply couldn't help herself, she turned to the file cabinet.

Her heart was pounding and her hands were sweating. She flipped through the files, and the names blurred before her eyes, and she had to start all over again. She found it at last. Johnson, Luther.

She pulled the chart out slowly and opened it to the last page. Quaid's spidery scrawl leaped and faded before her eyes and then became abruptly clear again: "June 30, 1:15 A.M.—Gunshot wound left calf..."

A wave of weakness went through her and she could hardly breathe for the pounding of her heart. A cold trickle of perspiration traveled from her armpit to her waist. She could not do this thing. How could she do it?

Voices echoed inside her head, blending into one another...

Someday you'll have to do something because it's right for you... The rules and regulations don't apply here... I can't help you with this one, Jaime...

Quaid was the man she loved. How could she not do it?

With a convulsive motion her hand closed on the paper and tore the last page out of the file. She slammed the drawer and she ran from the clinic.

THE PARK WAS QUITE DIFFERENT from the last time Jaime had visited it. The lake was crowded with brightly colored sailboats and racing speedboats; the shores were crowded with swimmers and sunbathers and picnickers. Children ran and squealed with laughter; a volleyball game was going on nearby. The day was hot and overcast and sticky, the very worst of New Orleans weather. But to Jaime it was lovely.

She had no trouble finding their bench, and almost as though by prearrangement it was empty. She sat down, and she did not know how long she stayed there, watching the crowd and tracing over and over with her fingers the initials carved inside a heart. JF and QG. She wondered how many hundreds of thousands of others would sit here and do as she was doing, wondering absently about the lovers whose initials were carved there, perhaps forming pictures of them in their minds. There was something magical and special about that.

For the longest time Jaime waited for the guilt, the shame, the paralyzing fear as at last the consequence of what she had done registered. None of it ever came. She felt, in fact, strangely peaceful and satisfied . . . and alive, really alive, for the very first time. And she was too overawed by it all, too content and free in the moment, to even wonder why that should be so. It was enough that it was.

She had been to see Mame LeCaree. The woman was sitting on the front porch, hands folded in her lap when Jaime arrived, and she did not look in the least surprised to see her.

Jaime had said simply, "I've come to make peace."

Mame LeCaree nodded. "I knew you would."

"I won't—interfere in your magic, if you won't interfere with my work."

A faint superior smile curved the other woman's lips. "And the magic—you have come to learn of it?"

"Yes," Jaime answered softly. What else could explain her recent behavior? "I understand about magic now."

Mame inclined her head beneficently. "You will do good here, child."

Jaime hesitated. "And—the curse? You'll take it off?"

"You bring the magic on yourself, you take it off yourself." And Mame LeCaree chuckled. "It was you, child, all the time. It's always you that makes the magic."

It's always you that makes the magic. The words echoed in Jaime's head now, and she liked the sound of them. She intended to make a great deal of magic in her life from now on.

She therefore was not surprised when she looked up, sometime late in the afternoon, to find Quaid standing a few feet away, just looking at her. How beautiful he was. How her heart swelled with the sight of him. How could she ever have thought, even for a moment, of leaving him?

He said, "The police were back. They took my records. Somehow I don't think they're going to find what they're looking for."

She searched his face, but she could find neither approval nor disapproval there. Her heart began to tighten just a little, wondering what he was thinking.

She said, "How...how did you know where to find me?"

He made a small sound that might have been a dry laugh, and his eyes moved lazily toward the lake. "*Chérie*, Lake Pontchartrain has been the repository for more so-called lost evidence than any other place in the world...except, perhaps, the East River."

She smiled a little hesitantly, still uncertain of what he was thinking, of what he felt. "Well," she said. "When I decide to break a rule, I go all the way, don't I?"

"Why bother with misdemeanors when you can go straight to felony?" he agreed easily.

Jaime took a deep breath. Felony. She was a *felon*. Would she ever get used to that? Would Quaid? Why didn't he say something?

Jaime said, after a moment, "I apologized to Miss Mame."

"Good." He smiled and held the broken talisman between his thumb and forefinger for her inspection. "Then I guess you won't be needing this anymore."

Her smile was faint and tremulous. "No. She said— she said we make our own magic."

"So we do," he answered soberly, and then there was silence.

He looked at her with eyes that were intent and searching and revealed nothing. Her nerves heightened and her muscles tightened, trying to read what he was thinking, but the silence went on.

"Well," she said after a while, nervously.

"Well," he repeated. He hooked his thumbs into his pockets, and he looked down at her thoughtfully. He didn't say anything else for a long time. And then he took another breath.

"So," he said carefully. "This is it. I'll never make more than twenty thousand dollars a year. My total assets include a cheaply furnished apartment and a worn-out motorcycle. I haven't had an uninterrupted Christmas or Thanksgiving in five years, and New Year's Eve is usually spent in the ER stitching up parts of people's bodies who are generally having more fun than I am. I have a tendency to forget birthdays and anniversaries, and I miss eight dinners out of ten. Life with me will be hectic, unpredictable and sometimes disappointing. And we'll fight. God, how we'll fight."

He shook his head slowly, as though in amused anticipation of the disagreements yet to come, and then he looked back at her, and the amusement faded. "I can't give you one good reason why you should marry me," he said simply. "Marry me anyway. Please."

Jaime got to her feet slowly, buoyed by a joy, a certainty so intense that it left her weak. She smiled at him. "Okay," she said.

He opened his arms to her and she stepped into them. He hugged her so tightly that it hurt, but she did not feel it, because she was embracing him with the same wonderful, fierce desperation. The fear was gone, and so was the confusion. Because for the first time in her life, she was exactly where she needed to be.

He pushed her away a little. His eyes were bright as they searched her face, hungry and adoring, yet mitigated just the faintest bit by a trace of disbelief. "You could do a lot better," he warned her.

"Ah," she answered softly, and she could feel the happiness dancing up inside her like bubbles ready to burst. "But I could do so much worse."

He laughed, and she laughed, and then their mouths sought each other's in a deep and passionate kiss. People were staring, but Jaime didn't care.

She didn't care at all.

HARLEQUIN SIGNATURE EDITION

Editorial secretary Debra Hartway travels to the Salvador family's rugged Cornish island home to work on Jack Salvador's latest book. Disturbing questions hang in the troubled air over Lovelis Island. What or who had caused the tragic death of Jack's young wife? Why did Jack stay away from the home and, more especially, the baby son he loved so well? And—why should Rodare, Jack's brother, who had proved himself a man of the highest integrity, constantly invade Debra's thoughts with such passionate, dark desires...?

Violet Winspear, who has written more than 65 romance novels translated worldwide into 18 languages, is one of Harlequin's best-loved and bestselling authors. HOUSE OF STORMS, her second title in the Harlequin Signature Edition program, is a full-length novel rich in romantic tradition and intriguingly spiced with an atmosphere of danger and mystery.

Watch for HOUSE OF STORMS—coming in October!

HOFS-1